THE NUCLEAR WINTER

A Reject High Legacy novel

Brian Thompson

Great Nation Publishing, LLC
3828 Salem Road #56
Covington, GA 30016

www.authorbrianthompson.com
E-mail: brian@authorbrianthompson.com

Printed in the United States of America

ISBN: 978-0-9891056-5-1

LCCN: 2019945587

This work is dedicated to the memory of Claudette Thompson and Margaret Harley

CHAPTER ONE

Since my fifth-grade year, Death has wanted to meet me. Three years, almost four, he'd followed me back and forth to elementary then middle school, chemotherapy, radiation treatments, the shower — everywhere. Okay, so maybe *stalked* was more accurate. Like ice dissolving in cold water, I eventually came around to see the inevitability of our appointment. My invisible stalker was harmless, though, because my life belonged to him. No rush. He'd claim me when the time came, and the inch-long pink scar across my left wrist reminded me I was on his clock not mine.

When I was born, my mother named me "Luciana" because nothing evil could coexist with light. She'd had me at seventeen, and my father wasn't around, so her hopes had to be wishful thinking. That explained the constant hovering over me and monitoring. At home, I kept to myself. Then, she wouldn't notice my behavior as much and have me committed against my will. Another visit to the mental floor of the hospital was a definite "no."

Tomorrow, I'd go back, not for an "involuntary hold of mental illness" but for removal of my Broviac lumen catheter and...I'd officially learn how long I'd have to live. It'd been the only thing I'd thought about since the first calendar alert chimed days ago. The goal was seeing the ball drop on the year 2030, which was a month and a half from today.

"Hey." Murdoch, a school resource officer who knew me on a first-name basis, pulled his police transport into my driveway. "Nice subdivision."

From the slick leather back seat, I felt his hazel-eyed stare and knew what he thought — I was a spoiled, rich chick with nothing better to do than cause trouble. Mom never said much about *where* she got the monetary units from to buy the house except that she'd inherited them, and an inheritance meant a person had to die for it to transfer, but who? We had no family to speak of.

He opened my door and repeated himself. "Young lady. I said 'nice subdivision'."

Under my breath, I'd admitted hearing him the first time. He gnashed his teeth. "Then, respond when I talk to you. Let's go."

I got out and stepped forward, eyes on everything but the broad-shouldered, bald white man who towered over my five-foot-three frame. My heart leapt with fear when he nudged my lower back with his hand. "Walking slow won't help."

Of course, it wouldn't. I buried deep the fact that he'd rattled me. He'd taken me off school grounds without administrator permission. Murdoch wasn't arresting me for smoking and letting a boy explore under my sweatshirt though I probably should be expelled. The guy flinched when, instead of my breast, he'd felt metal catheter prongs. That's when Murdoch showed up. "Loosen up," I told him. "What's the rush? It's not like I can outrun you."

He stopped me next to the dormant azalea bushes. "You'd prefer handcuffs?"

Of everything I'd done, meeting Mom in handcuffs wasn't one I wanted to try. "Faster it is."

When we crossed under the awning and stood on the rubber welcome mat, Murdoch rapped his knuckles hard against the front door. "Police," he shouted while repeatedly ringing the bell. Murdoch turned to me. "Is she home, Luciana? What about your dad?"

Hilarious. There was expectancy in his eyes. I shrugged and attempted to still myself, but the mid-November cold and Murdoch's closeness to my sweat-drenched body made me itchy. Tapping my sneaker soles against the concrete porch and biting my lip helped ease my nerves until I heard high-heeled footsteps across the hardwood living room floor. Anyone with a regular nine-to-five wouldn't have been home. Not Mom, who answered her holographic phone by the second or third ring. Whatever she did away from the house during business hours never took long. I'd found that out the hard way. Several times.

With no surprise in her voice, Mom greeted us, "Come in."

"Thanks, Mom," I joked, maybe for one of the last times before she vaporized me.

I plopped on our white leather couch. Mom stood close to me. Her dark brown hair in a bun meant she had finished lunch shift.

She rolled up her white blouse sleeves. "Shoplifting? Destruction of property? Fighting? Truancy?" Her face dropped when she leaned toward me and sniffed marijuana.

Though she'd sighed, I'd noticed no purple veins bulging out on her temples. She wasn't mad? Progress! I always told her. "Why be pissed at me? Doesn't change anything."

Murdoch sidled next to my mother and me. Every time we did this routine and the cop was a guy, he'd gaze at Mom with more than passing interest. She'd dyed strands of her shoulder-length hair silver and formally dressed to avoid it. Truth be told, with all that effort, she still didn't pass for a thirty-two year old. Her tanned skin was flawless satin except for multiple ear piercings she'd allowed to close. Before I got sick, I'd hoped to look half as hot as she did when I grew up.

She produced her driver's license and identified herself as my mother, Elayna Sandoval. He asked about my father, and Mom didn't directly answer him. Nothing to say about him.

Murdoch spoke matter-of-factly. I'm sure he'd delivered worse news than this to a parent before. "I discovered your daughter with drug paraphernalia and cornered by two senior boys at the high school."

Her perfect lips dropped a little. So far, she thought the worst thing I'd done in life was the weed. It helped with the nausea, and I liked not feeling miserable all the time.

The pressure from her stare could've drilled holes into the right side of my face. After this run-in, she'd wonder how many guys I'd slept with at fourteen. I'd let her wonder. The truth would've shocked her. She wouldn't have believed it. Not many guys want to have sex with a girl they thought might die in the sheets, and the ones that did I wanted nothing to do with.

"And..."

And Murdoch described the scene — nothing leading to something. They must've been medalists on Penn High's track team. I'd blinked and they were gone.

"Miss Sandoval, girls like your daughter don't need that kind of attention."

Girls like me. He didn't mean freshmen, or upper middle class, or Cape Verdean and Panamanian. I knew what he meant. Half-dying girls. Lonely, pathetic, desperate girls.

I swallowed my protests. *Everybody knows the surveillance cameras' range,* I'd have said. *Because I'm sick, everyone knows I'm a virgin, and I don't want to die that way.* But I held my tongue. Heart twisting in my chest, I battled tears. I didn't even like the guy. A month from now, who'd care about purity?

"You could've been assaulted," he told me. "Your life is important."

Right.

My mom crossed her arms. "Okay. What are her charges, Officer?"

Murdoch accessed the notetaking app on his holophone. "I'd like to have names or descriptions. I don't have children of my own, but I wouldn't — "

"She's got the point!"

Mom's arm tensed and cocked at the elbow as if she intended to slap me. She settled for a kick to my calf, which hurt enough, and said, *"Dile!"*

They looked at me. I didn't want to tell him anything, especially since I didn't ask for ID. Describing him meant he'd find out I was a well-endowed eighth-grader two weeks shy of turning fifteen, not a seventeen-year-old transfer student like I'd claimed. The tightness in my throat was unbearable. "Mom, I..."

"Luciana." Arms crossed, she stared me down.

"I told him I was seventeen. Murdoch will arrest him."

She clutched my slumped shoulders and squatted in front of me. "Name or describe him, okay? He *should* be in jail for stupidity."

True. But I still wasn't snitching. "It was a kiss, okay? He didn't..."

Mom's rapid hand flinging meant I'd exasperated her. "Your information, Officer."

He digitally transferred his contact information to her holophone. "Here's my private number. We don't have to make it official."

I wondered...would the head principal see it that way? Dr. Harris hated me as it was.

"Thank you."

"Call me when she's ready to talk."

If he had read my eyes, he'd know that'd happen right after the sun burned out. Who cared about my reputation or what people thought of me? I just didn't want to do it.

Murdoch showed himself out, and Mom voice-activated the locks. I expected a Hall of Fame lecture. The kind where I zoned out thirty seconds in. She'd demand to count my birth control. I skip a pill, and the cramp pain would kill me before the cancer did.

Instead, she knelt in front of me and teared up.

Let's face it. Say by a miracle I survived past next month. I had *no shot* to pass eighth grade. I'm not spending my final days doing schoolwork no matter how "normal" a life it was. I'd never have a job or a bill to finance. We'd inherited money, and all I had to do to get a big piece of it, impossible as it might seem, was stay alive for six more years. Nothing mattered. Why should it?

"What?" I finally asked her. "Stop staring! What do you want from me?"

"You're crazy!" she served back at me. "Two legal adults and *you?* I — "

"The guy recording was seventeen..."

"Recording?" She strung together several Spanish curse words. "They could've..."

"They *didn't*. Neither of them would have!"

Mom's skin lost color. I'd never seen her break down into sobs like she did at that moment. Her hands trembled, and she loudly wailed like she'd been personally injured by what I'd done.

Part of me wanted to erase it all. Not just my actions. My existence, too. "Y-you...you want me to be some perfect Catholic princess. Knee socks and pigtails with straight A's." Spit flew from my mouth onto her sweater. "That's not me. On my best day, I'm...*below average.*"

"No," she said between sniffles. "You're not. You're anything but. If you realized..."

What? My potential? I'm *special?* Parents were *supposed* to think their kids were special. I was not stupid. I was "not living up to my potential," or "not trying hard enough" or "bright but lazy." I knew myself. I'd hit my ceiling — a straight-C student with luck and hard work. And, if I didn't give it everything I had, I'd fail. Like I was doing now.

"So, I'm *special?*" I blinked back my own tears. "To *you?* I'm a pet you feed, clothe, protect, and keep from living."

Mom got to her feet. She looked as if she knew my feelings. Love, longing, and sadness mixed with regret and a dash of anger. *"Fourteen years."* Her voice cracked. "Murdoch could've reported you to the principal, thank God, he didn't. And fourteen years! *I've* been your mother and your father! And this is the thanks I get?"

I grabbed the sharpest emotional knife I had and plunged it into her heart. "Nobody asked you to be my father, too! My father needed to be my father, and where is he?"

The effect of my insult was sudden and dramatic. Tears rolled down her quivering chin. "Who cares, huh? How many events and ceremonies and 'muffins with Mom' have I been to? How long have I slept in your hospital bed, when you had nobody else, who was there, huh? And that's *nothing?* You treat me like *this?"*

Whatever. I didn't care what she thought anymore. I clenched my fists and stomped to the staircase. "It's not always all about you and how I treat you!"

"Young lady," she bellowed after me in Spanish. "I'm not done! Don't walk away from me when I'm talking to you!"

Mom had paused at the base of the stairs. I shouted over my shoulder. "Don't see you stopping me."

"The only reason I don't kill you right now is because you're already dying."

The half threat, half joke, sounded serious, but she'd never touched me in anger. I pushed her further. "Do what you have to do, *Elayna."*

Her nose flared. "No friends, holovision, or holophone."

There went my aspirations for Winter Dance Princess.

I slammed the door, backed against it and waited for a force to push it open. For a small woman, Mom was unnaturally strong. She didn't come. Instead, I heard her voice command to lock down the house. In sixty seconds, I'd be confined to my room like a prisoner. She'd activate the signal dampener as well. I'd have old paperback books and painted walls to keep me comfortable.

Right then, my stomach dropped and rumbled. I rushed to the toilet in time to flip the seat up and hurl. Good thing my hair hadn't grown back too far past my ears.

I lost my guts again, and the second time, it stung and burned, like I'd thrown up a small organ. Halfway through an ugly crying fit, a familiar arm surrounded my shoulders. How'd she gotten to me so fast without setting off the alarm? I'd have resisted her support if I'd had the strength. Most days, I had it together. Others, I didn't. Some, I tried to fake my way through.

"Mmmm..."

She understood my gurgling better than anyone. Her fingers squeezed my arm as I heaved and heaved and heaved until all I did was painfully groan into the toilet. Now empty, my stomach hardened like a stone. Whatever dignity I had left swirled around the bowl when I flushed it. I'd fought my mother and won and lost. I couldn't have gotten through a sickness like this without her. And she was all the family I had.

I wiped my mouth on a wad of toilet paper Mom handed to me. Then, she set a tall glass of ice water on my counter, like she'd always done. The first swallow would strike like ice daggers, but every gulp after that would be cool and refreshing — a swimming pool on a sweltering day. By the time I'd recovered enough to pry myself from the tile floor, she had left me.

A look in the mirror revealed the damage to my face. Black mascara had run in jagged trails down my pale cheeks. My red lipstick had blurred, and the black hair on my head looked like picked-apart straw. At least my brows were right.

As I washed my face and freshened up my mouth, my thoughts drifted to my closet. Buried beneath a mountain of dirty laundry was a duffle bag I'd packed with toiletries, what little monetary units I could stash away, and clothes. When the right moment came, I'd take it and run far away from this place. For my last days, I owed it to myself to see what kind of world was out there beyond my house, the school, and the bleak hospital walls.

Right as I got to the closet, my prepaid holophone chimed. I'd bought it a while ago to get around my punishments. My best friend, Natalee Gupta, had requested a face-to-face. Mom hadn't turned off the dampener.

I accepted it as a voice call. "Good thing you called the temp phone."

"Figured your mom had the main one when it went to voicemail."

No sense in searching. Off and going to voicemail meant Mom took it when I wasn't looking. The Indian accent turned from ethnic to East Coast when we talked. "What gives, Sandoval? Turn on the camera already."

I flopped onto the bed, holophone in hand, and remembered the girl I'd seen in the mirror. "Uh-uh. Face is busted."

"Face stays busted. What else is new?"

"I'll describe what I'm doing instead. I have not one but two middle fingers for you."

"Nice of you to go the extra mile." She paused so long that I thought the signal had dropped. No, she had been thinking of a way to bring it up in a way not to hurt my feelings. I'd tried to push everyone who cared about me away by mouthing off. Nat never left. "Umm..."

The video. "That bad, huh?" I asked her.

"Not really. You didn't let him do much, at least, and he didn't see your birthmark."

I licked my dry lips and sighed. "You're a terrible liar. How many posts?"

"It's a good night to be off Wi-Fi. Take the weekend. And, I didn't lie about the birthmark."

Memes, videos, pictures, of course. Good thing I hadn't taken my sweatshirt off like he'd wanted me to. Then I'd have to deal with jokes about the birthmark between my breasts and my stained white bra. My shape was one good thing I got from Mom's side, so no one would've talked crap about my chest. The stringy wires hanging below it were a different story. Tube-shaped with metal connectors, they transferred meds into my body. Not sexy at all. I hadn't intended to do what I did today. I was buzzed and didn't care.

Natalee, though, had a plan for everything. A few months older than me and way smarter, she was beautiful and petite with cocoa skin. I envied the wavy black braid that snaked from the back of her head over her shoulder and down to her belly button. Her father forbade her to do more than trim her broken ends. I'd thought it was a religious thing, they were Hindi or Buddhist, I think, but no. Mr. Gupta was a total control freak.

"They're removing the catheter tomorrow, right? Excited?"

I stared toward the ceiling to keep the tears from falling. "Yeah and testing. Finding out whether I'm special enough for a new treatment or immunotherapy, or dying for good." Talking past the lump in my throat required effort. "Y-yeah, I'm excited for that. I'm ready for that. All over that."

I pressed the red phone icon on my heads-up display to save her the trouble. More wetness dribbled from my eyes as I lay on my purple-and-white-checkered quilt and stared out the window. There, next to my bed, I imagined my father — tall and strong. He'd approach, curl behind me, and tangle his fingers in mine. I formed my hand into a fist and squeezed. My blinking slowed along with my breathing.

The next thing I knew, it was late. The room's atmosphere was dark. Jagged tree branches swayed outside my window, and rain tapped against the glass. According to the virtual reality clock, I'd slept for eight hours and it was two thirty in the morning. The almond soup Mom had left on my nightstand was room temperature, but I spooned it into my mouth anyway. She'd mixed too much garlic into it, but I was too weak to be picky. Heating it meant going to the kitchen, and the stairway was near Mom's room. She could be awake and waiting for me to exit. A sneak attack lecture would be the worst. Besides, I could've sworn the human-sized shadow in my peripheral vision hadn't moved. Death.

Was today my day?

I finished off the soup and crusty sourdough bread she'd brought me and fell back asleep.

The next day, I woke up, showered, and threw on a bra and a matching pair of underwear, both black, nothing frilly, a purple Zara Hristoff sweatshirt, black leggings, and a clean pair of black canvas sneakers. The muddy shoes I'd had were gone. Mom had taken them as a guilt trip. She'd achieved her purpose. I felt crappy, inside and out.

Morning light rays filtered through the kitchen window blinds. I'd gotten downstairs by seven thirty. My removal procedure was scheduled for nine, and the hospital was an hour away, so I had a minute to shove something in my mouth. We had cranberry bagels and cream cheese. I'd do one of those and green juice.

"No eating," Mom warned me from behind the refrigerator door. "Surgery, remember?"

I'd already eaten past midnight. She didn't know that, though, and tossed me a bottle of water. Good thing it was plastic because I couldn't catch. I dropped it onto the floor. As I knelt to pick it up, a tsunami of dizziness hit me. The cabinets swirled around like a brown and gold kaleidoscope on a Tilt-A-Whirl. When I hit the floor and closed my eyes, Mom considered it a call for help.

"Lucy!" she called out to me.

I swallowed hard and waved her away. "I'm good."

Though prayer isn't part of my daily routine, I pleaded with God, the Virgin Mary, Vishnu, and whoever else would listen to prevent me from throwing up again.

My mother crouched beside me, clutched my hand in hers, and resumed the praying. Whenever situations got too real or her temper fired up, she went bilingual on me. I'd taken Spanish in school, and it might've been the only class I hadn't miserably failed. When she said, "Amen," I felt a bit better. This time, she handed me the water bottle. All I'd be able to do is let it cool my mouth and spit it out.

"Salud," she said, touching her bottle with mine.

She drank while I swished the liquid around my mouth and spit it out into the sink. Mom had done a lot of good things for me and was unusually cool for all the things I'd said to her last night. I couldn't have knuckled up and fought without her. Didn't know if I would have wanted to.

A little while later, we were in her two-door Cougar transport and headed to the hospital. Mom turned on the satellite radio to distract me. Our musical tastes were worlds apart. She liked this station that played alternative and punk bands. I liked old hip hop and what she called "hood music." I forced myself to listen to the guitar riffs and radio snow until I couldn't take it anymore and activated my audial comm — a Bluetooth sound system topically implanted into my ears. A complete audio system would've sounded much better, but my treatment would've fried the circuitry. "Holophone? For music, I swear."

"Music." She opened a compartment in the transport and handed it to me.

Totally old school it was.

Right when I plugged in, a text came in from Natalee. She must be in first block by now. I glanced at it. "Good luck," it read, followed by, in caps, "Don't look."

My best friend knew me. She'd known I'd want to see the mockery, and she also knew I was going to look no matter what she said. "Thanks," I mouthed.

I'd forgotten my grounding, brought up all the social networking sites I could think of, and clicked on the profiles of people I knew hated me. Sure enough, there was an anonymous video. I waited for it to load.

Mom turned the radio down and calmly extended her hand. "Nope. Holophone, please."

I panicked. Hand it to her and the video would stop loading. She'd see the guy's face who I was kissing and get him arrested. "No way," I said, clutching the rectangular device.

Still driving, she pointed her finger at me. "Give me the phone, Luciana, or I will take it from you."

Beneath the calmness in her voice was an authority I rarely saw, and I didn't want to challenge it this time. Not in a moving transport. I obeyed. To my surprise, rather than toss it out the window, she swiped it off and stuck it in her pocket.

"A girl at my high school did something much worse than you did, and she found herself on the internet."

"They had the internet back then?"

She didn't crack a smile.

I held my breath. *Mom knows.* Even Murdoch didn't know about my starring role. Either that or he didn't say anything to Mom. Had one of the parents called her? I mouthed a curse word at the window and, for the first time in my life, wished we could get to the hospital faster.

"All right. What happened to her?"

Unlike all the other times she lectured me, I was interested in this story. My mother never talked about her high school days. My birth date was December 4, 2015. After I was born, she dropped out and received her general equivalency diploma in 2017. I didn't know much else about her past before those events. She didn't have yearbooks, and when I had her investigated, the website I'd paid sent me everything I'd already figured out.

The stream of vehicles in front of us slowed to a stop. Rush hour traffic. Mom throttled the gas and exited the highway. We were taking the back way to the hospital. At the top of the off ramp, she turned right and headed down the hill. Once we hit the straightaway, she continued with the story.

"This girl got involved with the wrong guy and lost her virginity on camera."

My skin flushed. People had become icons for having sex on camera, but I assumed that was not what happened to this chick. She agreed to it? Or she didn't know? The way Mom told it made me think the girl didn't know. Oh my God. A parent story I related to. "You watched it?"

Mom slapped the steering wheel. "No. Luce, you're missing what I'm saying. Be careful about who you associate yourself with. You stuck up for both of those boys, but when things hit the fan, did one of them stay and fight for you?"

We both knew the answer to her question though I didn't want to admit it out loud.

"You don't want a boy who won't fight for you." Her warm hand found mine on my lap. "You don't want anyone who won't fight for you. Do the right thing. Stay off the grid. Do you understand?"

I nodded. Do the right thing. Stay off the grid. Like I had much time left anyway.

CHAPTER TWO

We pulled into a parking spot at the emergency room entrance of the hospital. Dr. Keller was board-certified and one of the best oncologists on the East Coast. Of all the kinds of cancer I could have contracted, this one was a super rare and aggressive osteosarcoma. I'd been diagnosed in fifth grade, and I swear Mom cried for four days until her eyes dried out. I'd had all kinds of memories and mental pictures of her emotional disintegration over the years, but the one when I found her weeping on her knees to God stuck in my mind. He hadn't listened to her about healing me. Why, I wondered. Maybe He didn't listen because He didn't care.

My breath left my body as white smoke. Invisible icy daggers wormed between the buttoned gaps in my jacket and flew up my sweatshirt. Weather like this was common in November, and we often got snow. Last year, in 2028, we didn't use the heat until after my birthday. This year, we'd turned it on last night, which was three days before Thanksgiving.

Since I'd started chemo, I'd been affected by temperature drops. In the past, I'd loved drinking steaming hot green tea and sitting by our cobblestone fireplace. These days, I couldn't get warm by sitting in boiling water. Mom suffered along with me. She complained of joint soreness when the temperature dropped below fifty degrees, almost like she hadn't lived in weather like this all her life.

Right after we hustled into the red brick building, I experienced a lapse in time leading up to the actual operation. I'd told the doctors before about the memory gaps, but they waved them off as "anomalies or aberrations" and not a side effect of my treatment. I remembered entering the ER, Mom and her expensive peach-scented skin lotion, and her filling out forms on a tablet computer. That's all I recalled before they rolled me in a padded wheelchair back to a room.

I was asked to strip down to my panties and a gown. Soon, I was shivering in a full body X-ray. An injection in the bend of my arm to start an intravenous drip. Blackness.

When I awoke, I'd noticed Mom by the window jerking beneath a thin white blanket. The holovision played some sitcom where the little cute kid overacted every line. My chest felt like I'd dove onto a beehive. I wanted to pat where the incision was, but the clear bandage on top of it let me know that probably wasn't the best idea. Hopefully, my breasts were impressive enough to atone for the hideous pink scar on my light brown skin.

"Mom." I cleared my throat and called out with a little more strength. "Mom?"

She stirred and walked to my bedside. "Hey," she weakly sniffed. "How are you feeling?"

"Heavy," I responded. "Tired. Cold. *Buzzed*. Not that I remember what that feels like."

My wisecrack brought a smile to her face. She showed me a loose white tank top emblazoned with my favorite band on it and containing a shelf bra. "For when we leave."

Not a minute later, Dr. Keller came in to check on me. She was an older woman, late fifties, with a deep tan and crow's feet at the corners of her eyes. "How's the patient?"

Her thick Middle Eastern accent was always difficult for me to follow. "Itchy," I told her, "but otherwise, I'm good. Aren't you going to congratulate me?"

She and Mom shared a look. There was something I didn't know. "On what, exactly?"

Suddenly, I wasn't sure I should be smiling anymore. "I got my catheter out. That means no more chemo, right? Clean bill of health? Mets haven't grown...jump in any time here, Doc."

Dr. Keller opened a digital folder with my X-rays in them and projected them against the wall. Living X-rays always freaked me out. Your entire body was a beating, vibrating sculpture of blue bones of light and pulsating red organs. Tumors were black orbs. Where there used to be three or four small throbbing globes, I now counted sixteen all over my midsection. "Your cancer has progressed and spread," she said. "To your lungs, hips, ribs, and liver. I'm sorry."

The death sentence crushed what little happiness I'd conjured up over the past twenty-four hours. "So," I said, my voice broken. "You removed the Broviac because...there's nothing else you can do for me? Not the stem cell, immunotherapy...*nothing?*"

The doctor's brown eyes avoided mine. "Care from here on out would be palliative, to make you comfortable. Hospice in two or three weeks. Pain management at the end. Lucy — "

At the end. The end. My mother hugged me around the shoulders. I collapsed into her chest and sobbed. "I'm gonna die?" I repeated my question. "Like, I'm actually gonna die this time?"

Mom couldn't bring herself to lie to me, and she couldn't tell the truth. Instead, she cried with me and prayed in Spanish.

"Forgive me, Lord" was all I understood. Forgive her for *what?* He didn't prevent it, and He wouldn't take it away, so it might as well have come from Him, which was a reason why I didn't pray in the first place.

They might as well have been mumbling while discussing the options of my treatment. I didn't hear them beyond the sound of two different voices — one firm and the other shaky and high-pitched. When they finished, Mom helped me dress, and she set me back in the wheelchair. I followed wherever I was being led.

The trip through the white hallways reminded me of a maze, like the one on the back of children's menus in a restaurant. It did not matter how hard I tried to navigate those by myself. Even now, I'd still end up at a dead end by myself. I always needed help. Once someone started me on the right path, we'd finish it together. I guess that's what Mom and I would do now.

Outside, the midday air smacked me in the face and ran up my sweatshirt and tank top to my searing chest scar. We were outside, and my senses came back to me. The kind African-American nurse wanted me to wait for Mom to pull up in our silver Cougar, but I got up under my own power. Through blurry vision, I followed her to the vehicle and got in.

Mom handed me a tissue to blot my tears, started the ignition, and turned the heat on. We didn't move for a minute. I wondered why until I realized she wanted to talk. Since I'd been under the knife, she knew I couldn't run. The worst I could do was ignore her, and I didn't have the energy to be a jerk to her right now. "Go ahead. Say it."

"We'll find a way to beat this, Luce. Together."

How? She'd put me on a raw food and vegetable diet. We'd done surgery, chemo, radiation — nothing worked. There was no beating. I had a dozen and a half tumors, and I'd have reached into my body and ripped them off my organs and bones if it'd work. "I'm tired of ways that don't work, Mom. We did everything we were told to do, things we weren't told to do, and I'm still gonna die. Give it up. I have."

Mom faced the partially fogged-up windshield. She couldn't look me in the eye and tell me something different. I'd dropped truth.

"How long did he give me? When's my expiration date?"

"You're not a bottle of milk, Luce, you — "

I braced myself and watched her mouth for the answer. The words didn't come out. I read her lips. "Six weeks. We can't be sure. Maybe sooner."

I'd celebrate another Thanksgiving, my fifteenth birthday, and die before New Year's 2030. "I want to have a get-together, Mom. Tonight. At the house. Unchaperoned."

She didn't immediately answer. "You're hardly up for that."

"Please?"

"I'll stay downstairs in the theater. And you don't drink or smoke."

We shook hands.

From the transport, Mom called ahead to the house and had the cleaning lady come in and remove anything valuable from the ground floor for my "party." When we arrived, I freshened up in my bathroom. I couldn't shower or bathe until the clear bandages dissolved over my incision. Another case of the nervous sweats tonight and I'd start to smell bad fast. Would a sink bath kill me? I doubted it.

Dry parties sucked, but I'd convinced Natalee to bail on studying for an hour and to bring over some of her gifted classmates with no social lives. Anyone who'd attend. I'd ordered pizzas and we'd dance or play games. Lame, I know. Truth was, she was my only friend. Everyone else I suspected of making fun of me behind my back, including the people she hung out with. The only thing sadder than a girl dying of cancer at a dry party was one where nobody shows up.

Now what? I had a couple minutes to burn. Nothing meant anything to me. Holovision? Every minute I watched was sixty seconds I'd never get back. I had 3.62 million seconds to live, give or take, provided I dropped dead when Dr. Keller said I would. I didn't want to power nap. I'd lose that time, too. There were things I wanted to do, but I wasn't sure what they all were. Mom always liked to watch the sun rise and set — maybe we could do it from another country on the other side of the planet? Or, at least the West Coast. We'd never left the state, and when I'd ask why, she'd avoid answering me.

"We have each other, and everything we need right here," she'd say. "Why leave?"

I wasn't so sure about that anymore, and I didn't want to wonder what balmy weather was like at this time of year for the month and a half I had left.

At the edge of my room was a hand-carved rosewood storage case. In the bottom drawer was a pile of old school spiral notebooks I'd handwritten in. Mom called them "Wish Journals." The first time it looked like my cancer would be fatal, I started writing to the Make-A-Wish Foundation with the most outrageous things I could think of doing. Four wishes per page, front and back, for the entire year — practically the only thing I'd handwritten in years. There were three finished and the one I'd been writing in since New Year's 2029. I'd planned to burn them once I was given a thumbs-up by Dr. Keller.

With the time I had remaining, there was no way we could do all two thousand wishes before I died. "Maybe one," I convinced myself. I flipped open the cover of one. It smelled like a flowery perfume I used to spray all over myself. The first two wishes were to dance on stage with Justin Timberlake, which was weird because his son was my age and he stopped touring ages ago. The next two wishes were to kiss Billy Randall. I'd written my name with his last name a few times. *Lucy Randall.* Could I have been any more basic? He'd transferred schools after fifth grade, and I had no idea if he was hot anymore.

Without looking through them any further, I chose an older notebook with wrinkled pages and crooked handwriting and brought it to Mom's room. She was sitting on her bed, and when she saw me, she clapped her hands together to close the holographic browser display. Though her brown hair fell over her face and shielded it from me, I could tell she'd been weeping.

"What's up?" Her voice cracked, yet she pretended as if nothing was wrong.

I handed her the notebook. "Pick one."

Mom flipped through the wrinkled pages. The handwriting and number of words were the same on several different pages though it was too scribbly for me to read upside down. "Make-A-Wish does it, but they might need my help if it's crazy. Is it?"

I shrugged. "Don't know. I didn't look. That's why I wanted you to choose."

From the look on her face, Mom didn't believe me. "Right. You chose this book on purpose."

My eyes widened, and she slapped the cover shut before I could see what I'd wished for. "Totally random. Why? What is it? Justin Timberlake?"

Her bottom lip stiffened, like she was impressed with what I'd written. "No. No worries. I'll get started on it. What time are your friends coming?"

The time reading on the wall said 7:30 p.m. They were fashionably late. "Like now."

She tucked my notebook underneath her arm and stood. "I'd better get downstairs then. No drugs, no booze, no sex. Got it?"

"Why didn't you just say 'no fun'? It's less words."

Whenever I frustrated her, she responded by putting her hand on her forehead and rubbing it like a genie would pop out and grant her three wishes.

"I've never drank, and, despite what you may think, the closest I've gotten to sex was getting my butt grazed in the school hallway. Even if I got pregnant, I'd..." I wished I could've erased that last statement, so I didn't finish it. "What are you so worried about?"

"It's my full-time job." She patted me on the shoulder. "Have a not *great* time."

Five minutes later, Mom was safely in the finished basement and Nat was the first to arrive. We hugged, gently, as a full-body press would've hurt. She fingered the delicate gray-and-black-plaid scarf around her neck. "Done pacing?" she asked me.

My best friend could've charted my emotions. "For now. Where are the others?"

Natalee's lip twisted. Her expression said it all. "These others that you speak of..."

"None of them? Not even your secret boyfriend?"

She hushed me and patted her blouse down. "Father might've planted a bug on me. I only get an hour as it is."

Mr. Gupta wouldn't let her date, and he suspected she'd sneak behind his back. He didn't know what his perfect angel was capable of or what she'd already done.

"Anyway, I've got a little 'get well gift' in my bra for you," she told me. "Caught the dispensary right before it closed and bribed a guy on the way in."

Right then, my mood brightened. I grabbed her hand, and we ran upstairs. "Pizza will be here in ten. That's enough time."

Natalee rushed into my room and cracked the window. She handed me a poorly rolled cigarette and a lighter. "How did you get Elayna to vacate the premises?" she asked me.

I lit the slender stick, puffed hard enough to keep the cinders alive and burning, and passed it. The smoke warmed my body with a tingling sensation. "Here."

She held up her hand to refuse it. "Can't. I'll get killed coming home smelling like weed."

Another drag in, I came up with a brilliant idea. "Say you spilled something on your shirt. I'll wash and dry it. You can wear something of mine until it's done."

She gazed down at her black camisole and the white blouse she'd worn over it. "Nah. I had to wash and rinse three times before the scent left my hair last time. It's all yours."

An offer to smoke by myself? She didn't have to tell me twice. I heartily inhaled and only choked twice where she had to pat me on the back. My room felt hotter, bigger, and more circular. The carpet might as well be a fuzzy sponge. How far away was Natalee from me? A minute ago, I could've fingered her black French braid, and now she was ten miles away. Too far to reach out and touch.

"I'm dying, Nat," I said between hysterical giggles. "For real. I'm gonna die."

Her huffing meant she didn't believe me. I couldn't tell what Natalee was doing — crying, laughing, or floating in thin air. She fanned herself with a cancer wish notebook I'd left on my bed. "They removed the catheter. You're fine. They'll do the stem cell, and — "

"No. Like, I'll be dead. By December."

"Don't talk like that." Her words spun around like a blended smoothie in my brain. "And stop smoking. You're burning through it — "

My fingers tingled. "You said burning. Ha, ha."

" — and acting weird. You'll be here. Trust me."

"But what's *here?* Like here in this spot? Or everywhere? When you die, don't you go everywhere? Somewhere? Or nowhere. *Nowhere.* Where do you go? Do you know? Why am I rhyming so much?"

To me, Natalee's head stretched and expanded like a balloon. "This is the last time I buy you anything stronger than a multivitamin."

She confiscated the half-smoked cigarette from me, extinguished it on the sill, and threw it out of the window. I stumbled to the edge of my room to go after it, but she caught me before I could lift the window high enough to squeeze through. If my mother saw it in the bushes, she'd totally freak out. Or, the gardener would be happy.

"I jump out of this window and die tonight, I'm doing something with my life! I stay here, go to school, I'm doing nothing but what I'm expected to do. That's death every day, isn't it?"

Natalee squeezed me tight around the waist. I outweighed her by a good twenty pounds, but she'd positioned herself between me and the wall. "I hate it when you get like this."

Breathless, I brushed my hand through my hair and dropped to the floor in her arms. My heartbeat pounded up through my neck. I lightly patted my chest. The incision hadn't bled under my bandage. I was, however, sweaty and hungry. My armpits didn't stink, and I might be presentable in case a guy she invited came over and wanted to hook up. Who was I kidding? The guy I almost hooked up with was going to pass me around to another guys.

My best friend held me on the floor, and if she'd let go, I didn't know where I'd end up. I battled my emotions, and they won. I shook with uncontrollable sobs and collapsed on my rug. The soft fibers caught the wetness from my face. I was in no condition to party. I'd be better left alone. So, I lay in a half-fugue state and hoped she'd give up and abandon me. Her time had to be up soon. Natalee continued to comfort me anyway.

Another time lapse happened. I don't remember how I got in my bed and under the covers or how the delicious pepperoni taste got in my mouth. Natalee had left long ago. Mom was on top of the covers on my right with the pizza resting on the comforter. She was a neat freak. I'd seen her scrub a plastic shower liner once. She'd never have gone for me eating greasy Italian food anywhere in the house, much less in my bed, without a tarp and industrial cleaning spray nearby at any other time. Red sauce plus my clumsiness was a recipe for disaster.

Everything was different now. Say I broke a rule. What would she do, ground me? In weeks, I'd be a corpse. Who cared about rules and laws and things?

Aware of my cramping stomach, I wolfed down a pizza slice. I'd been eating raw food for months, and my body was not used to dairy or dough anymore. I could feel the revolt coming on hard. But it was worth the discomfort, and it wouldn't be fatal. It'd just feel that way.

"A half hour ago," she told me. "She said call or text her tomorrow. You can have your holo back although you have that base covered."

She'd found the temporary. "Okay," I said, almost choking on the bite I'd just swallowed. "Death sentences are a downer."

Eyes glued on the holovision display, she asked me straight up, "Was the weed good? This room smells like a gangsta rap concert. And, stop it with the spray. It doesn't help."

I sniffed my shirt, and the marijuana stench burned my nostrils. I'd passed out and forgotten to cover up what I'd done. "Ehh...kind of trippy. Sorry."

"Save me the 'for the pain' excuse. I didn't buy it the last three times, remember?"

I nodded out of respect. She was right.

Mom spoke slowly between chews. "There's no parenting manual. Especially single parenting. I know what the other moms say about me. 'Lucy's out of control,' and 'If she was my child, she wouldn't be acting out like this. I'd beat her like her mama should've.' Or, my favorite, 'It's because her father isn't around.'"

"You're special to him," she'd say. Yeah, I bet. Fourteen years and not one phone call, text message, or e-mail. But, I'm *special?* Sure.

"Your father...was my first love, and I was his. Everything after that...is *complicated.*"

Should I ask the obvious question — why tell me about him now? I decided not to for fear she'd stop talking and take it to the grave. Though I wasn't completely sure I wanted to hear the rest. I did turn my head and give her eye contact.

Mom measured her words. She'd have only one chance to tell me this story, and I'd memorize every syllable. "We thought there was no chance I'd end up pregnant because..."

I tried to control myself, but I cut her off. "Why not? What kind or protection did you use?"

She told the truth. "Nothing conventional."

"What does that mean? He..." I did a motion with my hand which she stopped.

"Can we start over?" she asked me. "There's a better way to tell this."

I tossed my chewed crust onto my bedspread, and it didn't even get a rise out of her. "Is there? Because all you've told me since I was born was that he's *alive*. I've had to assume the rest. He doesn't love me, he doesn't love you, and he doesn't want anything to do with us."

"That's not totally true, Luce. He loves you."

My stomach cramps took a back seat to the angry fire raging in my body. "He loves me?" Blood pulsed through my brain. "He's missed every holiday and birthday, and you're saying *he loves me?* Or you? Give it to me straight, Mom. I've heard worse."

She bit her lip. "You'll never forgive me."

I'd suspected the answer for a long time, and I'd force her to say it out loud. "'Never' is six weeks from now. Tell me."

Following a sigh, she confirmed one of my greatest fears. "He doesn't know you exist."

CHAPTER THREE

My father might've loved me and been there for the triumphs and awkward moments had he known I was on the planet. He'd *never* rejected me like she'd allowed me to believe. My entire life a thought nagged in the back of my mind. *He doesn't want me.* Nope. The person I'd trusted the most hadn't let me think differently.

"He doesn't know you exist" replayed in my mind on a steady loop. Nonexistence. Worse than death. With death, the certainty of life was there and then ceased to exist. Loss. But to him, whoever he was, wherever he was, I didn't exist. No gain. No loss.

A dull ache crept from the base of my neck up through my head. Though the throbbing was intense, I screamed, "Liar!" at her over and over until I heard my bedroom door shut.

I tossed off the covers and stumbled to my bathroom. I wretched until all that was left were groans. Then, I cleaned up and searched the house. Each room, every closet and imaginable hiding place. I'd driven her away by making her admit to the truth.

From my bedroom window, I noticed whitish-blue condensation drops on her transport windows. She hadn't driven it. No surprise there — the onboard computer had a tracking mechanism. "She walked out?" I said out loud. We lived in a safe neighborhood, but it was unlike her to go.

Later, she'd ask me for forgiveness. No. Heck no. I'd cling to my grudge like a death shroud, turn over in my casket, and die before letting go of what she'd done. I messaged Natalee: "You wouldn't believe what's going on over here."

Minutes passed and Nat hadn't responded. The time on my heads-up holophone display read 11:15 p.m. in large, blue script letters. Made sense. Mr. Gupta switched on their cell dampener at ten p.m. By morning, my emotions would be higher. Tonight was one of a million times I'd wished she'd hacked his system. She had the know-how. Computer science was her pre-high school pathway, and she'd never gotten an A-minus in her life.

I fought off sleep for as long as I could but lost the battle sometime in the middle of the night. Next thing I knew, my virtual clock's morning sun pried my eyes open. In the night, I'd forgotten to set the automated window's glass tint from opaque to blackout. No sense in doing it now.

In the sweatshirt and leggings I'd worn last night, I wandered downstairs to the kitchen. I'd heard movement there, and our cleaning lady wouldn't have arrived this early. Unless someone had broken in the house to cook, my mother was fixing breakfast. Pancakes and sausage from the smell of things. A full pot of strong-smelling coffee had been brewed, and a bowl of fresh fruit lay on the counter. What was this, a dream sequence on a freaking holovision sitcom? She'd untied my life last night and left me holding the strings. But I *was* hungry.

I sampled a plump strawberry from the bowl. The gush of cold, sweet tartness over my tongue whet my appetite for more. Two pineapple chunks and a few red grapes later, the refreshing sweet taste overcame the initial sourness. My thoughts overwhelmed me.

"He doesn't know I'm alive." The whiny hollow in my voice made me want to claw out my throat. My mother, the one who advised me not to chase a boy who wouldn't fight for me, never rang the opening bell for my father to leave his corner and swing.

Suddenly, my hatred for her reached another level. The life I had left had been turned upside done. What would a nutritionally balanced breakfast do for me? Nothing to the slow simmer between us. Not until I got answers. I repeated myself. "He doesn't know I'm alive."

"Lucy..."

"Does he?"

"No."

Her canary blouse ruffled as she poured batter into the skillet and waited for its skin to bubble.

My response was a colorful description of what she could do to herself for lying. I'd never used that level of profanity in front of her, and I half-expected a knife thrown at my head for it. Instead, she hardly broke motion and replied, "Let's try this again. Good morning, Luciana. Your bowl of fruit is on the counter. Kale smoothie in the fridge."

"Morning. *Liar.*"

"Luciana...*ponte algo de ropa.* Curse again and see what happens."

For a second, I thought she was commenting on my outfit. "I *am* dressed. You'd know that if you could look me in the face, *liar.*"

Mom turned around. "I'm gonna say this again in English so you understand. On all that is holy, you call me a liar one more time, you'll need Murdoch and five more cops bigger than him to pull me off you. Now, eat your freaking fruit."

Message received. I dialed it down. "How do you plan to erase fourteen years of lies?" I didn't call her a liar. "All the times I asked you about him. Remember what you said?"

I'd asked about his absence on a community playground once. Three-year-old Lucy wondered why the other girls had a dude helping them up the slide and she didn't. At eight, Lucy and her mom were in line for an animated movie. *Where was he?* she asked her. Every time the response was the same.

"Let me remind you what you said." My voice, unsteady and loud, wavered. "I ask, and you say 'He's not interested.' That was a lie, w-wasn't it?"

Avoiding my eyes, she crossed her arms and turned her back to me.

What was the truth? She was going to tell me. Here. Now. "Don't you think I deserve to know the truth?"

The clink of knife and fork continued against her plate. "Yes and no."

I bit my lip. "Not this time. Give me better. You owe me better."

She swallowed whatever food she'd chewed and resumed cooking. She cracked, seasoned, and scrambled two eggs. An egg hadn't passed my lips in months. What was she going for or trying to do by making actual food in front of me? Make me jealous? Temper my raging fury with breakfast? She could try but stuffing my guts into submission would get her nowhere.

"Your wish...the one from the book...is to meet your dad. It'll have to wait until the plane."

My next swallow of pineapple stuck in my throat. I choked it down. "Plane? To...I'm not going anywhere with you. Not without an answer. Can I even fly? As a matter of fact, I..."

Mom held up her hand to choke off my protests. "We're going to see him. Today."

Meet my dad? Right. Maybe she'd introduce me to a light-skinned guy with good hair and a murky nationality but not my actual parent. What a nice ironic sentiment. Living the last bit of my life, and *now* I get to meet him? Who *is* he? Or, better yet, who am I?

"When?"

"Flight is at eleven. Four hours, cross-country."

"East? Where is he *exactly?* And keep the answers short, please."

She fried the last pancake, turned off the stove, and slapped in onto a plate. Didn't take long for my will to break. I stole it and crammed it into my mouth. Hot and doughy cinnamon heaven.

"When you walked into my room last night, I was trying to locate him through the one person I know who can find him. Truth is, I lost track of them both years ago."

Okay, so that's why she pulled down the display so fast. My clammy fingers tightened around the kitchen island's marble surface as I munched on cantaloupe. "This is too important for guesswork. Give me his name. I'll find him. I've got websites I've bookmarked..."

"Neither of them lives under their given names. Your father hasn't for years."

The suspense tightened my insides. Screw the raw food diet. Figuring all of this out called for a pancake rolled around two sausage links with a syrup pocket in between. "Why?" I mumbled. "The hiding I mean."

She responded with "Chew before you swallow, please. All the answers are coming."

The constant questions and molasses-fast responses slowed my stress eating. As I inhaled my makeshift sandwich, my imagination ran wild. Okay, so he was what, a holovision star? Movies? An athlete? Millionaire who likes his space?

Criminal?

Mom forked a bite of pancake into her mouth and fixed me a decent plate of food. I'd eat everything she'd intended for herself and not pretend I was full to avoid the stares. I'd sip some coffee, too, and obsess more over my father and what kind of person he was.

"It's not a hunch. I know where my guy will be. Pack light, cool, and comfortable for three days or so."

Before I headed upstairs, I issued a warning. "By the way, I haven't forgiven you."

She lowered her head. I think she wasn't asking me to.

As I washed up, I mentally pictured him based on my face and body. My skin was about the shade of caramel. He's not white. Maybe African-American or interracial. The natural thread-like wavy texture of my hair had to have come from somewhere African. I straightened it for manageability. Couldn't be too tall. On my tiptoes, I was five-foot-five and close to eye level with Mom.

Her people were Central American. Apparently, women from there had pear shapes and fiery tempers. I had curves — hips, boobs, thighs. My anger was another thing. I'm a pressure cooker with no release valve. And what was with the pancakes? She'd always tell me to watch the carbs. Might as well fatten me up. A couple extra pounds in my problem spots wouldn't make the coffin weigh any more. Or the urn. I hadn't decided yet.

I layered a white cloth gauze pad between my old catheter incision and my bra, threw on a black long-sleeved shirt, and wiggled my way into a pair of tight ripped black jeans. I packed a small gray suitcase which would fit a couple days' worth of clothes in it. Beyond that, Mom would have to buy me outfits unless we were going to a place where we could do laundry.

"Where out west?" I thought aloud. Vegas? Utah? Washington? She hadn't said, and since airline companies had switched to advanced biometric scans for ticketing, I wouldn't know until we left. The airport was half an hour's drive away, and we needed an hour or so for screening, which didn't leave me a lot of time to investigate. I'd do an internet search on the drive instead.

Mom met me in the foyer in her amber Zara Hristoff designer sunglasses that cost a fortune and she'd never let me touch. The purple rolling bag next to her foot would fit in an overhead compartment, which meant she'd packed about what I'd had. Contrary to what I'd hoped, wherever we were going, we wouldn't be there for long.

But if she thought I'd meet the man I'd ached to see long as I could remember and leave him that quickly, she'd been mistaken. He'd ask to hold my cold, stiff hand while I took my final breath should I have my way, and I'd have allowed him to.

"Why are you looking at me like that?"

Being as I couldn't see my expression, I had to ask. "Like what?"

"Never mind."

"You okay?"

After unlocking the front door, she turned and said over her shoulder, "Why wouldn't I be?"

"He's your first love, right? Seeing him again can't be easy," I said to her back. "He's probably moved on."

A reminder she hadn't. When was the last time she had a date or a guy she was interested in? Had to be a year or more. And none of them stuck around long.

Mom opened the front door. "Set the alarm, and let's go."

I accessed the keypad and got out in time. We loaded our luggage into our transport's trunk and took off for the city airport. Mom turned on her annoying thrash music, and I played mine in my audial comms since she'd given back my holo.

"Plane leaves in two hours, right?"

"Uh-huh," she confirmed. "About that."

I checked the airport departure times on the web although I did not know the airline. Website after website. Turned out, there were a hundred planes going west and to various parts of the coast from the airport and dozens around noon.

Frustrated, I slapped my holo against my thigh and directed my attention to the orange digital traffic signs. We'd passed the exit for the airport miles ago.

Where are we going?

I pointed to the next highway exit. "We need to turn around."

"First, we make a quick stop. I'm getting makeup work for you."

Without warning, sharp, stirring pains hit my belly. Oh God! The decision to eat real food was coming back on me. I was going to lose it. Maybe it was not a vomit kind of morning, I hoped. "Why?" I asked her. "You heard Dr. Keller. I'm...why work for grades that won't matter?"

After shutting my eyes, I clutched my stomach, and I only wished for death to come twice. The mild shake of the transport didn't help with keeping the bile down. Deep slow breaths. Electric threads stretched from my wound into my chest and forced me into coughing spasms. At least, the revolt quieted above my waist. Though now, I wished I'd worn loose pants instead of skinny jeans. I'd been sicker and lived through it. But this was a heck of a way to die.

Mom's strong hand wrapped around mine. "You are going to bury *me*," she said. "Got it? It's not the other way around. You pick a nice day, find a high cliff over an ocean, and spread my ashes."

"Sure, Mom." Whatever got her to stop talking about death. He'd claim me soon enough, and I doubted she'd die in the next month.

The amount of time it took to park gave our location away. *Penn Middle School.* I opened my eyes. Forget about the bitter taste in my mouth or the clamminess between my thighs and under my armpits. Looking half as bad as I felt meant I'd become a social media icon again and not in a good way.

Regardless, I pried my body out of the transport, right leg first. Could I move on my own? I didn't have to — Mom pulled me forward with strength I didn't know she possessed. My body weight coupled with her force almost pitched me forward onto the parking lot. I steadied myself, used Mom's arm for leverage, and put one foot in front of the other. We reached the curb. Climbing it and the gray concrete steps might as well have been scaling the Alps.

"You can do it, *Mariposa,*" she said to me. "Five more steps."

She spoke Spanish now because she wanted to inspire me. Math homework, science problems, anything I struggled with. *Mariposa.* "Butterfly." Things might be easier if I could spread my wings, let the wind raise me up, and drift to the top of the stairs like a blue monarch. I'd be there. With the ability to fly, where couldn't I go? What then could keep me from finding my father? In my mind, it was settled. I'd have to grow some wings and fly away.

Mom steered me into the front office. While she gathered work that I'd ignore, I lingered next to the maroon leather chairs they intended to be comfortable. The old cushions with frayed edges were more rigid than soft. The administration used them as a pre-sentencing staging area for suspension students or potential new hires.

The front office secretary, a pleasant woman, with an aqua blue button-down sweater, approached the intercom system to call for a student. "Excuse the interruption, can you please send Bryce Parrish to the office?"

That name...*Bryce Parrish.* Who was he? Did I know him? Natalee wouldn't answer her holo, and I had no one else to text to pass the time, so I waited. Soon enough, I saw an athlete in a school jacket through the glass window. The spindly physique, tanned complexion, and bushy brown hair were familiar. It was "the" guy from my video. He'd lied about his age, too! He didn't see me until he passed the counter and dropped his body into a seat on sentencing row.

I waved my hand. "Hey."

Bryce glanced my way twice. Long enough for me to see a hint of recognition on his face. Yup. I'm *her*. The girl from the place between the schools or whatever the kids called me behind my back these days.

"What are you in for, Bryce Parrish?"

He didn't say a word or cop to anything he'd done. I wouldn't have either. You never knew who could be watching. But that was higher-level thinking for his knuckle-dragging people. He'd talk. I just hadn't found his pull string or the button on his chest yet.

"It's cool. Making small talk while I wait for makeup work. You remember me? I'm — "

"Whatever you thought," he said. "No. Stop talking to me."

I hated being interrupted, especially by nonsense. "Look, Bry. Trying to be nice here. I'm Lucy. The girl — "

"From the video. Video girl. Real sloppy kisser. Why didn't we do it a month ago? I mean, it's not like I couldn't have had you then, right?"

Small-time insults, to be sure, but they silenced me. Granted, he was higher up on the social food chain than me. Who did he think he was? Middle school athletes weren't exactly a commodity. Who was Bryce Parrish to make me feel this way? Truth was, I would've had sex with him. Not because he deserved my virginity. I had six weeks left to live and, short of handing out homemade tickets into my pants, my options not to die a maiden were limited.

The cracks in the office's white linoleum weren't wide enough to hide me. I'd have run out screaming if I had the stamina to make it to the entrance. Meanwhile, Bryce popped his gum, and the secretary glued herself to her computer screen. Neither of them could be bothered by the pool of sweat I was becoming before their eyes. My feet rooted themselves to the floor. I wanted to curse him and say how wrong Bryce was about me, but my trembling upper lip and stiff limbs wouldn't cooperate.

Bryce blew a lime green gum bubble. Satisfied he made his point, he left me alone.

The secretary called out, "The principal will see you now, Bryce."

On his way past me, he tripped on my outstretched foot. Everyone in the office had a laugh at his expense, including me. He cursed, and I imagine that would become part of his crimes.

As if on cue, Mom reentered with a handful of assignments. "You okay Luce?"

I'm sweaty. Hot. Sticky. Destroyed. "Yeah."

Exiting down the stairs would be considerably easier than going up. My symptoms had largely gone away, and I started to feel like myself again. The tingling at my neck helped me ignore the dizziness. What did you know? Bryce was good for something after all. Adrenaline.

Mom edged me away from the entrance. "Education is important. Remember that. One more stop in here."

By the direction her head bobbed, she wanted to visit my locker. "C'mon. That's a city mile from here. I'll get winded before the exit sign. Nat can bring over whatever is in there."

"Catch your wind. You'll need your transcripts."

Mom wasn't going to be deterred, and my books and transcripts weren't what concerned me. The locks opened for three people — me, an administrator, and a parent. She was the only one on record, and one day, I knew her access would bite me in the butt. This morning, apparently, was the one for butt biting. She'd see the writing, and I'd have to explain.

"Wait," I said to her. Mom always walked like a bill collector was chasing her with Ordnance. My pulse quickened as I tried to keep up. "Mom, wait!"

She didn't stop until she'd found my locker. How did she know it was mine? The red "CG" scrawled inside of a diamond must've given it away. I read her eyes. The backstory was simple, cut and dried. A guy vandalized the outside of my locker, hacked my biometric lock, and scrawled all sorts of colorful and inventive phrases about me on the inside.

"CG? For 'Cancer Girl'?" She chuckled. "Aww, c'mon. That doesn't even take effort."

The transaction didn't take long. I watched her get my scripts for classes I'd never attend. What was the point?

Hope? Faith? Mom had plenty of both. I had neither. She handed me my work and started walking.

"It's not always all about what you take, Luciana. Focus on what you leave behind."

CHAPTER FOUR

Once we left school and sped up the highway, I had no idea where we were going. Mom sensed my confusion and broke in with "Not going to International. I chartered a jet — "

"Wait, a *jet?*"

"From municipal. Last minute. We'll get West much faster."

A jet though? We were comfortable money-wise, sure, but we had *jet-level charter money?* Hmm. I'd have had to ask her to discover our location. Private jets had unpublished flight schedules. "I should've asked you for a bigger allowance than a hundred units a week."

"Could've." She sipped from her metal coffee cup. "Wouldn't have gotten it."

"Where are we going — exactly?"

She set the transport's autopilot, removed her black leather gloves, squeezed a small bottle of her expensive white lotion into her palms, and rubbed it in. "A place not far from my hometown. Small farming town called Walsh."

Another lie by omission. My mother *was* from the West Coast, and... "My father's a *farmer?*"

She repositioned herself in her seat and slipped her gloves back on. "Not at all." She laughed. "Visiting an old friend. He'll take us to him."

"An old friend who's a *farmer?*"

Every kid without a father around wanted him to be somebody important: wealthy, smart, sophisticated. Able to do the impossible without breaking a sweat. Obviously, my dad was all of this rolled together. Not some bum who spent a night or two with my mom and split like I'd once thought. That's why she'd never told me about him — she couldn't. This bit of background didn't do much to soothe the echoing emptiness inside me.

The autopilot parked us in the economy lot. We unloaded our bags and followed the displays pointing to a series of metal and concrete hangars. The walking got to me. "Charter a jet, but you can't cough up enough units for first-class parking?" I asked her. "You have handicap priority, so I *don't* have to walk."

Sounding a bit winded herself, she said, "Cougar won't get scratched there, and it's exercise...for the both of us."

I wasn't sure if "us" meant "you." I'd be dead soon. Exercise wouldn't change that fact.

The beige metal overhang painted with a black number five did nothing to shield us from the frigid temperature. Mom had her leather trench coat and insulated gloves on. I wished I had worn a thicker coat and gloves. My hand joints ached like they had been tapped with sharp, tiny hammers.

With my bag in hand, I followed Mom along the back side of a shiny white-, blue-, and gold-painted jet. The strong, fresh fuel scent stung the inside of my nose. I can be like a superstar for a day, I thought, or for a few hours until I met my dad.

A guy in pressed, navy blue slacks and a matching wool vest exited the jet and approached us. Carrying a black leather briefcase with gold locks, he saw Mom, and his face brightened. Great. Did he recognize my mother or want to sleep with her? This should be fun.

"Good morning, Miss Sandoval." His eyes took her in from head to toe. "Ready for warmer weather? Clear skies today for our flight together."

He's not the first guy to hit on her in front of me. Mom was beautiful in a way I would never be with her slender waist and her shoulder-length, straight brown hair that didn't frizz or flip at the top and refuse to lie down like mine did. Her appearance was always super glued together. Men loved her. Though she claimed she hated the attention, secretly, I think she *loved* it.

Mom pointed to her sunglass lenses with her index fingers. "Focus up, guy. My body didn't pay for the flight."

"Of course." He pointed at her and mentioned the name of a city I'd never heard of. "It's just...I was thinking...where you're headed...I grew up out there. You went to North High, right? Frank Moses, class of '19. Do you remember me?"

I laughed to myself. A black guy named Frank with a gap-toothed smile that bright? He must've gotten bullied. A lot. In fact, I would've bullied him myself.

She tucked her brown snakeskin handbag underneath her arm and checked the time on her digital timepiece. Frank annoyed her. Me, too. "I got my GED. I didn't graduate high school."

"Because she was pregnant with me," I chimed in.

"But you didn't go to high school at some point. North High?"

Maybe I didn't notice it as much before, but she had a way of answering questions without answering them, and he'd totally called her on it. But I was getting annoyed with his flirty conversation. "Can you just go ahead and scan us, dude?" I asked him. "We gotta go."

His fingers trailed a design on the glass of his computer. "I've found that conversation breaks up the uncomfortable silences while technology does what it does. Good enough." He snapped his fingers like it kick-started the memory in his brain. "Don't worry — Moses'll take you to the Promised Land."

He bugged me and not because of the corny catchphrase.

"Your name is Luciana, but you like to be called Lucy? Cute."

Nicknames, as far as I knew, weren't on our virtual files or credentials. Color me creeped out. And I thought he'd curb the questioning and small talk. "Yeah, so..."

"You know how everybody in the world must have a twin? Then, your mom's lookalike went to a place called North High with me. That girl was chunky, black hair longer than yours, hung out with a weird crowd. Her name was — "

Mom snatched the tablet from his hand. She'd had enough and was a tick away from cursing him out in Spanish. Her thumbprint against the reading plate turned the entire screen red. She handed the thing back so fast I was surprised Frank didn't fumble it more than he did.

"There seems to be an error with your computer," she told him. "Says 'no record'."

"Right. It couldn't possibly be you. My apologies. Let me reset."

He swiped down a screen, keyed a code, and presented it with a full handprint outline. "Try this. Sometime the system kicks out fingerprints. The full print reads better."

Mom hesitated before pressing her full hand against the screen. Again, it beeped with an error message.

"Uh-oh," he said with a nervous laugh. "Maybe it *is* you. One more error and it'll flag you for fraud. You won't be able to fly on anything, chartered or not, for six months."

My blood froze. This wasn't happening. *Six months? I had six weeks.* "Mom?"

Her voice quavered. "Can't do it by my retina?"

Frank wagged his finger and clicked his tongue. "No. Municipal has *two-step* verification. Without the fingerprint, it won't proceed to the retinal scan unless we do a full biometric."

There's no way she'd have consented to that. A biometric pulse would give Frank access to her physical history from broken bones to the duration of her last recorded menstrual period, and it would compare it to her medical history records for identification. Totally invasive concept, but since the government passed the law, terrorism on US incoming and outgoing flights had disappeared.

While he called into the plane, Mom whispered, "Mantén la calma" to me. I was calm enough. She wasn't, though, and I didn't know why.

"People book private flights because they think the security will be lower and they can sneak things through inspection: drugs, weapons. Is this your first private flight, Ms. Sandoval?"

Mom's icy stare meant I shouldn't say much. "First in a while."

"Excellent. Excuse me for a minute. I need another flight crew approval for a manual override. No need to be nervous since neither of you has anything to hide."

My mother swiped her bangs with her finger as Frank disappeared into the plane. That's when I noticed tiny sweat beads framing her brow.

"Are you okay?"

She turned away from the plane. "Stop talking. Get your bag. We need to go."

Did she switch my cancer meds with illegal drugs? *"Go?* What are you talking about?"

"I'll explain at home. Move!"

No. She'd explain right here. I crossed my arms. "We're not doing anything wrong. Are we?"

Following a strong sigh and a pause, she offered me no more of an explanation. "We need to go, Luciana."

"No."

"Now!" She said it like our lives depended on my obedience.

"I'm going to Walsh, with or without you."

Mom lunged at me and grabbed my arms. Frank's voice got closer. He'd be back soon. "Can't you do what I ask once without question?"

Not this time.

She dug into her handbag and squirted more lotion into her palms. The hangar was an ice cube. Could she even feel her hands to know they were dry? Maybe the brand was the warming kind?

Before I could ask for some for myself, Frank reappeared. After he finished conversing with a woman on the plane, he disembarked down the jet bridge and beckoned us to the edge of the staircase. Mom quickly tucked away the bottle back into her bag, as if moisturizing her hands was a criminal offense. This time, when Frank handed her the tablet, she did the handprint scan and it worked without issue.

"Funny," he said. "That's technology for you. Lift your glasses for the retinal, please."

She did so, and after a second, the scan confirmed her identity as Elayna Maria Sandoval. My scans went off fast with no problem.

"This is your only daughter?" he asked Mom while he finished scanning my eyes. "No other children?"

"Uh-huh. Why?"

He winked at her. "No trying for a boy?"

Mom said an angry Spanish phrase I couldn't translate. "Stay out of my uterus, okay, Frank? Thanks."

Hand up, he apologized. "Sorry. Especially to you, Luciana." He said my name with wonder like it was magical. "Following protocols. And call me Moses."

I saluted him and headed to the jet bridge alongside my mother. "Whatever."

"You have your mother's eyes," he said from behind me. "Brown. Beautiful. Soft like cotton. History behind them. Flecks of pain."

Why was he saying all of this? Was he buttering me up to get to her? "You know your adjectives," I said without breaking stride. "You got all that from a retinal scan?"

"Look in anyone's eyes long enough and you can see exactly who or what they are."

His words brought me enough discomfort to stop moving. There was a point he was trying to make. I was missing it. That was, until I heard the click of a cocked Ordnance.

"Your mom ever say you look like your father? Around the cheeks and chin."

My heartbeat stuttered. The chill from the air and the echo in the hangar faded away. Too afraid to move, I said, "You know my father, Moses? What he looks like? What's his name?"

I watched my mother with my peripheral vision. Over the years, I'd seen the range of her emotions. Every response was constant, almost rehearsed. When her nose flared, she was angry. Rolled her eyes? Annoyed. I'd never seen her this twitchy. This guy had a convincing bluff, or he knew my dad, and she'd gotten nervous about the information she'd thought he'd disclose.

Pointing my finger at him, I asked the obvious. "How does he know my father?"

"How do I know him, Elayna?"

Her face was expressionless stone. "He doesn't. Not personally, anyway." She placed her handbag atop her rolling suitcase, held her hands up in surrender, and slowly turned. I mimicked her actions with my own bag. "How many units are you being paid to keep us here?" she asked him. "I'll double it."

Moses aimed the silver Ordnance at her heart. I'd never seen a firearm up close before. Shiny. Boxy. Longer than I thought. Guys at school talked about wielding handheld Ordnance, but the way I figure, the ones who had one weren't really talking about it.

My mouth dried. Fear clotted in my chest. A relaxed finger on a shiny curved piece of metal was all that kept us alive. Mom seemed fearful. Not for her well-being but for mine.

"He knows you're alive, you know, always did," Moses laughed. "You want to stay that way? Turn around and go home."

Another gut punch. One more lie she'd told me. I didn't have everything I needed here, like she'd said. There was more, and this psycho wasn't going to keep me away from my father.

Mom's shoulders sagged. "My daughter is dying. Fly us to Walsh. Let me talk to him, face to face."

He pointed the firearm at me. *"Bone cancer?* Little young for that, isn't she?"

How did he know? And what, was I supposed to have gotten it later in life?

"Walk away, Elayna. Let her die. I'll pretend you never tried to leave in the first place."

"Can't happen," she replied. "She'll meet her father. I'll fly her myself if I have to."

"You? *Fly?*" Moses slid his thumb on the side of the Ordnance. According to all the holoshows I'd ever seen, he'd done so to switch the power to its kill setting. "Okay then."

Lip trembling, I interrupted them. "Are you going to...kill us?"

Moses holstered his weapon. "You said *twice* what he's paying me. Right, 'Elayna'?"

"Absolutely. Half now. Half when we get to Walsh."

The suggestion of flying to a cornfield town amused him more than it did me. Moses's exchange with my mother was frustrating. They spoke in enough generalities to be confusing to anyone else but themselves. Each time he said my mother's name, it was like he mocked her, and I started to think the "him" they talked about was the guy who could point us in the direction of my father. Why would he pay someone to keep us from traveling?

Swallowing my questions wasn't easy, so once we docked our bags on the plane, listened to the emergency instructions, and buckled up, I started a handwritten list. *What is my father's name? What is your name? Is he African-American or mixed? Where are you from? Where is our family from? Were you in love with my father? Is Luciana Sandoval my real name?"* The list continued. *"What did Moses mean by bone cancer already? Who is going to find my father? Who died and left us that kind of money?"*

And who is she?

Sitting across from me, Mom must've noticed my dedication. "What are you doing?"

"Writing." I realized my answer was more sarcastic than I meant it to be. Keeping my hand steady as we taxied was even more difficult. "Coming up with questions to ask you so I don't forget them."

"Hmm. Looks like a decent start. Can I see?"

I continued with my list. "I'm not done. I don't know if I ever will be."

While Moses and his assistant prepared for us to fly, Mom placed her hand on my knee and glanced at my list, which was numbered in the high teens. "Still going?"

By question twenty, I ran out of gas. The list was comprehensive. I handed it over.

"The name." She spoke under her breath and removed her hand from my leg.

I reminded her of her promise to give me answers once we were on the plane. Aside from the unintended wrinkling of her nose bridge, there was no way I could tell if she was telling the truth.

Even though Moses and his accomplice were out of earshot, she lowered her voice to a whisper. "Anibel."

"What?"

"Oh God, Lucy, I'm not saying it again. Not even your father knew my real first name."

Anibel? Who names their kid Anibel in the twentieth century? "Tell me no one ever called you that."

"Only your grandmother Ruby and only when I was younger. I wish you could've met her." Mom dabbed a cocktail napkin underneath her shades. "I went by Rhapsody."

Rhapsody. Okay, what? My mouth and the mouths of the butterflies of my stomach dropped open. "S-she's dead?"

"Don't know." She sniffed and blotted her nose with the napkin's corner. "She's not where I left her."

"Which was?"

"Panama."

"Grandma liked to party?" I liked this game of "truth or truth" with my mother. Forcing her hand and making her uncomfortable entertained me. Like spinning a hamster wheel with the hamster running in it or throwing imaginary balls into a field for a dog to chase.

"It's where she's from — where the Martinezes are from. You're a fourth Panamanian and a fourth Cape Verdean. Your dad is African-American. That's the other half."

This was the longest conversation we had had in months. The most honest one, too. Not once had she told me a lie or the convenience of an omitted truth. I'd have to web search Cape Verdean. Neither of us noticed Moses approach us from the cabin with a tablet computer. "Wire me two million units."

Brushing her hair behind her ears, Mom said, "I said half now. Half later."

He steadied himself from our latest turn and pushed the computer toward her. "You also said *twice* what he was paying me. Two million."

I had to know. Would he tell me? "Who's he? And whoever 'he' is, he's cheap."

Moses showed his gapped teeth. "You're not ready to know, sweetheart. Two million, or we turn this thing around."

Two million units was more money than I'd see in two lifetimes. After a few authorizations, the deed was done.

"Thanks. Ruby."

Ruby? She'd faked my grandmother's identity? God, every time I got one question answered, five more popped into my brain.

Moses happily returned to his seat at the front of the jet. He was a millionaire. Four hours later, he would have doubled his take. What was his deal, anyway? Okay, but, like, what do extortionists do for a day job? He didn't strike me as a minimum-wage kind of dude. He had Ordnance stashed under his suit jacket. I wasn't the swiftest person in the world. Tackling and disarming him was out of the question. What could Mom do? Was she hiding any secret fighting skills?

Mom gasped at the brief turbulence. "Don't like flying?" I asked her.

"Haven't done it in ages," she groaned.

The rising sensation thrilled me like a roller coaster climbing toward the sky. Nerves on a first flight were normal, but this? My skin was fever-hot, and my eyes burned no matter how much I blinked to produce tears. Even worse, the quarter-sized circular vent above us did nothing to blast away the warmth radiating throughout my body. Could human beings melt? I might be close to finding out over the next several hours.

Once we were established in the air, I heard a thunderous roar and sniffed a troubling burnt smell. I continued to wonder and clutched the armrests until my fingers numbed. My questions remained inside me with their answers barely an arm's reach away. How did Mom maintain her cool in this luxurious deathtrap? What was she thinking? What would she say next? I didn't know my father's name. Should have started with that question. And where to find him — Walsh? Do I shout in a cornfield until an African-American guy with my chin and cheeks responds?

I yelled until my face tingled and veins bulged in my neck. "Mom!"

She rolled her head in my direction, nonchalantly, like I'd asked her for a piece of gum. The plane was in obvious distress, and she couldn't be bothered? I tried reading her lips. "Lucy?" she asked me. "You all right?"

The cords in my throat strained. "What's his name?"

"Huh?"

"What is my father's name? Need to know before I die!"

Mom opened her mouth and bared her teeth and, in slow motion, said his name. The jet shook and yawned too much for me to understand what she said. She repeated his name. What was she saying? Did it start with a G or J?

The jet moaned and crunched near the entrance door, like a giant hand had wrapped around it and squeezed. My pulse throbbed in my ears. The in-flight instructions covered a crash in the ocean. Grab the seat and float. That much was simple. Not whatever was happening. The seat cushion didn't have wings, and the inflatable slide would be a useless air sock. At this height, I'd be sucked out and land somewhere over the mountains.

An orange flame exploded from the cabin door and blew it off the hinges. The resulting vacuum sucked Moses and his cohort out into open air. I remembered in the Bible Moses never led his people to the Promised Land, and now, he wouldn't take me to mine.

Yellow masks dropped from the jet's roof. Mine smacked me in the head twice before I was able to pull it over my face. At my left, Mom hadn't used her mask. In fact, she seemed fine. Almost unbothered. She unbuckled her seat belt and knelt in front of me. How had the current, which had ripped the flight crew out, not done the same to her?

She embraced me. I wrapped my arms around her back and squeezed with everything I had. Our last embrace. I needed more time. But I didn't have it. My questions would go unanswered, at least on this side. On the other side, who knew? Whatever or whoever was there might have mercy on me.

I did the sign of the cross with my right hand and said as much of the Hail Mary prayer as I could remember, including the end: "Mother of God, pray for us sinners, now and at the hour of death. Amen."

My life's moments didn't flash before my eyes the way I expected them to. Instead, every thought in my mind had to do with regret. I'd spent the past three and a half years fighting a disease I couldn't defeat. I'd clashed with my mother over many things and won by submission. Would I get an after-death trophy or championship belt?

Deafening gusts of wind whipped at my face like a fleet of belts. I forced my eyes shut. Whatever came next, I didn't want to watch. "Goodbye," I whispered into Mom's shoulder.

She unlatched my lap belt, and the next thing I knew, my world turned cold and soundless.

CHAPTER FIVE

I woke up with a gasp. Before I could spit out the nauseating blood taste, a pair of fingers swabbed the inside of my mouth dry. Straps at my wrists held me down against a flat, forgiving surface — a bed?

The last thing I remembered was an explosion brighter than a thousand suns.

How had I gotten here?

I opened my eyes to a dizzying blender of blinding lights, and I quickly shut them. By cracking my eyelids open and then slowly lifting them, I could focus. My head and ears burned and stung, and the second I tried to talk, the steel wool sensation in my throat made me wish I hadn't tried. This wasn't death. That much was for sure. Hell would've hurt more.

A shadow resembling my mother's shape hovered over my face and spoke. The voice's harmony matched hers, but I couldn't be certain. Being thrown out of an airplane didn't improve my already horrible lip-reading skills. A minute later, a white sign with black print appeared with a little of Mom's handwriting on it. I squinted to read it.

"Hi," it read. "We're safe. Rest."

A stiff, sharp object pricked my arm. Darkness.

Whatever had happened to me, I recalled staring into bright whiteness. My right cheek sank into the softest pillow, I think, I'd ever slept on. The pain in my skull had changed from agony to a heavy, grinding ache. I'd been out, asleep or drugged.

In any case, I surveyed my surroundings. I mentally took note of a window with simple tan curtains muffling the sunlight. Three or four feet in front of me was a round, wooden table littered with used white Styrofoam plates and cups. Based on the number, we must have been here for a day or more. On either side of the table were matching chairs. I'd never been inside of a room so retro and simply decorated.

"Mom?" My voice sounded worn and ragged, but at least my hearing had returned.

She stuck a cup near my face and angled the red and white straw into my mouth. "Try not to talk much."

That was not a promise I could keep. "Your clothes." I pointed to her shredded yellow blouse. "Where..."

"The Alleghenies. Don't worry about my clothes. Save your strength."

We'd barely gotten across the state line before the crash. Except we hadn't crashed. The exit door exploded, Moses had led us to the mountain, gotten splattered over it, and we'd somehow survived.

My body tingled with numbness beneath the weighty black comforter covering me. I lay on my back, which I was used to doing because I couldn't sleep on my catheter. I maneuvered to a sitting position and assessed my condition. Weak and functional was how I would've described it. My mouth was blood free. The bend in my right arm was bandaged and sore. And right now, I wanted to know what kind of food had been on the plates and whether I could eat any of it. Mom must have noticed me eyeing them. "I saved these for you. Happy Thanksgiving."

The plastic container she handed me had six spicy tuna rolls in it. Our tradition — Chinese food for Thanksgiving. I plucked one and stuffed it into my mouth. The fresh lush velvet with rice and ginger was heaven against my tongue. I ate until the box was empty.

I guzzled all the water and asked for a refill. Mom left me and returned with a full cup. Strange. Hunger and thirst were different now. Prior to my illness, I had a list of favorite foods — sushi, pizza, chicken wings, and a rice and sausage dish called *jagacida* my mother rarely cooked. After cancer, I was happy to keep anything down.

I'd been asleep for a day. "How did you know I'd wake up? The sushi is cold."

Mom laughed. "You don't miss Chinese Thanksgiving."

Nope, not even the year we ate a bad batch of Moo Shu pork and threw up nonstop for two days. I couldn't look at the stuff anymore without remembering the stench of bleach and noodle vomit.

Mom placed her hand on mine. "Focus." She sounded insecure. Reluctant. "Focus on what I'm about to say."

"No more," I groaned. "...*lies.*"

She nodded. "The truth — is a lot to take in."

My desire for answers at this point outweighed my need to be right, so I shut up.

She fidgeted with a large hole in her slacks. "In 1859, no...wait...that's boring. Important, but...let me not start that far back."

The starting and stopping, well, I wished Mom had a fast-forward sensor on her mouth I could use to get to the good parts. Whatever she had to say was crucial, and there was only one way I was going to get to hear it.

I couldn't be myself. "It's okay," I whispered.

"We survived the explosion, Lucy, and I was able to get you fresh sushi because I have — I haven't used them in a bit — I have special abilities."

She didn't say anything about mouthing questions to her. "What kind?"

"Watch."

Mom reached into the air. My mouth dropped as the distance between her palm and the room's ceiling grew shorter. She could *levitate? Fly?* Meanwhile, her other forearm and hand vanished for a second. Good thing my voice had crapped out. Otherwise, as Mom descended and reappeared, she would've heard every curse word I could think of.

At the end of it, I asked the most important follow-up question known to man. How?

Solar flares, a radioactive mineral called beryl, and AB negative blood with a rare antigen were the answers. What? Wait! Did I have the antigen? I pointed to her and demanded to know the truth. Mom shook her head and the air escaped my lungs. "Less than a thousand people on earth have it," she told me. "I never had you tested."

Right, because with Death knocking on my door, what good would a superpower do? My mother had them. Assuming my father did, wouldn't my blood have this antigen, too, although it was type-O positive?

Determination must have shone through my facial expressions. "Even with the antigen, there isn't any beryl left from the solar storms to give you powers."

Of course. The girl dying of bone cancer can't catch a break there, either. Solar flares? And what is beryl? "Where's yours? The beryl."

"Blood transfusion. I don't need to wear one. Beryl's a gem. All goes back to 1859 — Carrington solar storm. The part that'll bore you."

Considering what I'd just witnessed, what could she say at this point that I wouldn't listen to like my life depended on it? Blood antigens, invisibility, floating — it made more sense than the buttoned-down, uptight, plain oatmeal personality I thought she had all these years. With the retro hardcore rock music she listened to, and the way she slung curse words around, I knew there had to be a wild animal stirring deep down inside her.

I'd say the moments afterward, the laughs and the memories we shared, were awkward. They weren't. They were comfortable, like we were old friends. I didn't prod or push her to share anything, but her confession rolled down like an avalanche, and I couldn't keep up with all the details. Solar flares, colors of beryl, powers, deadly enemies and friends — she hadn't told any of this to another soul in fourteen years. I listened the best I could. It was the one thing I had the strength to accomplish by myself. When the sun dropped below the horizon, the bedroom we'd been in got progressively darker. Mom didn't seem to mind the blackening atmosphere, and without a light or lit candle, soon we wouldn't be able to see one another.

She ended our conversation with an odd request. "Can you walk?"

Was she kidding? My limbs were lead. "Where to?"

"We need to leave. This cabin was abandoned, and we're — "

"Squatters?"

"The place wasn't up for rent. We're not safe anymore."

I'd been sitting so long that the lower half of my body had gone pins and needles on me. The threat of imminent danger did nothing to motivate me out of the bed. On a pitch-black mountain or under cotton sheets, Death would've found me soon enough. "Can we wait until morning?" I asked her. "Just a few hours. Then, I'll be good to go."

It was like she'd forgotten how rapidly spreading bone cancer sapped my energy levels. Mom rested her chin on her hand. "Okay. A couple hours."

I closed my eyes and sighed. Mom was with me. I rested easy.

Pressure at my shoulders woke me out of a deep sleep. Mom was shaking me, and, though I couldn't see, her tense grip informed me not to speak. I swung my legs over the edge of the mattress and tapped my feet on the hardwood floor. Eventually, I located what remained of my shoes. There was sole, a little fabric, and shoelace. Not much else. But, being barefoot in the Pennsylvania mountains wasn't an option. My heart raced. What was happening? Mom's fingers wandered down my elbow and clutched my hand. Who was sweating worse, me or her?

The floor creaked beneath heavy footsteps, two or three sets. From the size of this room, I imagined the cabin was small, and we'd soon be found out. Mom could turn herself invisible, which could help her escape, but what about *me?* I had to be worth something to her alive. Otherwise, she'd have left me in the jet to die or here to be caught by whomever. I'd do whatever I had to do to survive past this moment and find my father.

I watched the bedroom door and expected it to burst into flames or fold onto itself. It did neither. I held my breath, and Mom squeezed my fingers. I looked at my body and saw *nothing*. She'd turned me invisible. The door swung open, and right when I thought I'd get a peek at who was behind it, I found myself standing next to a tree and freezing. My sweatshirt was hoodless and tattered. Damp weeds slapped their moisture onto my legs as my mother dragged me through the woods. "I need your help," she said.

What? My help?

The two of us stumbled over a slick group of rocks and landed flat on our backs. The bed of wet leaves did little to cushion our fall. I groaned and rolled to a sitting position. Rubbing my sore ankle would not keep it from throbbing, but I massaged it anyway.

Mom brushed off her slacks and stood. "There's no outrunning them. We'll have to fight."

What did that mean? We? I couldn't fly, turn invisible, or pass through solid objects. Or *could I?* I reached my hands forward and shook them like something would blast out of my fingers. What could I do? "You said I didn't have powers."

"No, I said I never had you tested. The antigen and the radioactivity may be in your blood."

That was a truth I could've used. Say I had powers. How did I use them?

"Get up. Let's keep moving."

But she said we couldn't outrun them! She obviously could not do it alone. We *had* to fight.

Her eyes darted back and forth with panic. I was right. For some reason, she wouldn't let me do anything. I wobbled after her, thinking the stubborn attitude might break. She'd change her mind and teach me how to access my ability, whatever it was. By the time we'd reach the small clearing what felt like half a football field away, my hope had dissolved to nothing. Win or lose, I'd have no part in the outcome. Had we done the impossible and outrun them?

"Can you feel that?"

What, the bugs?

She waved her hands. "The heat. Electricity in the air. They're *here*."

For the third time in the last few days, someone or something might kill me. Great. The threat of death robbed me of words and conscious thought. Fight or flight was all I had. I'd have run a marathon if it would've saved my life. But if my mother could float in air, turn invisible, and pass through solid objects, what could these people do to me? The possibilities...oh God! I was going to die.

With her hands locked on my arms, Mom shook me. "Listen to me. Think of the most powerful emotion you have, whatever gets your adrenaline moving..."

Killer clowns, darkness, rabid animals with gory fangs, extreme heights, betrayal, dying alone and unloved — every fear I'd ever had or gotten over bubbled up to my mind's surface. Any second now an Ordnance shot would pierce my anxious body and relieve me of this constant stress.

I had cotton mouth, my body temperature was blazing hot, and my heart thumped so badly I checked my left arm for feeling. Mom looked into my eyes and seemed to approve my condition.

"Project it."

Good advice for someone who could think straight. "Okay. Then what?" I waited for an answer and heard nothing though I called out her name. I felt a presence behind me — a definitive *evil*.

The edges of a sharp blade stuck on the right side of my neck and made a straight line to the other side. I should be dead in seconds. Choking on reflex, I clutched around the wound. What did death by a slashed throat feel like? A shock of pain, the rush of blood, gasps for air? None of that happened. No blood had passed over my fingers, and I stopped gagging. My neck was fine. Unmarked. The blade hadn't touched me. Matter of fact, *it had passed through me.*

Yet another thing beyond what I could've thought was possible. I'd inherited Mom's powers after all! He jabbed an Ordnance through my intangible back and fired his weapon. The shot passed through me and entered the darkness. He didn't get another chance to kill me. His body weight slumped to the ground.

Mom's words replayed in my mind. "Get it in your mind and project it." I had a hot stirring in my belly, but when I knelt and jumped, my feet barely left the ground. I did the next best thing to fighting and ran for cover behind a thick-trunked tree. All the action took place where I couldn't see it, so I leaned on my ears. Blows crashed into body parts, grunts, snapping branches or bones, and body weight hitting the grass — one after the other — and then quiet.

"Lucy!"

The shrill whisper of Mom's voice startled me. I stepped out and came face to face with Moses! Aside from his missing sport coat and tie, he appeared the same. Unharmed. He drew his weapon from behind his back and fired twice over my shoulder. My insides tensed. I didn't dare turn around to check his target. Apparently, he had good aim, because another body dropped. I didn't get it. What gives? Wasn't he trying to kill us a few days ago?

In this instance, her voice was a warning. "Turn around. Slowly."

Hands in the air, Moses did as she said. "Your transfer didn't process. You knew that already, didn't you?"

"Bank flags large, over-the-phone transfers for voice authorization."

He rubbed the back of his neck with his right hand. "Yeah. Well, your mistake looked like an inside job. Which it would've been, and a successful one, had the units transferred. Instead, you get to keep your money, and my custom jet gets blown out of the sky."

Which raised questions I had to ask. "How did whoever know? How did you survive?"

"People like us can be particularly difficult to kill," Moses said. "By the way, unless they find our dead bodies among these, they'll keep coming."

Good to know. Mom wasn't convinced, though. "It took you fourteen years to find us. I could kill you here, and we'll go into hiding."

I'd never considered my mother to be a murderer, and her threats were mostly harmless. Here, surrounded by unmoving bodies, I had to believe that person, the one who couldn't bake cookies without burning them, didn't exist anymore. Elayna Maria Sandoval was dead, the way I'd come to know her, at least, and I didn't have the time or space to mourn her. She'd never be the strict mother or the "mom/friend" either. I'd have to settle for this highly-trained, superpowered assassin and hope her pancakes were as good as Elayna's.

Moses' hearty laughing made me want to punch him in the face. He stopped laughing long enough to recite our social security and holophone numbers, and bank account amounts. Man, Mom was *super rich*. To add insult to injury, he listed our body measurements and how much we weighed to the pound. I couldn't believe it. He ended with "Tell me. How are you going to access your money without dermal lotion? The little bit Lucy has saved won't get you cross-country, and the second she uses her handprint to access her account, you'll be discovered."

Mom licked her lips, like she wanted to face the challenge. "We'll fight."

"You'll lose. You need me. And, as I understand it, she's on somewhat of a tight schedule. Promise me the four million, and I'll deliver you to him *alive*. We don't make it, and I get nothing."

An interesting point. A battle inside me raged between believing him, the double-crosser I'd known for a half hour minus a plane explosion, and going with my mother, who had lied to me my entire life. Why would he bet everything with no leverage, another double-cross? Would his boss give him more for bringing me and Mom to their doorstep? After witnessing what she was capable of, I could see why they might want her, but why me? I wasn't special at all.

Part of me wanted to call the whole thing crap and walk away from them both. Dying alone scared me, but I could rely on myself and the malformed cells in my body to do the job. Moses and my mother didn't have to do anything. I could die right here by myself without help. My thoughts were a mess, and the truth was, I didn't know what to do. I didn't trust either of them.

Fortunately, Mom wasn't searching for input. She extended her right hand.

CHAPTER SIX

What? They had a *deal?* How had the last weeks of my life been decided by two people I largely distrusted and in less than ten sentences? I wasn't going for it. Nope. Absolutely not. They could be a happy couple, jet across the country together, and rendezvous with my father. He didn't know I was alive, breathing. And a month from now, I'd be worm food. Not like he could regret what he never had, could he? He wouldn't miss me.

Nobody would.

This is what adults did to me. They argued topics of enormous consequence to my life and never involved me in the conversation. I watched them do it. Mom and Dr. Keller had figured out the best treatment plan, like what was the most likely to simultaneously kill the cancer and keep me alive. She and my counselor discussed how I could recover my missing credits before my catheter got removed, and today's subject was how to escape whoever was after us.

"Call in and buy us some time with him," she told him.

He beat his fist into his chest. "I'm not the point man. You broke his neck back there."

"Do it," she said. "Lie. BS your way through. Just give an excuse and sell it."

Moses left us, mumbling about women and their ways and whether it was worth four million freaking units to deal with my mother and her impossible demands. Once he turned his back and walked beyond earshot, she pulled an ink pen-shaped object from her pocket and clicked it on. She slowly circled around until the thing let out three high-pitched beeps and displayed a holographic set of coordinates. She disengaged the device before I could memorize the rest. I tried to sound disinterested when I asked her, "What's there?"

"A mountain that way" — she pointed beyond a range in the distance — "and my bag. Or what's left of it. It shouldn't take me long."

What was so important in her luggage? No time to press her further, because Moses wouldn't be on a call forever, and she intended to leave me alone with him — and the corpses littered around the clearing — to get it. Waving at my mouth didn't help the words come out faster. Neither did gulping down air. Being in an above-ground graveyard made my skin crawl, and I couldn't unzip it and step out. Dealing with dizziness and the stabbing tremors in my limbs was one thing, but to do so alone, for however long, would be torture. I wanted her to hold my hands and squeeze the terror out of me. She would if I asked, but I wasn't going to ask. Those same hands had snapped the necks of a half dozen people and had blood on them. On the flip side, she was completely capable to protect me.

I pleaded with her. "Take me with you."

"I'm not strong enough yet. I'll be back in a minute."

My mother leapt into the sky and flew away. She. Flew. Away. What alternate reality had I stepped into where my mother was a holo game character? I tracked her movement until the darkness became too thick. Moses was busy feeding his superior a lie to keep him in the dark. I forced myself to approach the nearest dead guy. After kicking his Ordnance away from his dead hand, I picked it up and ran downhill as fast as I could without falling. The branches I couldn't push aside smacked cold dew and leaves into my skin. Putting enough distance between me and whatever was going on back at the clearing was my goal. Eventually, I'd end up at a road where I could hitch a ride back to my house and live out the rest of my days in pain and safety.

The hot stabbing in my side forced me to stop. How long had I been running? I turned my head over my shoulder to see just how far I'd gone, and I blinked away sweat dripping down my brow. The next thing I knew, I was at the clearing standing next to Moses without the Ordnance. What was that smell like rotten eggs? Had I blinked myself back to where I'd started?

"Have a nice jog?" he asked me.

An irresistible urge hit my stomach and I threw up sushi and water next to Moses's shoes. He cursed and jumped back, barely avoiding the spray from my mouth. By the time I finished, everything inside me returned to normal. Strange. Usually my nausea had unpleasant residue, like unsteadiness and spasms in my belly, but not this time. I slumped to the ground in front of my vomit pool shaking and uncontrollably weeping. Then it hit me. I didn't have powers, and I hadn't done a thing. Moses pulled me back here. This was bad. How was I supposed to escape when he could yo-yo me back to him at will?

I couldn't.

I was trapped.

No different than the five weeks and change I had left to go. Closing my eyes didn't make it go away.

All of this was real.

Moses knelt in front of me. "Gotta give it to you. For a dying girl with wide hips, you're fast. Look, I'll be a millionaire after taking you to see an old man. You're not leaving until I get paid."

He had blackmailed the wrong girl. "And if I die first?"

The brevity of his chuckle let me know he hadn't thought of the possibility that the cancer might drop me before he got his money. After all, the deal hinged on taking me west, and Dr. Keller made no promises about the progression of my illness. Who knows when my appetite would drop out, I'd lose my "wide hips," and I'd be barely able to move? Rolling me out on a stretcher or hospital bed to meet my father for the first time had no romantic appeal. I'd die early just for spite, and he could try strong-arming my superhuman mother into paying up.

His voice hitched with uncertainty. "Touché. Okay, then. You'll be there tomorrow."

"Yeah?" I told him. "No jet and stranded? Good luck with that."

A loud boom exploded above us. *A sonic boom?* Then, my mother softly landed near the spot she'd left me minutes ago, bag in hand. The lid of the suitcase had been torn off, but the contents, whatever they were, appeared to be secure. "What happened here?" she asked me while sniffing the rotten egg smell. "You're a *teleporter?* How is that even possible?"

Moses revealed a necklace below his collar with a gold-colored jewel hanging from its center. "Long story" was all he said about it. Mom had told me about the different colors of beryl and what they did. Which one was gold?

My eyes bulged. "How'd you know?"

"The scent. I was gone, what, five minutes? I told you to stay here."

She told me to do lots of things: clean my room, stop cursing, count my carbs. I did none of it. Because what were rules in the context of death? Would God really judge me for a messy room or for being a size eight? Okay, maybe for the curse words. But, suppose He made me after all. My disorganization and body chemistry shouldn't be a mystery then. I win. Rules are garbage.

"First, you tell me to stay here with dead bodies of the people you've killed and a stranger you're paying," I argued. My brief pause for breath didn't give them time to interrupt. "And, and, a-and...you don't ask me what I think or how I feel about whatever, being left here. Alone. I have so many questions you don't or won't answer, and I don't want it anymore. At all. Screw you and screw my father for not being around."

"You're going to stop disrespecting me, Luciana, or —
"

"Or what?" I pointed to the dead guy I'd stolen the Ordnance from. "I'll end up like him? Whatever. Hey, Teleporter Guy. You can 'poof' me back to my house, right?"

Moses stuffed his hands in his pockets. "Make it worth my while."

Though he hadn't revealed the amount of his "while," he'd already extorted a promised fortune out of us. Nothing mattered to him. "How much more?" she asked.

"Quarter million. I get two million plus that when we arrive. Whether or not you survive it." He scratched his ear. "My benefactor wanted to make sure you and your mother stay off his quadrant of the country. Obviously, you weren't going to do that, so he'll kill you to save himself the trouble. Your house is the first place anyone with a brain would check."

"And why do you care?" Mom asked him.

"Four million, sweetheart. I have a vested interest in keeping you alive."

She motioned her hand like she was trying to wind up an explanation. "Why do you want to go back? It's dangerous and doesn't make sense."

The person who used to fix me peanut butter and jelly sandwiches with the crust cut off had *killed people* and *flown*. The guy standing next to me could *teleport*. I wanted to run, but this time, with a superhuman parent. That and a change of clothes. What I wouldn't give for the boring life I swore I hated. "Máma. Please?"

"Quarter of a million each way," he repeated. "Four and a half million total."

I wasn't asking for a round trip. One way worked for me. Whoever wanted to kill me could try. My mother was capable of handling them, and Moses could defend me, too, if he wanted his money. Little did he know I intended to bolt. I nodded to my mother and said, "Thank you."

The next thing I knew, I was standing in the middle of my room. All I'd been doing for the better part of my adolescence was throwing up my guts, but after we teleported and when the urge hit, nothing came out. Home. I quickly stripped naked and jumped in the shower. The hot arcing streams did wonders in helping me forget the events of the past three days. I lathered until the wonderful aroma of cucumber melon soap covered the stench of sweat and medicine. The last shower I'd taken was days ago — and I had smelled like it.

When I finished drying off and moisturizing, I slipped into comfortable clothes easy to run and hide in — black leggings and a black hooded sweatshirt. Orange and yellow light shone through my window. The sun was coming up on Saturday morning. Too early to call Nat and say goodbye even with my terminal cancer patient you're-allowed-to-bother-me-anytime-because-I'm-dying thing. Or the fact she had text messaged me fourteen times since Wednesday morning wondering how I was and where I'd been. Knowing her home situation, she might want to join me if I asked. "Hey," I typed on my disposable phone. "Sorry. Been off the grid. Headed out for a while. Don't know when I'll be back. Love you."

I settled on the edge of my bed with my back to the window. Without warning, Moses shoved the door open and stepped inside my room. He lingered near the edge of my stressed wood dresser and tapped his fingers against its surface. Ignoring the rhythm spent my patience. What he had to say, I guessed, was judgmental or critical, but either way, I didn't want to hear it. After a minute or so of constant tapping, he finally said something. "Nice costume change."

Coming from an older guy, I'd usually take it as a compliment. "Thanks."

"How long do you intend to live in this Norman Rockwell painting?"

"Who's Norman Rockwell?"

"How old are you?"

"Fourteen. Why?"

"When are we going? Apparently, you call the shots on this one."

No wonder. Mom was in no hurry. I wouldn't want to see my first love, the guy who'd left me behind a decade and a half ago. Especially without being sure what he looked like, who he was with, and if she was prettier than me. "Fifteen minutes," I told him.

Moses rubbed the back of his neck, cleared his throat, and said, "Ten."

"Fifteen. What do you need four million units for, anyway?"

Moses picked at his fingernails and avoided my eyes. "Nobody 'needs' four million units, sweetheart, except the people who don't have four million units. And it's four and a half now."

"You're broke, huh?"

"Fifteen minutes," he said while walking out.

Healthy people like him and Mom assumed all us terminally ill folks wanted was to live longer. Meeting my father at the risk of early death wasn't worth the expense with someone else at the controls. Death could come for me, but when I met him, it'd be on my terms.

I pocketed my extra holo, went to my closet, and discovered the bag I'd packed was missing. I dug underneath the pile of clothes I'd used to hide it. Everything I could've needed was in there — a couple thousand tangible units, clothes, hygiene stuff, and a knife. In about ten minutes, I'd be back on the road with my homicidal mother and her high school classmate.

Near tears, I realized Moses had told me I had fifteen minutes to get myself together about five minutes ago. Was that someone knocking? No, it was the holovision, or was it? My biometric lock wouldn't keep either of them out longer than a second, but I activated it anyway. I walked along my wall over to the window, conscious that the floor might creak beneath the pressure. When I opened the window, a gust of crisp morning air cooled my fingers.

"Soundproof on."

Mom's voice startled me. I turned around and dropped my bag. "We don't have much time," she said. Her eyes wandered to the luggage on the floor. "I need you to trust me."

I had nothing to say. Honestly, who would blame me? "Trust you? I don't even *know* you. You're a murderer I happen to look like."

"It was either them or us, and — "

"I'm going to die anyway. You didn't have to — "

"Not today you're not. Not if I have anything to say about it. Are you with me?"

The woman who pushed me out was a safer bet than a mercenary, I guessed, but by how much? She saved my life quite a few times already. I nodded yes.

"You're going to need these." She threw a heavy knapsack and a hooded black bodysuit onto my bed. "Lose the sweatshirt and put that on. Keep your shoes."

"Why should I?"

I'd pushed my mother long enough to know the exasperation on her face. She'd spent half a million units for almost nothing on my word. By her wrinkled eyebrows and unmoving eyes, I had two choices: go with *her* or go with *them*. Leaving on my own wasn't an option anymore, so I pulled my sweatshirt off and slipped on the bodysuit over my sneakers. Complete with gloves, the suit had material with a soft, pliable metallic finish, and the hood was a *mask*. Weird. Seconds after Mom helped me zip it shut, the suit made a sucking sound and fit skintight.

"Here." She pulled the mask over my face and pressed a panel on my glove. The suit turned transparent — I could see my clothes! What was all this?

I repeated her action to deactivate the cloaking. "Where's Moses?"

"Downstairs." She sounded annoyed. "I got what we needed from him."

Oh no. Another corpse, and this time it was in our house? "He's — "

"Alive." She dismissed my insinuation with a hand wave. "Soundproof off."

Heavy footsteps boomed up our staircase. Mom tossed me the bag she'd brought. I put my arms through the straps. We hurried into my closet and shut it from the inside. The strong funk of my sweaty clothes stung my nose. A lot of good skipping laundry did to hide my intentions to run away. She'd known about it anyway.

Was the airflow hissing in my mask audible to anyone else but me? Didn't matter. I only inhaled when the burning in my chest from holding my breath overwhelmed me. Mom grabbed my hand in hers, and we vanished into thin air. Waiting them out here wouldn't work, would it? Then again, I wasn't the assassin with superpowers. She'd thought this out more than I had. There had to be logic in Mom's actions, and against my better instincts, I needed to trust her.

A loud crack let us know they had entered my room by force. My mind raced. The sounds of what they did were distinct. The heavy plunks were my mattress and box spring being dislodged, and the rattle, clank and *whoosh* were my curtains and window dressings. The walk-in closet was the last believable place in my room for us to be hiding. Mom's hand squeezed the circulation out of mine, and then it released. The next thing I heard were the clicks of Ordnance being cocked and deafening blasts. I thought I'd hemorrhage and bleed out through my ears because of the noise. I watched bright bursts of bluish light pass through my body, singe my hanging clothes, and burn into the wall behind us.

Mom dropped us through the floor into the kitchen, which was beneath my bedroom. I quickly caught my breath from the roller-coaster-like, descending sensation, and we materialized. Though no armed men were stationed there, there were three I saw outside the breakfast nook windows scrambling to the front of the house.

We were trapped.

"What now?" I whispered.

She bent over, hands on her knees. For the first time, I noticed she, too, had a knapsack on her back. I heard a bell-like ringing and deep breathing, almost like Mom was gasping right next to my head. The mask must've had connected comms built into it. "Just a minute," she said. "Need EpiPen from my bag. Help me."

Instead, I grabbed the largest knife from our cutting block and tucked myself in the corner between the refrigerator and the hallway entrance to the kitchen leaving Mom to fend for herself. It was the first time I ever wished myself to have a smaller body out loud. I mean, I always wanted to be skinnier, but to say it and hear my voice pronounce the words made them more real than thinking them. The backpack didn't help. Mom frantically motioned for me to drop the blade, but I waved her off. I didn't want her to die any more than me.

I tightly clutched the knife's wooden handle in my gloved hand and steeled myself to use it. Whoever came this way, I had to be prepared to take him out without second-guessing. Either him or us. I debated myself to muster the courage — I could do it. No, I couldn't do it. There weren't enough Our Father prayers to erase the stain of slicing a person to death. No, I could do it. Self-defense. Protecting this house and our lives normalized everything, and my brain wouldn't get hung up on what I'd forced it to do. From that point on, my thoughts cleared.

A cylindrical Ordnance barrel poked into the kitchen. The person aiming it hadn't passed through yet. He couldn't pivot the weapon in my direction until he entered, and Mom had taken shelter behind the island. I passed the blade handle to my gloved left hand and held my breath.

From the corner of my eye, I saw the rounded edge of a black boot. Jabbing the steel into his leg wouldn't disarm him, and as he was right handed, there was no easy way to get to his chest. I lowered my arm's level enough to reach his midsection and stabbed the mesh spot to the right of his stomach. He groaned in pain and rapidly fired at the kitchen's far wall. I pushed the blade in farther until he collapsed facedown onto the Italian marble.

CHAPTER SEVEN

The emotional rush was fantastic and awful. The man at my feet writhed and moaned from the wound I'd given him. Mom grabbed my hand and pulled me away from the refrigerator. I tiptoed over the body and tried ignoring the bloodied butcher knife he'd taken out of his side and the pooling blood. He hadn't died. Not yet. I wasn't a killer, but the gash might be fatal if left unattended.

Lucky for him, the shots he'd fired had drawn reinforcements. A five-member team sidestepped their fallen comrade and filed into the kitchen. Two of them docked their weapons and helped the injured guy out of the house. The remaining three trained their Ordnance on us, and the one running point on the attack ordered us to surrender.

Mom announced her actions first. She raised her hands. I did the same. Of course, this was the headlining act to our show. Soon, they would fire kill shots, the ammunition would pass through us and destroy the kitchen she'd so carefully remodeled last year. Big deal. Dropping two million units plus on extortion meant she had the money to fix things around here. I'd never see the tile at the kitchen entrance the same way again. Doubtful she'd rip up all of it for me.

"I can still see you," I whispered through my teeth. My heartbeat throbbed in my ears. "What are you waiting for?"

The delay tensed my entire body. The first time she revealed her powers, I experienced a sense of shock and awe. Upstairs, it turned into wonder and now terror.

Were Moses' abilities this unreliable? They didn't seem to be. Finally, she pronounced two words syllable by syllable. *A-dre-nal fa-tigue.* Adrenal fatigue? Adrenal glands could get fatigued? My legs weakened. She'd needed my help, and I'd ignored her. She'd been rendered powerless. We were screwed.

"Freeze. Both of you," the point man barked at us. "You so much as twitch and we'll shoot."

A lump formed in my throat, and I couldn't swallow past it. Why hadn't they opened fire like upstairs? Had their orders changed, or were they more afraid than we were? Their hesitation meant to me they had no idea what Mom was capable of or what they may think I was able to do. Neither did I. Acting out of fear meant either us or them could end up dead. This was the part where Mom bargained to save our lives and offered boatloads of units like she'd done before.

No. She was a silent statue.

Moving anything but my mouth might get me made into a human piece of Swiss cheese, so I urged her on with my voice. "Say something," I whispered. When she did not immediately do that, I stepped up and improvised. My raised arms tingled and ached. "Okay. Okay, look. Put the Ordnance down, and we'll all walk away from this alive."

One of them adjusted his weapon's setting. "That thing's threatening us."

I'd been called many things in fourteen years, but a genderless *thing* was not one of them. Maybe I'd seen better days, but my hair wasn't boy short, and I certainly wasn't shaped like a dude. Regardless of his insult, I walked back my previous statement. "I meant you'll go home to your families. Tell your boss mission accomplished. Leaving was my idea in the first place, and I don't want to go anymore. My mother and I will stay put here. You have our word."

I'd bluffed way bigger than this, like convincing Bryce Parrish I was older than fourteen. The important part was he'd *thought* I was telling the truth. The mask hid my facial expressions, which was a good thing in case I had a visible tell, and they couldn't see the sweat trails rolling down my face quicker than the suit's cool interior could dry them.

The Ordnance barrels never moved from us. We were at their mercy. Trigger-happy guy worried me the most. He adjusted his fingers around his weapon's handle a half dozen times. The others stared us down through their targeting scopes. I wondered why the heavy artillery. What they were carrying could've mowed down a few dozen people in seconds. "We have a deal?"

"Lucy? Miss Sandoval? Are you here? Are you okay?"

Oh God. Natalee.

She'd ignored the destruction and walked inside of our busted front entrance. Though I'm sure she stepped carefully, I heard what I assumed were glass shards crunching underneath her feet. Any normal person outside of this science fiction action film would've turned around, ran away screaming, or called the police. Not my best friend. She had to see for herself what had happened. Her other friends used to call her a dumb blonde until she lectured them about how offensive it was to consider her brilliant and hardworking because she's Indian or use the stereotype that blonde girls were stupid.

The point man mouthed "Do not respond" to us.

"I've called the police, and — "

The jumpy guy who'd thought I'd threatened him turned and unloaded a couple shots in Natalee's direction. Then his friends opened fire on us. I shut my eyes, expecting to wake up on the other side of eternity. Instead, I heard a piercing scream and a hard thud and a sound like sifting sand and sizzling bacon. And I smelled burnt clothing.

Oh God, I was *dead.* I'd skipped purgatory and ended up in Hell. My body was sweltering hot. This wasn't happening. I mean, I believed in God more or less.

Wasn't I supposed to go to purgatory first and get a second chance?

Mom jabbed me in the ribs. "Lucy!"

She'd been sentenced here, too? She hit confessional every Tuesday night like clockwork, and *she* didn't make it into Heaven either? God must be stricter with sins and other crap than I imagined Him to be. The worst thing I'd ever known her to do was lie to me before she killed those men in the clearing, but she also had a different name and another life I knew nothing about. More skeletons were likely lining her closet.

I decided not to look. Eons could pass, and I'd never see the tormented for myself. The raging fire coursing inside of my body was enough. I deserved all of it. Unlike my mother, I hadn't had my confirmation yet, and I'd altogether been a terrible Catholic. But I'd said a prayer every time — okay, *sometimes* — I'd done something wrong, which was often. Apparently, that wasn't enough. Could I say it down here? Would God hear me?

A strong pair of hands shook my masked face. "Get a hold of yourself. Natalee's been shot."

What the — We were still in my house?

I cracked my eyelids. The three armed men furiously batted at their legs, arms, and puffed-up reddened faces. My stomach quivered. The bacon was *their skin.* One by one, they dropped to the ground screaming in agony at their simmering flesh and hair. Their weapons lay on the tile and had melted at the triggers and handles. Right before my eyes, the Ordnance dissolved into black and gray simmering puddles. A second ago, I remembered thinking those things were hot but still functional and they needed to be useless. The heat, the burning...it was *me.* I was doing it. *This Hell on Earth was my doing.* White flames burst from their limbs in bright flickers, and streams of black smoke formed a cloud above our circular pot rack. The rising temperature had charred the wooden outlays of the kitchen's island and caused the white ceiling's paint to buckle and peel.

Small orbs of fire formed in my palms. I screamed and clapped my hands together. The orbs burst and spurted flames worse than before. My skin had a stinging sensation, like I'd lost circulation all over and not like I had become a living, breathing candle.

Mom's voice caught my attention from the hallway, where she checked on Natalee. "Dial it back."

"I can't!"

"Calm down, Lucy — "

"I. Can't."

"Deep breaths!"

Easy to be calm when your body wasn't on fire. "Yelling doesn't help!"

"Focus!"

"I mean, I don't know how," I shouted. Any wonder I failed everything in school?

Yelling turned into shrieking. "Picture the flames going away in your mind and project it. *Breathe. Picture. Release.*"

Mid-panic attack, my eyes stung. I rolled them and blinked again and again. My vision wouldn't steady. Everything was hazy yellow. Two gaping holes appeared in the kitchen ceiling up through the floor in my room and the roof. The kitchen walls and ceiling, the hallway, foyer walls, a swath of the living room carpet, and a white cargo transport parked outside caught fire. Great. Heat vision? I was one more stupid thing away from crapping my pants. With my luck, the crap would've been flaming.

Mom tossed Nat over her shoulder, dodged the pillars of fire, and rushed in front of my flaming eyeballs. Instead of igniting her for challenging me, my inner spark immediately quieted. Everything returned to normal. Except for the fact I had heat rays coming out of my face and I had razed half of my house because I couldn't control them.

Our attackers yelped and lay next to pools of smoking metal. Part of me thought I should help them until I remembered how they had shot my best friend and almost killed me.

Mom gently set Nat into a kitchen chair and propped her up against the wall. The heat was worsening, the house was becoming an inferno, and we coughed like lifelong smokers. She wiggled out of her bodysuit and fearlessly plunged a needle into her thigh. After the shot revived her energy, she redressed. Her motions were quick-action, pinpoint-like muscle memory. She'd done this before. Not much about her was familiar to me anymore. This was the real person who had given birth to me, not the domesticated alter ego I was familiar with.

The sight of my unconscious friend bleeding and slumped against the China cabinet unsettled me but not more than the hideous monster I'd become. Nat hadn't asked to be a part of this madness. She was my only friend, and I'd unwittingly dragged her along for the ride. Dropping her off to get medical attention would be wrong, but I didn't see much of a choice.

Mom hefted Nat into her arms and motioned her head toward the double French doors at the back of the kitchen. "Follow me."

We hurried out of our burning, soot- and debris-covered kitchen into the grassy backyard. The fresh, autumn air was a relief. There, on one of our concrete benches, was...*Moses?* It appeared he had been sitting there for a while bent over with hands folded. What was he doing? Contemplating the universe's mysteries? He didn't appear to be the type of dude to meditate, pray, or think about something beyond himself unless it involved money. All the money-motivated guys I knew like him were one hundred percent tunnel vision and useless for anything else. Maybe he was mentally calculating how much he could make off helping us this time.

Mom set Natalee next to him on the bench. That was the first time I got a good look at her wounds. Two Ordnance rounds had tagged her beneath her left collarbone. Her white blouse and button-down blue sweater were singed at the sleeves and drenched in blood. She grimaced and let out a tearful moan. Still alive.

Behind her, our home was collapsing. How many times had I taken it for granted? Not many people I went to school with could afford to live like me. With any luck, the approaching emergency vehicle sirens could save it, but I knew I'd never see it like I remembered again.

Moses slowly placed his arm around Natalee's shoulder to steady her wobbling figure, and he looked to my mother for instruction. The end of his nose was clotted with blood. "Twelve ten Meredith Avenue. Dayton, Ohio," she told him. "Take her around the back of the building. Knock four times."

He nodded and immediately teleported them away. I swatted at the foul-smelling golden cloud they left behind. "Dayton, *Ohio?*" I asked out loud.

Mom turned her back to me and made a holo call. "Yeah. You need to see Rhapsody. ETA five minutes,"

Who was she talking to, and what was she talking about? My best friend is bleeding to death. "How are we getting there?"

Mom grabbed me under my near my ribs. Her grasp was tight. "Arms around my waist. Don't let go, and don't forget to breathe."

Oh God.

I followed her directions and squeezed her side.

The next thing I knew, we rocketed into the air. Flying fast and invisible. The drop in my intestines was sudden, and I held my breath to compensate. Her advice came back to me. "Don't let go, and don't forget to breathe." The pressure glued my arm to her side. I couldn't let go if I wanted to. Inhaling through my mask was surprisingly easy especially considering how quickly the air whipped past. The back of the mask's material had solidified and kept my head from moving too much in any direction.

We were soaring high as well, I guessed, to avoid birds and insects but low enough to dodge aircraft. Everything I saw was baby blue and white puffiness, and our forward thrust sort of froze my head into place. From the corner of my eye, I saw Mom. I had no idea she was keeping this massive level of information from me all these years, but now, I needed to know it all. Wherever we were going, I assumed an explanation had to be close by. Otherwise, judging from what I'd just done, I'd be like a walking lit match in a building made of C4 explosives.

Mom squeezed my ribs and spoke through my earpiece so clearly it was like she was inside of my head. "Hold on."

We shot forward so fast I temporarily lost my hearing. Thank God we flew in a straight line. Otherwise, I would've gotten sick inside of my mask. I lost consciousness once or twice. The last time, when I woke up, we were on a gradual arcing descent slow enough that my body didn't revolt. Soon, we landed behind a lone building in a parking lot. The impact of Mom's feet shattered the road surface and sprayed large concrete chunks into the air. I had no time to process anything that had happened. She ghosted — her word not mine — us through the locked back door and pulled her mask off. Her face was flushed red and sweaty. I took off my mask and imagined I must look the same or worse.

The room was, I guessed, about ninety feet long and wide, painted gray, and dimly lit. The wall we had passed through had a ginormous medicine cabinet stocked with vials and various sizes of labeled bottles. At our left were five maroon cushioned chairs. To our far right was a circular white curtain and medical monitoring equipment. I'd seen them before in the hospital. That's where Natalee must be. Moses was nowhere to be seen.

The reality of how we'd arrived washed over me. We'd *flown* hundreds of miles away in less than an hour. The math didn't add up. Ten miles a minute or more had to mean...we went faster than *seven hundred miles an hour*. Considering the events of the past few days, it was the most amazing thing to have happened but not the strangest.

My muscles and my bones were tight and sore. I knew no amount of massaging would help this, and there was no time for real rest. Still, Mom settled into one of the chairs and sighed. My back and leg muscles wouldn't unlock, so I folded my body the best way I could into the seat next to her. "Where are we?" I asked.

She patted my left knee. "The stiffness goes away. You'll get used to it. What about your feet and hearing?"

This was not a normal conversation, but she made it sound as if I'd slept in an awkward position with no pillow instead of traveling on a plane-less supersonic flight. "Fine."

"How are you feeling otherwise?"

Going through chemotherapy meant hearing "How are you feeling?" on a loop, but who wanted to know the truth? Nobody wanted to hear "I had my guts cut out, microwaved, and put back in" or "Feels like I've run a marathon, and at the end, someone shot me with a flamethrower." Not to mention the condition of my best friend. "I'm good."

"We couldn't leave her in a hospital. She's seen too much. So, I had Moses bring her here."

"Where's 'here' exactly?"

She licked her lips. "A pharmacy storage unit run by someone I trust. She delivered you."

My eyebrow raised. "She *who?* An OB/GYN?"

"It's complicated. She knows how our biology works."

A random, regular chick helped deliver me? "Explain."

The chair squeaked as she repositioned herself to better face me. She mentioned the basics about radioactive beryl and how the rare blood protein we have processes it. Adrenaline turns on our abilities, but my prolonged labor weakened her adrenal glands. There were four adrenaline booster shots she carried around in case of emergencies like today.

"Focus directs what you can do," she added.

I didn't want to be a weapon of mass destruction. I'd rather have had a harmless ability, like *living*. Instead, I'd destroyed my childhood home and given third-degree burns to men who were trying to murder me. "I don't want to do anything, focus on anything. I want to be *me.*"

"Listen," she said to me. "That look...the way you look right now. I never wanted this. It's — "

There was a time and place for this discussion, and it was not now. She'd given me the most information I'd ever had about my life, and I wanted more. "Can we check on Nat?"

"No. Let Isabella do her work. She'll give us updates when she can."

"What do we do while we wait? Sit here?"

With a smirk, she replied, "We eat."

CHAPTER EIGHT

The suggestion that I desert my dying best friend for brunch sounded heartless, but the second Mom said eat, my stomach reacted with an angry grumble. Like, how dare I discover I was inhuman, barely evade death, and neglect to feed my face? I discovered what she said was less of a good idea and more of a necessary command. Our abilities stressed our systems and made us slaves to our body's cravings. We *had* to eat or suffer the consequences. Still, I resisted. "Not leaving."

"Okay. You'll want to know what'll happen next. Your insulin levels will crash. You'll get cold shivers, won't be able to think straight or walk. Isa will start an IV, and I'll be back by the time you wake up."

No fair using my hatred of needles against me. Her sketchy doctor friend would've had to dig around in my arm to start a drip. The hospital nurses meant well. None of them could pin down my veins. When they tried, the bruises took weeks to heal. Looking back at the drawn curtain, I concluded that I'd do no good unconscious. With time, she'd be in better condition, and I'd be able to get her to safety far away from us dangerous mutants.

Once she knew I agreed to her proposal, Mom ghosted us through the wall and onto the street. The bright, midmorning sun made me reach for my mask. Its blue heads-up display reminded me of my first holo, and the eye visors automatically yellow tinted for environmental glare and brightness. Its filtered air flow tickled the inside of my nose like a slow-building, never-culminating sneeze.

By the end of the first city block, my balance wavered. Mom clutched my right elbow and pointed at the corner. "Easy. We'll go there."

We'd walked several more blocks to the Chicago Liner Diner. In the shape of an old-fashioned train car, the thing looked like a gray tube that a strong enough wind could blow apart. High-speed travel had come a long way since this relic was made, what, twenty years ago? I'd never known her to be sentimental or interested in history, and we could've hit a fast food spot and eaten. "What kind of food?" I asked her.

Mom helped me up the stairs and opened the sliding metal door. "I'm guessing diner food."

Suddenly, she's sarcastic? This should be fun.

I trudged inside. The smell of cooking food hypnotized me so badly she had to nudge me forward. Coffee. Eggs. Meat. Waffles. Pancakes. I kept myself from jumping the counter and eating whatever I could.

I walked down the narrow aisles of green padded booths. There were four older couples eating, and one deeply tanned man, who had haunting green eyes and a cane, sitting alone and drinking from a coffee cup. Those people occupied the few tables at the front. The open first booth I saw had dirty plates on the table, so I passed it and took the last available one at the back of the restaurant. I groaned and folded my body into the booth seat which is when I saw Mom had not moved from her post at the front of the car.

"What are you doing?" she mouthed to me, hands open. "Takeout!"

Wasn't it obvious? I mouthed "Getting ready to eat" and glanced at the menu, to which she said, "We're not staying" and repeated, "Takeout."

The scent of cooking eggs and bacon distracted me from using an inside voice. "Why not?"

Mom waved me back to the front, and I made the same motion with two hands. She shuffled past the stools and tables to meet me. The way she eyed the front and checked over her shoulder didn't help my anxiety at all. "It's not safe," she said in a hushed whisper. "Moses' boss is searching for us. Besides, there's no emergency exit."

She could pass through solid objects. "Oh yeah, there's an emergency exit — "

"That's subtle. No. We're getting takeout."

Is that why we got takeout? All these years, it was the one thing that made her cooler than most other parents. Especially when she found the vegan spot that delivered. And we weren't going to dine at home. Was I supposed to comfortably chew from a disposable container while sitting at my comatose best friend's bedside? "It's a diner in a freaking train car. A freaking old diner train car that you picked — "

"I have a feeling we shouldn't. We're getting takeout. Period."

"C'mon Máma, please? Sit down. I'm tired. You're tired. Look, I hurt everywhere, and we'll get a chance to talk about things."

She didn't outright say no, which meant she was considering it. She loosened the straps of her knapsack. Mine was already on the seat next to me. I called her Máma when I really wanted something. I'd won her over.

"You're not slick. And stop speaking Spanish. Your grandmother would siphon her blood from your veins if she heard you speaking our language sounding like a gringo. We eat fast."

"Lightning. Yep. Got it."

She made a half-circle motion with her finger. "Let me sit there."

"What? Why?"

"This is not a negotiation. I need to face the door. Move."

I wished she had said something before my bones and muscles had unwound a bit and relaxed. With a groan for effect, I clutched my bag, got up, and switched booth seats with her. Right then I realized all the times we'd gone out as far back as I could remember she'd done the same thing and watched the entrance. My entire life, she'd been in protection mode. All this time I thought she suffered from OCD, needed a date to unwind or a strong drink.

By the time the bald waiter with diamond stud earrings got there with a steaming coffee pot, in my mind, I'd switched orders ten or twelve times. My DEFCON 1 hunger made me consider shoving the greasy laminated menu in my mouth and calling it a day.

"Hi, ladies." His obnoxious gum chomping furthered my irritation. "My name's Charles, uuh-huh, and I'll be taking care of you this morning. What can I get you?"

Mom pointed to the silver carafe Charles carried. "We're PMSing and running a marathon later today — "

"Mom!"

"So we'll be carb loading and eating our feelings. There's a big tip for you at the end if you can keep up without asking too many questions."

His raised eyebrows and eyes read annoyance and "what does that have to do with me?"

"Start us off with a few regular coffees."

He reached over the diner counter for two white mugs, poured dark liquid into them, and placed them at our hands. Oil sludge from our transport's conversion engine couldn't have been darker. My lips puckered at the thought of letting it pass my lips without intense dilution. Four hazelnut creamers and five spoons of sugar did the trick.

Charles waved his hand. "I'll give you two a few minutes to, you know, mmm, figure out your situation and what you two are gonna eat, okay?"

He walked far enough away not to hear what I said to her. *"PMS and a marathon?"*

While I sipped, Mom leaned in. "I needed an excuse for how much we're gonna order. A woman would offer us ibuprofen and sanitary napkins. He's not going to wonder now."

My new powers didn't include the ability to dissolve into the floor. Otherwise, I would've used it. "Yeah, well, let me make the excuses next time. Yours are terrible."

"Go heavy with protein — eggs, steak, and chicken. Twice as much as you think is normal."

I'd do what she said, but I didn't think I could swallow that much and keep it down. Chemo had sapped my appetite. I never lost much weight because of it, and whatever I lost, it came back once I resumed eating. No one said "I wish I lost more weight because of my cancer," and I felt ashamed and shallow for thinking it. But seriously, all the vomiting, radiation, chemo, starving, and raw food dieting I'd done, and ten pounds was it? No more than half a dress size and not an inch off my hips? Fine. I'd gorge myself more than ever before and see what happened.

"Can you put a call into your friend and check on Nat?" I asked her. "I'm worried."

Mom folded her hands. "I know you are. Me, too, but Isa's good at what she does. She's taken care of me after some bad scrapes. We have to let her work, and neither of us will be worth much of anything to either of them unless we refuel right now."

I didn't doubt that, so I patted my suit's pockets down for my holo. "Then, let me call Mr. Gupta real quick to let him know her condition."

Mom gave me a cutoff sign and a stern warning. "Don't."

"Why not? He could think she's — "

"He's better off thinking that way until she's no longer in danger. Trust me."

"Not likely."

"I know what I'm doing. Your geolocation — "

"I'll turn it off. Problem solved."

"Won't matter if the police set up a trace. We don't want that attention. Until you learn your emotional triggers and how to control them, you're like a bomb with a short fuse."

Valid points, but Mr. Gupta would be climbing the walls over Nat's whereabouts.

"Any decent parent would want to know their kid is alive."

The irony of my words wasn't lost on me considering my search for a father who might or might not be worth the salt I thought he should be. Mom clinked a spoon against her cup, as if she knew I was talking about both Mr. Gupta and her ex-boyfriend. Nat could've left a note or a message that pointed to us. Then, Mr. Gupta could go to our place, see the destruction, and already think she was dead.

Say I reached him. "How's she doing? Is she alive?" he'd ask.

What could I tell him, besides "Sort of, I think?" What would he do after discovering she was hundreds of miles away? Call the cops. And I *hate* cops. I'd end up burning them like I had done back at the house. Mom was right. I bit my lip to keep from admitting it or cursing.

"Shouldn't we at least — "

"Acting on emotion will get you hurt."

I didn't miss the waver or the crack in her voice. I'd never seen my mother emotional. Then again, I didn't really know her or at least this version of her. Throughout my life, Mom hadn't expressed anything toward me beyond anger, disappointment, and the occasional flash of warmth. However, the more time we spent with one another, the more sides of her I saw.

"Is that what you did?" I asked her. Were they the reason her and my father's relationship never made it? Or did her actions drive him away? That's what I had assumed until she explained.

"He would've been there for me, for *us*, if I had let him be."

I tried pushing without sounding as pissed off as I was at her for her decision. "Why didn't you?"

She sipped coffee so long I wanted to slap the mug clean out of her hands. "He was in love with another girl.

I didn't want him staying with me or coming back out of obligation or because he thought he should because it was the right thing to do. Once the opportunity to set him free presented itself, I took it."

Over the course of time, I'd imagined acceptable reasons why he was absent from my life. He was at war or a foreign diplomat — some occupation where human contact was unreasonable. When Mom told me he didn't know I existed, I did the same for her. Maybe he had another family behind her back or he was a criminal. Because she did not want him to be around had never crossed my mind, and it was unacceptable. Under normal circumstances, I would've lost my appetite, but I was hungrier than ever.

Finally, Charles returned. My mother gave her order first and listed enough food to feed three people: nine scrambled eggs with cheese, three side orders of bacon and sausage links, three orders of hash browns scattered with onions and ham, a side of chicken fried steak and an orange juice. His eyes bulged as he scribbled especially the part where he wrote to the bottom of the sheet and she indicated that was for *her* and not *us*.

I hadn't ordered yet.

Despite my better judgment, I copied her order except for the chicken fried steak which I substituted with a medium well T-bone.

"All right," he said after filling the second sheet. "I'll be back in a minute with more coffee."

I waited until Charles was out of earshot. "Whether you think I did or not, I deserved a father," I hissed, "*and you took that from me.*"

My words stabbed her as deeply as I had intended them to. "I did what I thought was best."

"Best for me or best for *you?*"

Mom's eyes drifted to the silverware wrapped in a napkin near her left hand. "Both. But that's not all you wanted to ask, so ask."

I paused mid-swallow. "Ask you *what?*"

"The questions behind your eyes. You haven't looked me in the face since the cabin."

Hadn't I? Maybe she was telling the truth. I traced the brown pattern in the table with my fingers. At its center was a vintage photo of the Chicago Transit Authority train from thirty years ago and a short, typewritten history about how an unnamed benefactor had restored it following a derailment. Not any derailment ---the 2013 CTA Fourteen terrorist derailment. The food scents I inhaled were hypnotizing. I'd almost forgotten to ask her. "This was *you?*" I asked her while pointing at the laminated history.

She nodded. "Your father and a couple friends. Six, not fourteen. Clones don't count."

Clones? "You're a freaking terrorist?"

"No."

My stomach clenched. "What else aren't you telling me?"

"The media didn't understand what we were, so 'terrorist' was the label. It wasn't us. Dangerous man we had to stop. We lost good friends that day."

We continued to chew in silence. Media or not, my mother was an at-large terrorist.

"You've used your powers to spy on me, too, haven't you?"

From the twist of her lips, I could tell I'd offended her. "Let's discuss this later in somewhere not so public."

The silverware rattled when I slammed my hand against the table. "What else is there to talk about? A discussion means you're adding one more thing to the long list of things I can't do with my own life."

"You don't get it," she angrily whispered. "This...our lives...isn't a game — "

"So, it's okay if you did it?"

"Yes," she spat out. "Whenever you'd had chemo and bio-locked your door, I had to be sure you weren't dying."

I suspected I wasn't alone lots of times. How many times was I not alone? What about after I showered and shaved, stood in front of my floor-length mirror, and moaned about my thigh fat? That's sick and way creepy. My ideas on how deep this could go stacked on top of one another like layers of dirt on my skin.

"And when I *wasn't* in the middle of a chemo cycle?" I managed to stutter out.

She bit her lip and stared into her coffee mug. "Not much."

I leaned in and lowered my head. "That's it. I'm out of here. Get Nat home safely, please."

"Wait." Mom set her mug down. Her face said I really didn't need to be alone as much, which was unacceptable. "Use *more*." She slid the sugar across the table. "This stuff is rocket fuel. And on your grandmother, I swear I watched you maybe five times besides that."

Yeah, right. I challenged her. "Name them."

The list read backward like this: she'd quantum tunneled, or ghosted, through my wall most recently to help me when I got sick a week ago. The other four I immediately mind dumped as unimportant. The last one, which was the first time she'd said she spied, was three years ago when I'd had my first period and barricaded myself in my room because I thought I was bleeding out. I believed her, not because I trusted her but because she was a horrible liar on the fly. I, on the other hand, was a pro who had lied my way out of countless citations and disciplinary referrals.

"You have major trust issues," I told her while bottoming out my mug. Sugary whitish-brown slush lined the cup's insides.

Mom took a sip from her cup. "So do you. You get that from me. Your mouth and stubbornness, too."

She continued lecturing me as I stared through the square window to my right. The parking lot was empty except for a compact transport and a rusted blue pickup. Strange. All but a booth or two were full with patrons. I guess they had walked up like us. "Yeah? What do I get from my father?" I asked her.

"Your temper," she said without hesitation. "And your heart."

Not a minute too soon, Charles arrived with backup to deliver our food. By the time they finished jamming the plates onto the table, we had no choice but to pile food on a few plates and eat our way from the top down. Which worked out well once I figured out how to stack them. I had three mountains of hash browns and cheese eggs with bacon and sausage layered onto my steak. Charles happily refreshed our coffees and laid the check next to Mom's mug. I was surprised he didn't insist we pay before eating. The way his eyes bulged, he probably thought we'd die before we could eat all the food.

Mom led me in a prayer and the sign of the cross. Then, she added pepper to her eggs and started eating. She ate at a steady methodical pace, and before I had time to assess how she'd done it, one of her plates was completely clean. This phenomenon was too much for me to handle, so I took a forkful of egg and swallowed it. They were good, but I didn't feel anything special. I kept eating and swallowing until my plate, too, was empty. I was still hungry, like I had eaten a couple of crackers and not three eggs and the equivalent of a full entrée. Excited, I dove in for more and conquered my second plate in half the time of the first.

Charles placed his hands on either side of his face and opened his mouth at what Mom and I were doing to our entrées and sides. Holo in hand, he encouraged me to pose, which I did with a forkful of steak and a smile, I'm sure, had ketchup-doused egg on it. I didn't mind. After this, I didn't anticipate bumping into him, and my internet presence couldn't get more negative than it had recently become. I resumed eating until he motioned at me. "Came out blurry," he said. "Can we try it again, sweetheart?"

This time, Mom noticed us. "What's that?"

"Nothing." I had a mouth full of hash brown, ham, and onion. "He wants a picture of me."

Her smile had a hint of hesitation to it. "Why are you taking pictures of my daughter?" she asked him. "She's fourteen, Charles."

I shot fire from my eyes. A guy taking a picture of me was the least of my concerns. He was harmless, but neither his response nor his tone sounded harmless. "For my boss. He wants proof that one of the CTA Fourteen is here before he arrives."

Mom reached across the table, grabbed my hand, and thrust her shoulder hard into the diner wall. She couldn't ghost through it. Her strength alone should've blown a wide hole in the train car's surface or at least dented it. Pain registered on her face. Ramming into the wall had hurt her? I don't think her adrenaline boost wore off that fast. Something else was at work. I didn't know an emotion to kick-start my powers, and fear wasn't working.

I fought back tears. "What's happening?"

"Goshenite." Mom winced and let go of me. "White stone that takes away our powers. They must have some."

They? The well-meaning elderly people?

"Run!" she shouted.

The group stood and crowded together to block our path to the front exit. Wait, had they gotten taller? I was near Mom's height, but they appeared to be at least six and a half feet which was a foot higher than us. I noticed the similarities in their long, thin graying physiques. Wiry but solid and intimidating. Their bloodshot eyes stirred fear deep inside of me. Perhaps it was my hunger when we first arrived, but I'd glossed over their appearances.

We could take them, though, right?

Mom had missed it, too. Or she hadn't. A feeling was how she described it, and I didn't listen to her. Again. And it had gotten us in a bad situation. I hated when she was right, but I *really* hated it when I was wrong and there was no way around admitting it.

"Are we gonna die?" I asked her.

"Not today," she told me. "Don't move."

How was I supposed to do that? Tingling flowed up and down my fingers. It had to be my powers. They disabled Mom's abilities, but mine were operational. I clenched my fists and hoped smoke wasn't coming out of them to give my secret away. Eight of them formed a two-person deep barrier between us and the exit. Trying to melt the train car's wall enough to escape would be risky even if I could burn hot enough to do that.

Whatever I had inside of me, I had to unleash it and burn our way free. "Give me a — "

"Wait."

Behind them, I saw the man with the cane had moved so that we could see him through the crowd. He nodded at us. Was I supposed to know what that meant? Mom mirrored what he'd done and whispered, "Don't."

I closed my eyes, quieted my arguments, and backed down. After all, if I wasn't going to admit she was right, the least I could do was obey her without question. Once.

Suddenly, I detected the scent of rotten eggs. Gross. I lost my balance. Next thing I knew, I'd been handcuffed to a chair in an unfurnished loft apartment above the city's skyline. I bent over and threw up, thankfully, into a trash can between my legs and not onto my feet or the wooden floor. The older man wiped my mouth with a facial tissue and pushed a peppermint candy between my lips. The minty freshness helped my breath and stopped my nausea.

Beside me, Mom sucked in deep breaths and struggled against her restraints. The afternoon sun shined through the wall-length windows until he commanded them to blacken. Good idea considering an angry gang of muscular senior citizens was after us.

"What is this?" I asked him. "Who are you?"

The disguised form of the man we knew from the diner suddenly melted away into Moses. He had changed clothes as well — the airport uniform blues had become a black set of cargo pants, gray combat boots, a white shirt, and a black utility jacket. He wagged his finger at my mother and tapped his temple. "Won't be getting up here again, Anibel."

Hold up, my mother did something to *his mind?* I flashed back to the way he followed her directions without question back at our burning house. Mind control. What other superpowers was she keeping secret? One more to the growing list of reasons not to trust her. I yelled and yanked my wrists apart. The binds bit into my skin, and I cursed a blue streak.

"Where is he, Moses? He wanted to kill us so badly — let him do it himself. Where is he?"

Her face flushed as she growled and yelled. Behind us, someone cleared their throat.

Using my legs, I rotated the chair around until I faced him. He'd been behind us the entire time. He leaned on his cane's handle and limped between Mom and I while struggling with a wet sounding cough. He hacked into a white cloth handkerchief covering his left fist. So nasty.

"Didn't recognize me in the diner? His wheezing, high-pitched voice warped like he'd swallowed a tall glass of acid. "Burns healed over, and cancer chewed my muscles. Made me like this."

Man, the guy had to have been through a war or *five.* Life had dragged the crap out of him from the way his wrinkled brown skin laid across his bones and his gums pulled away from his big yellowed teeth. I'd never seen a person so old and broken down before not even in the hospital. He had to have been born during the Great Depression if not earlier. A hundred years ago wouldn't have been a stretch. But what did he want with us?

"Who are you?"

Old Guy spun my chair around as if I wasn't in it. I weighed at least one hundred and — how did he do that? He stared at my face from beneath his ball cap and didn't blink. I caught a whiff of his breath which smelled like strong medicine. Beneath his shirt was a large, pale yellow jewel on a short chain. That was...I couldn't remember the name for gold beryl, but even money it kept him alive. For some reason, him being so close made me uneasy. Afraid.

"You knew the rule," he said to my mother while staring into my face. "You should've killed her in utero. No legacies."

What? I spat on Old Guy and called him names I'd never regret. He smiled. Of course, he did. What did he care how many multi-syllabic curse words I called him? I struggled to wrangle myself free. The sharp-edged handcuffs wouldn't budge. Pretty sure my wrists were bloody beneath my bodysuit from all the tugging. Mom needed to kill him for what he'd said about me. If she hesitated, I would.

CHAPTER NINE

Old Guy hobbled to a rhythm: the *thump* of his cane's brown rubber bottom against the hardwood, quickly followed by the *click* of his right shoe's wooden heel and the *scrrrch* sound of his left foot dragging across the hardwood. *Thump, click, scrrrch.* He paced between Mom and me. Old Guy's staggered stride measured a couple seconds which left me a small window to eliminate him. Once my powers returned, *if* they returned, I couldn't hesitate.

My belly trembled from the brief thought of *murdering* this man. Murder. Not badly injuring or knocking him out so he can later make a full, healthy recovery. I was thinking about separating his soul from his body — literally removing a human life from the planet. Was I crazy? Seriously, I wasn't a *killer*. Once we got free, he'd be easy to overpower. I'd do that instead.

Suddenly, a sharp prick hit my lower back. Too thin and long to be a knife. Cool liquid oozed into my muscle. Warmth flooded my skin, and I shook. What I really wanted was to curl up and fall asleep, which I fought if that was what the shot was designed to do. Moses injected Mom with the same drug. She gritted her teeth and exhaled, but otherwise, she appeared to be normal.

"An adrenaline suppressor, I'm guessing." She gasped for breath. "No powers."

Meaning it canceled out her boost. Made sense why she wasn't as affected as me. Her condition made her used to it. "Good thing," I slurred. I thought he was drugging us for something far worse, like a black-market organ auction, a sex trade, or something. "Why?"

Old Guy wagged his finger. "Needed you more cooperative."

Cooperative? "For what?"

Nobody answered. I groaned all the cuss words I could string together in one labored breath. "Tell me the truth. Or on my life, I'll burn this whole place down."

He motioned to Moses, who unlatched our cuffs. The padded inside of my gloves were slick with blood and sweat, and I couldn't wipe them off. We were free! Sort of. Neither of us was in any condition to fight, and Moses could teleport. We'd be swinging at air. And the senior citizen had a gold emerald. All I remembered about those was they granted the wearer an ability. His, obviously, wasn't teleportation.

But if he had, say, strength, he could end the fight before it got underway. Nothing about his demeanor suggested he'd hesitate to punch a woman or a teenage girl in the mouth. Powerless, my bark was way worse than my bite, and everyone in this room knew that. He ordered Moses to secure the outside perimeter downstairs.

Moses vanished in a column of gold smoke. The lingering rotten egg smell made me gag again. No amount of hand fanning made the stench go away.

Still sitting, I rubbed my wrists through the bodysuit armor, and the cuts stung. "Geez. At least your son has manners — "

"What?"

"Moses...Frank. He's your son, right? Looks like you around the nose. Must get the rest from his momma."

Old Guy whirled around and swung his cane like his next move was to brain me. It was the first time I'd gotten a good look at it. There were chips, dents, and flecks of dried blood up and down the black shiny surface. Either he liked to gnaw wood or hit things, or people, hard. At its end was a jewel...*a fading green emerald.* Uh-oh.

"Nothing," I said.

Spit particles flew from his mouth. "You said something about *my son!*"

Arms stretched out, Mom left her chair and positioned herself in front of me. "Swing that cane at either of us, Peters, and your next breath will be your last."

She'd never defended me before. For all the times Principal Harris called her about what I'd done in school, she'd immediately blamed me. Yes, I'd done it. Never stopped anyone else's parents from blindly standing up for them no matter what they were doing. She didn't do that. Cutting class? She'd believe that. Smoking, too. Defacing property, cussing, sleeping in class, mouthing off, holo-messaging — I'd really done all of that. The only other thing that got her temperature rising was when I got caught kissing Bryce.

I guess she did love me after all.

He froze in position like he thought about following through on his threat. To kill or not to kill. Mom could fight, and I could roll out of the way and cheer her on. I guess it depended on how strong he was. From the looks of it, he couldn't fight a strong wind. But looks could be deceiving, especially with two emeralds, not just one.

The cane slowly eased down his hand back to its original position in his palm. I breathed again. Mom helped me to a standing position, but I used the chair to bear my weight. I hadn't been cancer weak in days, but I guessed my time was running out. "What's your problem?"

"We used to call them...you...*legacies*. The children we weren't supposed to make because of the danger. Every one of you has turned out defective. Jade, Iain, *you*."

His insult stung. *Defective?*

"Not defective, Lucy. With problems. His sociopath son was one of them."

Okay, I called Moses his son by mistake, and he's ready to slaughter me, but she calls him a sociopath and he does nothing? "What kind of problems?"

The words were hard to hear. Other than being crazy, he said his son, Iain, had suffered from multiple sclerosis and Jade had split personalities. And then, there was me.

What was my problem? So, I was a little overweight, but who isn't?

Oh, right. *That.*

Wait a second? I had bone cancer because of my bloodline, and *she didn't want to tell me?* All of this was too much to take in. I'd experienced it up close and personal, and I hardly believed it. My flamethrower hands, Mom's flying and strength — I could be losing my grip on reality. Or, it could all be *real,* and I lacked the ability to deal with it.

"I want to go home. Now."

"That's not possible, Lucy."

"Fine, Mom. You can stay here. I'll run away, go into the system, live in a group home or on the street until I die. I'll figure it out. I'm done."

I moved to the door. The steel rectangle didn't have a handle. Not much use for one, I guessed, when you had a live-in teleporter. I patted the walls to locate a hidden emergency escape and, to the best of my ability, I couldn't locate one. None of the empty rooms had exits either. I peered through the darkened window, and all I saw were the tops of buildings and an open skyline. We had to be fifty stories in the air. There was no escape.

"You're wasting your time," Old Guy said. "I wouldn't have gone through all this trouble just to set you free. We need one another."

My head dropped to my chest and tears flooded my eyes. "For what, man?"

Nothing made sense until Mom pieced it together. "To find your father."

I pounded my fists against the window, and the reinforced glass didn't budge. He was using me as bait. "Good luck with that. He doesn't know I exist, and he thinks Mom's dead."

Old Guy grinned. If his teeth weren't rotten, he either soaked them in mud every night or never brushed them. "That's what she wanted us to think. He knows she's alive. He always did. I figure he has a clue you're around, too."

I could only hope.

Mom's hands flared at her sides. "I don't know where he is! I was going home to find out."

"He hasn't been there in years. You don't follow the news much, do you?"

Old Guy cast projections of online articles and blogs in front of us. *Dozens* of them. Each headline told a story of a miraculous, unexplainable event. A three-story office building had caught fire. No casualties. Barely any injuries. A commercial flight had lost both engines and somehow made an emergency landing without incident.

Explosions, shootouts, robberies, natural disasters — the list continued. No matter the situation, there were minimal losses. The locations were spread across the United States: Washington, Texas, New Orleans, Maine. From the foreign countries, I made out places in Russia, Africa, and South America. No pattern to follow except he stayed away from the northeast or our part of the United States.

On top of knowing Mom was alive, was he avoiding her *on purpose?*

"The entries stopped in 2034," he said. "Since then, he's been a phantom."

Miraculous saves are what my father did for other people? My thoughts about him were validated. "Where is he now?"

Old Guy rubbed the stubble sprouting from his chin. "The Carolinas. I have a lead."

"Vague much?"

He limped across the room, his back toward us. "It's all you need to know. We're not the only ones after him."

My father had an archenemy like in the movies? "Who?" my mother asked him. "The Collective is dead except for you."

"People far worse than you thought us to be. Politicians. Military. To them, you're nuclear deterrents, militaristic weapons: a means to an end."

"What's so wrong with that?"

"Nothing" — he exploded into a coughing fit — "if you're on the right side."

I'd seen my mother be unconvinced a hundred times before. She'd put her hands on her hips and look down although she was barely taller than me. Because Old Guy had a little height, she couldn't look down at him. Skepticism filled her eyes. "What do you get out of it? No one's around to pull your strings anymore, and you're too old for women."

"Something," Old Guy said before snapping his left wrist to chest level. He eyed the large, black timepiece strapped to his arm and frowned. "Perimeter checks take six minutes top to bottom. He's been gone eight."

And? "He had to take a whiz, or he called a girlfriend. Relax."

Old Guy called Moses on comms and paused far too long. His wrinkled face tightened with worry. Mom appeared to sense the tension and asked him, "How long does the suppression drug last?"

"An hour," he growled. "Too long for what you're thinking."

She rummaged through her backpack and counted the epinephrine shots left. Three. Who knew if one, or even two, could jumpstart her adrenal glands? Getting to Isabella wouldn't happen anytime soon, and it was not like she could go to the local pharmacy and buy them. I read her nervous movements as she gathered them into her hand. She must be thinking the exact same thing. No powers meant we're dead. "Give us the antidote then! I know you have one."

Old Guy pushed down Mom's hand holding the syringes. "There is none."

His eyes never wavered. Maybe he was telling the truth. After all, if we were bargaining chips to him, what good would we be dead? "Save the shots. We've been compromised." He pointed to the immovable door. "The service elevator is this way."

We followed him as he staggered toward the front of the apartment. He leaned forward and forced his shoulder into the metal. The thing buckled in the middle and sounded as if a human-sized sledgehammer had struck it instead of an old man's bones. There was enough separation between it and the frame for us to squeeze through one at a time. Down the hallway and to the right was the service elevator. The button lit up when I pressed it, but I continued to push it. According to the digital display above it, the elevator had stopped on the twenty-fifth floor. The regular elevator was moving up from floor thirty-three.

Whoever was in that elevator was going to get to us first. "Stairs?"

Mom and Old Guy eyed me. I wasn't stupid. I had seen him walk. We stood a better chance of surviving without him. However, he had information we needed. He must live as well. I stood on my toes and bounced up and down until my calves burned. We were fifty-two stories up according to the bronze plate affixed to the wall. The regular elevator stopped on the forty-first floor. The service elevator was on the thirty-fifth floor.

"Hey, Old Guy?"

"Call me Peters."

I liked Old Guy better. "Who are these guys? Government? Black Ops military?"

His eyebrows raised. "Something like that."

That didn't compute. "Wouldn't they be in the regular elevator *and* the service elevator? That's what I'd do."

We'd have to take the stairs. And, with a guy this old, nobody would expect us to have gone that way. It made sense, and I wasn't crazy after all.

"I can't go down that many stairs," he said.

Circling around to Mom's back, I unzipped her bag, removed an EpiPen, and plugged Old Guy Peters in the stomach. His green eyes widened, and he convulsed. A second before I thought he'd drop dead, he put his cane under his arm and took to the exit. We followed him, Mom behind him with me bringing up the rear. He was always a half level in front of Mom and a full one in front of me. The burning in my side was out of control. I'd have to stop in the next couple of steps.

Mom paused on the landing between floors. She turned and faced me. "Hold on for a minute."

Mind racing, I leaned over the curved gray metal bannister and tried to breathe the best I could. My heartbeat pounded in my ears, but I still heard the pained groans in the background followed by the unmistakable snap of bones. From there, I matched Mom's pace and held my stomach when I passed a lifeless, bloodied body. *Moses.* Hardly knew the dude, he'd borderline assaulted us, and his death saddened me. Weird. Mom paused before she knelt and grabbed his discarded Ordnance beside a pool of blood. I found a firearm, too.

"Luciana!" Mom stopped walking and faced me. "Put that down! You're fourteen years old, and you think I'll let you shoot at people?"

I was honest. "You don't have a choice."

Despite her misgivings, she let me keep it. Old Guy Peters exited the stairwell about ten floors too early and waved us through a gray security door he'd smashed open. The gust of frigid wind told me why he'd done it — a parking garage on the tenth floor. Either the people following us hadn't checked the building's blueprint before they stormed it, or they were on their way. We trailed him to an old-school black Cougar transport with four doors. He tossed a set of keys to me...*keys?* How ancient was that thing to work on a key system?

He snatched the Ordnance from my right hand. "You can drive, right? It's not a stick."

I clutched the keys in my left hand, figuring the long one would start up this steel dinosaur. What was a "stick" anyway? "Totally."

"No! She has to finish Gail's Law, and she doesn't turn fifteen for another two weeks."

I pressed the button on the key until the transport unlocked. Old Guy Peters opened the passenger door behind the driver's seat. "It's a dumb law. She's not a drunk idiot who'll plow through a group of kids, all right? What, you'd rather have her shooting?"

He had a point. Who was to say I'd live to see fifteen anyway?

Mom circled around to sit next to me in the passenger seat. The way Old Guy Peters collapsed into the leather seat signaled to me that the adrenaline shot was wearing off, and he'd be back to normal speed soon. "Are you lucid?" he asked me from behind.

"Lucy. Short for Luciana."

Once he sufficiently rolled his eyes and sighed, I figured out I'd misinterpreted what he'd said. *"Lucid.* Clear. In other words, are you going to kill us all driving?"

"Y-yeah. No, I mean, I'm lucid. Not going to kill us. That's what I meant. Nope. All clear."

He reached his withered hand forward and touched a jagged-looking slot. "Long key goes here. Turn it clockwise. Be gentle. It's a 2019."

I did as he said, and the engine fired up with a thunderous roar. Its powerful hum sounded different than anything I'd ever been inside. Looked different too — the inside was less digital than I was used to. How did I shift into reverse with no touchpad console? The knob near my wrist? If "P" was for "Park," which is the gear we were in, then "N" was for...

Mom knocked my hand aside and pulled the knob back to reverse. The transport lurched backward until I stopped it. "Figure it out on the go," she said. "We're short on time."

I tapped the brake to give myself time to adjust the mirrors, and I backed out of the spot without hitting anything. Proud of myself, I put the knob to "D" and accelerated. The engine's ample power raged underneath me, and I fought the urge to push it. Instead, I followed the yellow signs painted on the concrete overhangs pointing to the exit. Mom gave me directions. I didn't need them. My sweaty hands slipped on the wheel, but my other tour guide had given me one direction to follow, and I had to master it.

I whipped around the first few turns so hard the tires squealed. I slowed down and readjusted my approach. Near the garage's exit, Old Guy Peters said, "Stop." I abruptly did it, and we all jerked forward.

"Switch the setting from stun to kill," he said to my mother. "Know how to do that?"

"Yeah." She fiddled with the Ordnance controls before locating the correct switch.

At least I knew that about her. She attended a marksmanship class twice a month with her girlfriends. I always thought it was pointless since she didn't own Ordnance herself, but apparently, she was just refreshing her assassin-level skills.

"Twenty round charge." He pulled off the inside panel frame near the window and motioned she should do the same. Air flooded the transport. He'd hollowed out part of the chassis to give them space to shoot. "Aim true. These guys don't miss often."

Their faces darkened. They understood what I didn't. We might get caught, and I had no idea what those consequences were. Torture? Death? Could anything be worse than death? Live dissection?

He coughed — the same kind of phlegm-filled way he'd done when I met him. "Forget what I said before. Ram through and right turn outside the garage."

"Glass is charge-proof, right?" I asked him.

He answered me with "Resistant."

Resistant? What the —

"At best. Mash the gas, turn right, and clear the opening. Go!"

Mass vehicular homicide and then turn right. Got it. Unlucky for us, there was a line of transports checking out. At the front was a group of policemen and men with white shirts and black ties and slacks conducting eye scans for identification.

This was a real problem. I was breaking several laws. Mom's fake identity would pass. God knows what the old man's eye scan would turn up.

He opened his window. "Two at twelve o' clock. One plus the eye scanner. Both armed."

"Four on my side," Mom told him as he rolled up the window. *"Armed.* They're moving back in the line, Peters. No chance we're getting through."

"What happens if we get caught?"

Old Guy Peters leaned forward and placed his hands on the sides of our seats. "Back up, Lucy," he whispered. *"Slowly."*

The transport eased into reverse without incident. But we couldn't climb the incline. Not unless I hit the gas, but the pedal was stuck. Frustrated, I used more muscle and the engine gunned. We zipped backward until I heard them yelling at me, and I regained the presence of mind to brake. The tire squeals drew the attention of the guard on my left side who pointed in our direction. I shifted back into drive, floored the gas, and zipped around the line of transports. Blue Ordnance fire cracked the windshield. A burst of light flashed past my right ear, and pain seared my temple.

We crashed through the yellow and black security arm on the entrance side. The metal clunked against the transport's chassis and dropped onto the street. It was a small miracle I didn't hit anybody. For a good five seconds, I was in the wrong lane. I swerved to the right, adjusting enough to avoid oncoming traffic, and course corrected. Clouds of gray tire smoke wafted behind us, and I smelled the rubber through the vents. Peters let out a howl, like I'd won a gold medal for driving, and my mother said nothing, which was odd for her.

My right eye stung, and the corner of my vision was cloudy. "I can't see," I said to nobody. Neither of my passengers said a word.

We rolled through a green traffic signal and continued at a regular speed up the hilly street. When I glanced at the rearview mirror, I noticed a wicked slash mark on my face. I'd been shot, grazed, really, which explained the smell of burnt hair and the hot stickiness and stinging at my ear. My first battle wound. I wouldn't get a badge or anything better than a crazy story to tell my friends. *Natalee.* She'd hear it. I'd get back to her. First things first. "Everybody okay?" I asked them.

Old Guy Peters moaned and rubbed the back of his wrinkled neck. "The car deflected most of the blasts, and of all the..." His voice trailed off. He leaned forward into the space between the seats. Steady, calm, but firm, he told me, "Pull over."

The road didn't have a clearly defined shoulder. Only a rumble strip and a bike lane. What was the emergency? I didn't ask, but I did as he said just as I'd gotten into a driving rhythm. Why did adults make things always sound hard? "Wait until you get to middle school. Things are harder."

No, they weren't. I could've handled a little more of my classwork if I cared or if I wasn't in and out of the hospital with chemo treatments and checkups. Driving was no big deal even in an old school "car" like this one — I could handle it.

I put the transport in park, unbuckled my safety belt, and readjusted myself. Mom was slumped down against the window. Three Ordnance holes had burned through her bodysuit, and its cloaking device was rapidly flickering on and off.

And her body wasn't moving.

Everything became blurs of colored light and slurred words. She was *dead.* Dead. I had nothing left to live for. For all the fights we'd had, and the times I'd said I hated her but didn't, I wanted to go with her. She'd be in purgatory or Heaven, and I'd be here. The guy who'd shot me should've aimed a couple inches to his right and put me down. I wished he had. Sure, the woman annoyed me a good sixty percent of the time, but what would I do without her? I'd have no connections to speak of.

I rested my hand on her lifeless arm. Frigid air whisked through the transport's cabin. A force pushed Mom's seat so hard it shook once. Then twice. In my stupor, I snapped back to the present. Peters had jabbed her remaining epinephrine pens into her leg. The sight of syringes dangling from her thigh muscle brought me back to reality. That was the answer. Kick-start her abilities, and the healing process would take care of itself. Except she still hadn't budged. "Did it work?" I asked him.

He pressed two fingers into the side of her neck. "No."

"Do something!" I screamed.

"Get in the back," he told me.

I did it as if my life, and not my mother's, depended on it. Once I got there and secured myself, Old Guy Peters limped to the driver's seat. He dropped down, rested his cane near my mother's feet, and slapped his Ordnance into my hand. "Don't be shy with this," he told me. "It's either you or them."

He gunned the engine, and we sped off zipping around transports and ignoring traffic signals. After a few miles, we attracted the attention of one police cruiser. Then two. The flashing lights and blaring sirens were magnets. Three, four cruisers. I stopped counting. The word about us was out, and we were in a full-on, high-speed chase.

My heart beat hard. Should I try to shoot out their tires like people do in action holofilms? Besides the shake of my sweat-drenched hands, the transport kept hitting bumps. I was lucky I hadn't already shot myself.

Gathering up the courage, I located the homemade turret in the transport paneling. As soon as I had poked the firearm through it, the policemen opened fire on us. The transport's blast-resistant chassis deflected many of their shots. The few that hit the glass cracked it. Old Guy Peters cursed and shouted for me to return fire. I closed my eyes and pulled the trigger. There was no telling where that blast went. The kickback pushed my hand against the chassis' metal, and I almost dropped the Ordnance onto the street.

Taking a deep breath, I readjusted, aimed for the closest target, and squeezed off three straight rounds. Sparks flew from the front of the transport I'd hit, and it disoriented the driver enough that he crashed into the transport next to him. Now confident, I emptied the firearm and hit nothing else. The return fire continued. Another direct blast to the fractured rear windshield would probably break it.

Our transport zoomed onto a highway on-ramp. Old Guy Peters steered us to the angled concrete shoulder. The policemen ceased fire but continued following us. He sped up, the vehicle hit another faster gear, and the distance between us and them widened.

He'd done it. We were escaping!

"Hey!" I shouted, looking up ahead. "Might want to actually get on the road there!"

He ignored me. At the rate of speed and direction we were traveling, we were going to crash into a pillar supporting a bridge. In about thirty seconds. No big deal except the senior citizen was playing a game of chicken with an inanimate object. My fingertip edges tingled with hot pins and needles as I gripped Mom's headrest. She hadn't breathed in a couple of minutes. If Old Guy Peters didn't turn off though, it wouldn't matter.

I cursed at him. "Get on the road!"

He still said nothing. *What am I going to do?* Jumping out of the back seat meant I'd surely die, run over by a fleet of policemen. Staying here meant I *could* die, not that I *would*. The old man was toast, and Mom was...I didn't want to think about it. Her safety belt was secured, and so was mine. The paneling looked as if it may contain self-inflating airbags. All transports had those, right? I resigned myself to whatever injuries I'd sustain from his crazy plan. At least there was a possibility I might survive.

I closed my eyes and waited for the inevitable sound of crunching metal and shattering glass. Instead, I heard a large explosion. A *boom* shook and rattled the transport, but it was still moving. We slowed down and proceeded on a downward angle almost roller-coaster steep. I cracked one eye open then the other. Our surroundings were dark — an underground tunnel. Liquid splashed beneath the tires, and the headlights illuminated just a few feet in front of us. Not too long afterward, Old Guy Peters parked the transport on a platform. I followed his lead and stepped out. An underground cavern? A cave? The ceiling was high, and the walls were curved and seemingly made of stone.

"Come here." He motioned me over to the passenger side of the transport. After unbuckling her, he put his hands beneath Mom's arms and grunted as he positioned her body out of the seat. I grabbed her feet. Together, we got her to the cave's cool metal grid surface. The interior lights shone on her face. Being half Cape Verdean and Panamanian, I'd thought she should be more naturally tanned than she was. Still, her skin shocked me by how white it had become. I refused to believe she was dead.

Old Guy Peters tossed the used needles aside, and he performed CPR. I recited as many Our Father prayers as I could. The thought of his lips touching my mother in any situation freaked me out more than him pumping her chest with his fist, but I let him do it.

Good thing, because I heard her gasp.

CHAPTER TEN

Her next breaths were short. Shallow. Ragged. I struggled to catch air myself while anticipating her chest's rising and falling. Eventually, it did. This continued. Though I couldn't keep time, it passed like three years in slow motion. All we'd been through together, after everything, I couldn't lose her. I *couldn't*. It'd break me.

The humid air smelled of stale water. We were in Ohio, underground. I had no idea how we ended up in a rock cave. From what I remembered, we had nearly crashed into a concrete highway pillar, and *then...what?* I accessed the communications display in my mask. No signal. Crap. Old Guy didn't say much, not even when I needled him about whether Mom would live. He said superhuman biology was enhanced, complicated, and "tough to quantify."

Not a week ago, Mom told me my survival odds were "hard to accurately calculate." My bone cancer behaved erratically. As the tumors got bigger and spread, Dr. Keller still wouldn't commit to survival odds. Until last week when my case suddenly went terminal. Whatever the situation with my sickness, Mom spared little details with me. Aside from the situation with my father, she told it how it was. She knew me. I needed that. If there was a slight chance I'd win a fight, then I'd scrap like an animal. Otherwise, I'd give up. No sense in fighting a losing battle.

For that, she deserved the same treatment from me. I stood at Mom's feet. "Answer me. Is she going to live or not?"

Old Guy opened the transport's trunk and grabbed a vintage flashlight from the storage space to examine our surroundings. He talked to me, I think, but all I heard were the gruff echoes of his mumbling voice and dripping liquid.

"Hey!" he yelled at me. The stench of his liquor breath arrested my attention.

"Huh?"

He pressed a square on his yellow and black flashlight. Its bulb flickered dull orange. I hadn't paid attention to the blackness. Except for that bit of illumination, we were completely in the dark.

"Light it up."

I turned my attention away from Mom's condition to hand him a death stare. "What?"

"The power cell in this thing is dying, and I don't want to waste the car's battery."

"What's a 'battery'?"

"Forget it and make some fire!"

After giving him two one finger salutes, I let him know what he could do with his desire to see. I'd rather be in the dark, I told him. Would light help my mother's breathing? No. Then, why help him? Anyway, his sketchy drug suppressed my adrenaline and *hadn't* worn off, which irritated me further. All of this was his fault.

Halfway through my angry tirade, my hand's bones burned like fireworks were inside them. The building sensation shut me up. His shot had finally worn off. He'd given it to us at around the same time, so Mom's powers should return soon, too, which had to be a good thing.

"Concentrate," he said with force. "Let your power stretch and unfold inside of you."

How? I tried it. Deep in my belly, the fire flared like an invisible twisting rope I tried to wave at and grab. Raising my arm into the darkness like I was in class, I cursed and squeezed my fist hard. Ironically, that's when it happened. Orange sparks crackled between my fingers, and then they engulfed my hand. My suit glove didn't melt. No pain.

"Stop screaming!" he growled. "Focus and hold it."

I looked at Old Guy, expecting him to give me another level of instruction beyond six words. Instead, he opened his trunk, threw the flashlight inside, removed a shiny metal flask, unscrewed the top, and poured some liquid on the ground before taking a swig. Perfect time for a drink, at least in his mind, I guess. I was thirsty, too.

Meanwhile, I admired my torch of a fist. "Is that flammable?"

"No worries," he said after another swallow. "You couldn't light a match right now."

Out of anger, I cupped my hand and tried throwing flames at him. He laughed when nothing came of it. The next time, I closed my eyes and imagined a ball. I gasped when I opened them. A clear orange and yellow orb the size of a large marble sat in the center of my palm. It moved in my hand as if it was solid and not a fiery circle of nothing. Rolling it into my fingers, I chucked it at him, and he flinched although I'd missed him by a wide margin.

He chuckled. "Practice. You throw like a girl."

I did as he said. After two dozen failed attempts, I was on the verge of giving up. That's it. I didn't have the power to stop whatever was after us. *I throw like a girl because I am a girl.* We were gonna die. All three of us. In my boiling frustration, I saw Old Guy eyeing my face. He saw tears welling in my eyes. I blinked them free, and he turned away, as if to dismiss my feelings. I had to do the same.

Around trial number thirty, I grew the fire to the size of a baseball. Couldn't throw to save my life, but I kept at it, winging shots into the darkness. Their arc curved to the left. Had to be my wrist. I adjusted to compensate. Once I accomplished that, the next challenge was speed. Did it matter how hard I threw? Kind of. When I released, a small flame trail followed and gave it extra push. I did this until my arms were sore, my stomach rumbled, and my throat was dry. Water was above us, and we couldn't drink it.

Old Guy had batted one of my errant fireballs to ignite a makeshift torch of dirty rags and a short metal pole. He lit and aggressively puffed a cigarette like it had made him angry.

"Got another one?" I asked him.

He pulled a slender white stick from his pocket and waved it at me. "You're *fourteen,*" he said.

"I've smoked worse."

"And it's a bad habit. They can cause cancer, you know."

I snatched it from him and lit it on the fingers of my smoldering right glove. "That's not funny," I mumbled. My face perspired from my hand's residual heat.

He stated the obvious following a lengthy drag. "Wasn't meant to be. It's fact."

We would never be friends, but for a tiny second, I'd forgotten everything he'd done to us. Except put Mom in the condition she was. We had one thing in common. I had terminal cancer, and if he was as ancient as he said he was, he'd be in stage four hundred by now.

"What do you think he will be like when you find him?"

"Who?"

"The great Jason Champion. Your father."

His name. I finally knew his name. *Jason Champion.* Nobody could take that away from me. Luciana Champion. Lucy Champion. Either would take getting used to. I'd been Lucy Sandoval my entire life, and, come to find out, my last name was fake anyway.

What did I think he would be like? My greatest hopes and wildest dreams. He'd call me "Lucy" from jump and run to hug me, long and hard, and it would be like he'd never missed all my life's important moments. I'd trade them all for that. I'd never have to wonder where he was again. The explanations would be overwhelming and thrilling. No room for negativity. Not even my mother knew all of this. I'd hardly describe all of that to someone I did not trust. "I don't know."

A smile escaped his wrinkled face. "Try not to care so much. Makes you *weak*."

Caring made me *weak*? "That's stupid."

He recited a long list of people he'd lost over the years. Men and women of different ethnic backgrounds. Parents, his wife and son, girlfriends — *a lot* of girlfriends — acquaintances, friends and enemies and how he'd lost them. He'd made his point. The ones who hadn't died violently he'd certainly outlived. "Even in fiction," he continued. "Name one person of significant power, and their loved ones have faced threats. Why do you think you have no 'family' to speak of? None of us do! And — "

"Stop."

"Your mother — "

"Stop!"

Old Guy paused and blew a smoke ring into the wispy clouds we'd created together. "She was Jason's weakness. He was hers. They were...no good together."

As Mom fought for her life in this Godforsaken cave, I got the urge to defend her life choices. "They were good together at least once."

He chuckled. The pole torch flickered out. He pointed it toward the ground, and I winged a fireball at it. Direct hit. My aim had improved. Once the flames picked up, he put it back over his shoulder and continued smoking. "Maybe, but instead of having just your mother as leverage against him, now they've got you, too."

Great. Another thing to worry about. I puffed the cigarette and let it relax my nerves. When Mom recovered, both of us could defend ourselves. "Who's they?"

"They." He laughed. "They are anyone not in this cave. Everyone who knows about what you can do."

That was disheartening. "You know about Moses?"

"You don't say." He let out a healthy cough. "Moses, my servant, is dead. Pooling blood and broken neck gave it away."

That wasn't my point, and he knew it. "He was their leverage on you, wasn't he?"

"Just a friend" was all he said. That, and a word or two about seeing the Promised Land.

Now, I felt bad for making fun of him and calling him Old Guy's son. Turned out they had a relationship deeper than boss-henchman. "How'd you meet?"

Old Man huffed again. "How friends meet."

"Coffee shop? Dating app? Roleplaying game with inappropriate avatars..."

He chucked the used cigarette butt onto the ground. His bloodshot eyes narrowed and focused on me. "Jason sent Frank to me."

He name-dropped him again: my father, Jason Champion. Luciana Champion. That would take some getting used to.

I wondered, him? My father sent Moses to Old Guy and not us? Why? To find Mom? To fight whatever was coming after us? She would've come if he directly approached her. At least, I thought she would.

He answered for me. "She's the one who walked away from him, not the other way around. I trained them both."

"Trained them?" I tossed away my cigarette. "You call kidnapping *training?*"

He motioned to Mom. "Whatever works. You're alive and your abilities work, don't they?"

Drugging people and dragging them across the northeast United States wasn't training. Only a psychopath would think of captivity and torture as instruction tools. But I was trapped. I crossed my arms and watched him smoke as I practiced being a human flamethrower. Hey, I wondered to myself, could I set my whole body on fire? Not sure I wanted to give it a shot.

Pleased with himself, he leaned against his transport's chassis and finished. After he tossed the wrinkled butt on the ground, he popped the trunk open and handed me several packages the size of my palm. "Eat these," he said as I stomped out my cigarette. "You need your strength."

My right glove melted the plastic wrapping. They were the color of mud and had the texture of wet bread. I bit into one without questioning what exactly "it" was. The first one tasted like an explosion of fruit — peaches, grapes, apples, bananas, mangoes, and a few other sweet tastes I couldn't distinguish. The second one tasted like steak, mashed potatoes, and gravy, and the third like a Caesar salad with croutons. Forget the other stuff. How had the manufacturer copied the taste of croutons? These were amazing!

Clearly, I had eaten these out of order, but I was full.

Just then, several thunder-like cracks struck hard and shook the cave's foundation. Pebbles and dust dropped from overhead. What was that, a battering ram? Tank? Before I could ask, Old Guy handed me a black leather suitcase from his trunk. "Change out of that relic and put this on. There's not much time."

Quicker than I was used to moving, I stripped out of the bodysuit I'd been wearing. Its white pads stuck to my skin, and I almost had to peel the thing off. Inside the suitcase was a new bodysuit — sleek and the exterior was milk white. I failed to see how this would be stealth, but I slipped into it anyway. Once I zipped the thing up at the neck, it shrank to my body's contours and turned transparent. Although there was no visible padding, the thing was as comfortable as my robe at home. "So, we're going to fight them?"

There was an extra suit in the suitcase beneath mine, and since Old Guy didn't respond to me or ask for it, I put it on Mom. The incessant pounding outside the cave continued, so I rushed. Mom lightly moaned when I undressed her and forced her limbs the way I needed them to go. It was like dressing a one-hundred-and-thirty-pound sleeping baby. By the time I was done, Mom's eyes fluttered open and she eased to a sitting position. "Hey," she weakly said.

"Hey. Can you stand? We kind of need you."

She wiggled her feet and bounced her legs. "I think so. What's going on?"

With my help, she got to a standing position before another blast hit the cave. This one made all of us struggle to keep our balance. She was in no condition to fight, which meant we'd have to run. "Which way is out, Peters?"

He pointed toward the front of the transport. "Twenty yards that way. The back axle is broken. You'll have to get out the hard way."

You'll not *we'll*? "What are you going to be doing?" I asked him.

He pointed to his prized vehicle. "Moving *that*. You'll need it."

I put my arm around Mom, and she leaned on me for support. Behind us, Old Guy pushed the transport. The shattered axle scraped the rock surface as it rolled forward. The only thing louder than the grating were the blasts, which tightened in frequency and strength. Old Guy's torch in my free hand lit the way, and when we reached the cave's end, it was nothing like what we expected — a large mound of rocks.

"How are we supposed to get through?" I asked. Thinking back to my internal flame, I said, "How hot do I have to burn to get through rock?"

"If you *could*," Old Guy said, "you'd kill yourself and everything around you."

That couldn't have been the plan, right? Mom was in on it. Sure, she was. From the look on her face and what I could tell, she'd figured it out. "How do I find him?" she asked.

"You can't," he replied. "Moses was the only way."

He rounded the side of the transport and poked beneath the chassis until he heard two metallic snaps. I sniffed the strong scent of fluid. Old Guy had popped the combustion engine's fuel and oil lines.

"Give me thirty seconds," he said while snatching the torch from my hand. I used my left fist to light our way. "Hit the lines and overheat the battery. They'll blow and trigger the self-destruct."

Make the transport explode in this small space? "Are you insane? We won't survive that!"

He coughed for a minute. "The second part..." He stopped to spit on the ground. "The second part of your job is to *survive*. Rhapsody can do the rest."

In her condition? She could hardly stand. "Why can't I wait until they come in and blow it then — take out a few of them in the process?"

"Listen. This isn't the time to improvise," he said. "Not here. Not now."

He and Mom approached one another. They exchanged looks I could not decipher besides deciding what they weren't. Not love or sentiment and barely like. In the absence of those, I think there was a shared level of respect between them — enough to shake hands. This relationship had to be complicated, because I didn't see myself giving the man who had kidnapped me and said my daughter shouldn't exist a good second of my attention.

"Goodbye," she whispered as Old Guy limped away. "Thank you."

I counted backward from thirty, and with each second, I watched the torch grow smaller and smaller in the distance. The last thunderous blast blew inward so far that pebbles and dust clouds pelted the transport's bumper and taillights. After brushing the debris away from our masks, we glanced at one another.

"There's no way this guy buys us fifteen more seconds," I thought out loud. I conjured a pair of fireballs and lengthened them into foot-high columns. All I had to do was flip my palms and shoot into the hood and the fluid-soaked rock foundation. "You trust him?"

"No." Mom held up her hand. "But you don't live almost two hundred years and not know what you're talking about."

The afternoon sun shone into the cave. Only the suit's visor with automatic brown tint helped me see through the dust clouds. The eye shields zoomed in to the front of the cave. They'd brought about twenty people, and they had no weapons. How had they gotten inside without explosives? Red outlined their bodies, and the reading on the side of my heads-up display was 13.5 kRad. Whatever kRads were, I assumed that's why Mom's mouth gaped. I called her name three or four times, and she did not answer. The hand keeping me from acting, however, had not moved.

Ten more seconds.

Old Guy yelled and attacked them. I had no idea he could move so fast. He dropped a group of them until one overcame him and forced him to his knees. He cried out a shortened, "Now!" when they yanked the heliodor from his neck. He disintegrated into a pile of bones and dust.

Fire engulfed my hands and arms and then my shoulders as I shot it forward. Orange and yellow flames licked up the fuel. No explosion yet. I clenched my teeth together until they hurt, focused on getting hotter, and anticipated the thing exploding like a balloon blown up past its capacity. I closed my eyes. Sweat dribbled down my face. A strong pair of hands wrapped around my arms. He or she was too late.

Nothing could stop me.

The next thing I knew, I was lying on my back, sore and out of breath. Medical diagnoses flashed on my display, but the stabbing and white flashes in my eyes and my ringing ears made it difficult to read. *Mild concussion.* Thanks. I didn't need a computer to tell me that. To my left, amidst the transport's flaming wreckage, was a blackened skeleton with no hands. Its charred fingers were still on my left arm! I shrieked and shook, wiggled, and slapped my forearm until the rattling things fell.

Oh God!

I was a *murderer.*

I never meant to kill anyone.

What had he done to deserve death?

Besides getting too close to me?

Would everyone close to me die?

I rolled my head in the other direction. More melting transport parts and scattered fires. Mom was to my right, propped up against the wall and unconscious. At least she wasn't dead, too. Old Guy's — Peters' — suicidal plan had half worked. Past Mom was sunlight. We had an escape route. The explosion had done what he said it would and opened a passageway to freedom though neither of us was in the condition to use it. Two of the ones he hadn't crawled our way. No flames from my body. Must be the concussion.

Too far to reach Mom, I stretched my arm in her direction and hoped our communication systems were connected. "Mom." My weak voice resounded inside my head. Was I even talking? "Get up, Mom."

She was breathing. The suit outlined her body in green. She was alive but unresponsive.

My muscles hurt and weighed me down. I called her again with more strength this time. She gasped and coughed. Everything her mentor had said came back to me. Of course, she was a *weakness.* Like it or not, I cared what happened to her. I hated that Old Guy was right, and now that he was gone, he wouldn't even have the satisfaction of knowing I was wrong.

Without warning, the two men approaching us stopped. One had black hair and a goatee, and the other had short brown hair. Assuming a fighting position, they jumped past us to fight whatever or whoever it was I couldn't see. The rock foundation at my back shook. Who had the advantage? All I saw was a silent movie of flailing limbs and exchanged blows. There were two teleporters. One per side, good guy and bad, I assumed, and I was thankful the mask blocked most of the rotten egg smell given off. I couldn't tell anything about the other two fighters. Too much darkness, and my concussed haze didn't help. Mom was a couple yards away. She might as well have been ten thousand.

I blinked and found myself lying across her legs. Specks of green dust floated around me. Good teleporter or bad teleporter had put us together. We were *packages*. It was easier to move two things when they were close together. And, let's face it, we were *things*. None of them would see us as *people*: a mother and a daughter. Mom and I were two super beings, and if what Old Guy said was true, someone wanted to control us and use what we could do. With both of us, anything was possible.

Mom grunted. "Were you always this heavy?"

I almost shifted before I realized she was joking. "*Now* you have a sense of humor?"

The fighting continued, but the other guys, the ones we'd been warned about, were bringing reinforcements. A new group of men appeared at the makeshift entrance to the cave. I rolled to my side and forced myself to my hands and knees. "Can you move?"

"No," she mouthed. "Stay still."

Her hand was iron on my shoulder. Besides breathing and shifting to keep numbness from creeping into my legs, I did as she said. We were supposed to sit here and let the superhuman battle decide our fate? Did we have a choice? Neither of us was in the condition to protest. Natalee once had boys get in a fight over her, and when it was over, she did not go out with either of them. From her perspective, it wasn't her fault, and she felt no obligation to reward "savage behavior." Wasn't that what we were doing by lying here?

We had to do something!

My voice was weak and raspy. I rubbed my gloved fingers. Could've been the concussion fooling my eyes or I conjured up a spark of flame. I repeated the action, and, as luck would have it, a tennis-ball-sized fireball popped into my palm. I flung it sidearm at the teleporters and tagged one of them. His covered face focused on me for a split second. The glare from behind the black material stirred fear in me, like an evil presence aware it could do whatever it wanted to me, and I couldn't overcome its will. He returned to the fight. In the darkness, the blow by blow and the winning side were impossible to track.

One of the transporters caught the other off guard and made his hand disappear and reappear into the chest of the other guy who dropped dead. My stomach tensed. No good guy I'd ever seen would kill so mercilessly.

The killer knelt and grabbed me by the throat with his bloodied hand. Thus far, I envisioned myself dying any number of ways — from a fatal infection, alone, on the bathroom floor. Maybe in a hospital bed from complications or even at Old Guy's hand — but not like this.

Before he had an opportunity to do anything, a man snapped his neck and dropped him to the ground.

He shouted, "How long?" to no one in particular. He was cloaked head to toe in black body armor, and all I could tell about the man who had presumably rescued me was that he had a British accent, his voice didn't carry the wear of age, and he wasn't tall or overly muscular.

"Wait!" I yelled at him and pointed at her limp body. "Her, too."

He followed my finger downward to where my mother lay. "No time."

My abilities made me a force. "Then leave me. I'll save her myself."

Or so I thought. He lifted me like I was nothing and flew — *flew* — me through the opening the explosion had created and into broad daylight. He and I floated two stories above the ground. With all the strength I had, I beat my fists into his chest and squirmed to get free. I might as well have been punching concrete. He might not have been a jacked-up bodybuilder, but he was *solid*. "How do you feel?" he asked.

What was this, a therapy session in the sky? Pissed off. Worried about Mom. What did this fool think? Who was he? How did he think I felt being kidnapped *again?* A flock of birds flapped in formation near us, and I hoped not to get crapped on. "Go back and get her!"

Suddenly, my insides boiled. I slapped at my stomach to stop it and screamed in agony. I was melting alive.

His next words to me were "They might've pinged you. Hold on tight and keep breathing."

We shot straight up into the air. Miles into the sky. I must have blacked out from the quick change in altitude, because the next thing I knew, we were hovering among the clouds. Apparently, my suit was insufficient to accommodate this kind of altitude. Its breathing apparatus wasn't helping much. I could tell from the burning in my lungs and my lightheadedness.

"We're out of range now," he told me. "Breathe."

Not a problem. My chattering teeth and shivering upper torso made anything else impossible. We soared across the sky for several minutes according to my mask's display, and the whipping drag winds assaulted my ears. This high-tech suit needed a soundproof setting. Did it have one? I whispered "soundproof," and the pressure on the sides of my head relaxed.

Once I did that, the man held me tighter and thrust us forward through the clouds. An exhilarating experience if not for the lack of sound and the fact I kept entering and exiting consciousness.

The landing was gradual, like a bird finding its footing after gliding, not abrupt like the takeoff. I knelt and flexed my aching leg and arm joints. The incessant pounding was bearable — I could think past it — but focus was an issue. My unaffected pilot circled me while I groaned and stretched. It occurred to me that he might have been talking, so I gave my suit the command to return sound. My ears popped, and I could hear again.

"Where's my mother?" I slurred.

His lips moved, but his voice was difficult to make out. Was he whispering? I think he said "accelerator" and "infirmary." Situated around us were tall brick buildings, like a military-looking complex with no soldiers. Behind it was a mountain range — the Appalachians? We weren't far enough west for it to be anything else, meaning we could be anywhere along the upper East Coast. He took me by the arm and led me to a white rectangular building with metal walls that, from the outside, looked like a warehouse.

A handprint on a biometric pad later, we were inside of it. The security system recognized him by name — Liam Thomas. Beneath the lights, I got a good look at him. Liam couldn't be more than five feet ten inches and two hundred pounds. From the sleekness of his caramel skin, he was young, nineteen or twenty, with a thin beard and brown eyes. Cute but unremarkable besides his arms — man, *those chiseled arms* — and a tiny, bluish moon-shaped scar on his right hand near his thumb.

I followed him down a corridor, a right turn at the end, through another corridor, and into a row of hospital-like rooms. Memorizing the path was important in case I needed a quick getaway. In the middle of the row lay my mom. She was hooked up to machines and sensors. Eyes closed, she appeared to be at peace. I remembered Old Guy's speech about leverage. Threaten her life and they could get me to do pretty much anything.

At that moment, it occurred to me that maybe we hadn't been rescued at all.

CHAPTER ELEVEN

Liam wanted to escort me all over the shiny, white industrial complex. Everything was white — even the light fixtures, digital ceiling cameras, side railing fixtures, and baseboards. The slick hallways, wooden cabinets, handles, and counters had to be bleached or repainted daily to stay this clean. The air didn't smell like paint or strong cleanser, though, less of a bleach burn or gentle aroma in my nostrils and more like a sterile freshness.

What also struck me was the contrast of black wheel paths worn into the otherwise perfectly waxed floor on the pathway leading to Mom's room. They were deep enough for my feet to feel a difference when I stepped on them. She was far from the first person to be attended to in that room. Rolling beds shouldn't be that heavy, should they? Why were the trails so distinctive, and why had no one bothered to fix them? How many had been there? With so few people around, the custodial staff must not be large either.

I needed to explore who was housed here and why. But right now, I wanted to stay put next to Mom without Liam. His stiff body movements said he'd rather be anywhere else than with me by her bedside, but he stayed.

I settled down into the room's white leather padded chair and curled into a tight ball with my hands clutching my ankles. Mom's body looked deathlike in her paper-thin gown with printed blue diamonds. The quilted blue blankets covering her up to the midsection were warm to the touch for now. I fingered the holes to touch her skin. After a while, the air would chill her, and the covering would provide little insulation. Being unconscious, she might not know the difference...but I did.

I yanked the slack in the cotton mesh blankets from the bottom, covered her below the monitors attached to her chest, and returned to my position beside her. After about a half an hour, Liam left me alone and returned with a steaming Styrofoam cup for me.

"What's in yours?" I asked him as he offered it.

"Water. We're out of tea." He jostled the cup in his other hand. "Caffeine makes me irritable."

Guys used the word "irritable" to describe themselves? Was it a British thing, or was he one of those high-maintenance dudes who drinks with his pinky sticking out while reading stock market predictions? For me, I didn't want the coffee especially fearing he'd dosed it to knock me out. A refusal might arouse his suspicions. I accepted it and slowly slipped. Whatever was in it, cream, sugar, artificial sweetener, poison — I wouldn't swallow enough to damage my system. Soon, I'd say I have a thing about cold coffee and use it as my reason not to finish.

As I fake sipped, Liam checked the time on his antique wrist piece. Pretty old school. I preferred the wall clock setting for my holo so I knew how to read it: four p.m. on the mark. The thing made a cute beeping sound. He fished the largest, darkest-colored pill I'd ever seen out of his pocket, tossed it into his mouth, and chased it with his cup of water. His Adam's apple bobbed up and down, so he'd somehow swallowed the monstrous thing without choking.

"Little late in the day for a vitamin," I joked.

"Not this kind."

He tossed the cup into a trash can behind him, which made me remember to fake sip again, but this time, I took a little in. I continued to push to know more. "What kind of vitamin is black anyway?"

He chuckled but didn't elaborate beyond "It's dark brown, not black."

Fine. Be mysterious then.

I repositioned and glanced over my shoulder. Mom's room and the corridor we'd taken to get here were closed off to the outside. I hadn't noticed that before. The observation windows were tinted yellow. Bodies walked past them too fast. I couldn't make mental note of its appearance beyond white clothing and the tan or whitish-pink skin hue. Most were men or mannish-looking women.

Why was everything white here? Was color banned?

My companion groaned and eased himself onto the chair across from me. "Comfortable enough?"

"The chair pads are soft, but no matter what I do, my right butt cheek keeps going numb."

"Ha." He pointed to the hospital bed. "Your mum's improving."

"How do you know that? She's unconscious."

He licked his lips and said, "Her vitals are steady. They were erratic when she arrived."

I didn't know where to begin with the questions. The clear-door refrigerator full of blood bags was a start. "Vampire fridge is for a transfusion?" I asked him.

He nodded. "Worse case, yeah. What blood type is she?"

"I don't know." Hopefully, my shrug was convincing.

"Well, what blood type are you? It could be the same."

Having powers meant I had to be AB negative with the antigen, didn't it? "I don't pay attention when nurses draw my blood."

"Hmm." He stood and stretched his legs. "We'll figure it out, then, yeah?"

Didn't look like the explosion had left her with many injuries, but we could only see the surface, and they'd scan her body to be certain, which could uncover more than she'd want them to know. Protecting her was my number one priority with escaping this place a close second.

Liam waved his hands in front of a wall panel. A blue, holographic, three-dimensional image of Mom's skeletal system appeared. "Mild to moderate concussion," he said, pointing to a throbbing red mass in her skull. "Worse than yours. Your rapid blinking gave it away."

Meaning we couldn't fly to escape.

He also explained the small blue knots dotted along her spine — muscle contusions — and the crooked line on her ribcage was a hairline fracture. How had I caused the explosion and barely suffered a scratch?

"Try to relax."

I stopped fidgeting and noticed I'd spilled coffee on the floor. "Oh. Sorry."

He waved me off, bent over, and blotted the spot with a napkin. "No worries."

"Why all of the white? Black would be easier to hide stains."

He laughed at my suggestion and tossed the napkin into the automatic trash can. "You'll have to ask," he said while dusting himself off.

"Who? When?"

Liam rubbed his hands together. "Soon enough."

The way he said it sounded like I was going to the VIP section to shake hands with a celebrity. I'd been there and done that enough to be somewhat fearless though the authority figures I'd met weren't powered. "Where are you from?"

With a twirl of his right index finger he said, "Across the pond. Nowhere special."

"And you're *my* age?"

He crossed his arms and repositioned himself in the chair to face me. His smooth and comfortable body language did nothing to ease the rising tension in my chest. "No. I'm legal."

Again, he was nonspecific. His dark lips were kissable, but he wasn't my type — that's not why I asked his age. Over eighteen meant he'd chosen to stay superhuman. According to Mom, on December 4, 2042 — my eighteenth birthday — I'd be forced into a similar decision: keep my abilities or be "normal." Even now, I felt conflict about it. Superpowered people don't get recurrences of bone cancer and die from it. Normal people don't shoot flames from their hands and wear tech-outfitted body suits.

"Where are we, Liam?"

"That's classified."

I cleared my throat. "Are we still on the East Coast?"

"Classified."

Fantastic. Escaping would be more difficult. One direction would take me near home while others could send me to another coast or across the Atlantic.

Liam gulped his water and gave me a wary look. "Plotting an escape?"

To keep myself safe, I overexaggerated my reaction to his question. "Escape? *Me?* From *here?* Are you holding us hostage?"

"No. You're free to leave whenever you'd like." The tone of his voice suggested the opposite was true. "I'm hoping you and your mum will listen to our pitch, first. To join us."

"Who's us? Government?"

He nodded. "Of a sort."

What would it take to get a straight answer longer than three words from this guy? I leaned back in my chair. "Are you this vague with your girlfriend?"

Liam laughed heartily.

"You don't have a girlfriend?" I asked him. "Or, you do, and she's an idiot."

"Any question you've asked, have I not answered?"

"Okay, a boyfriend?"

His voice raised in pitch. "I have not lied to you, Lucy."

Crossing my arms over my breasts, I continued stomping on his nerves. "You haven't told me the entire truth. We can leave whenever we want, but we don't know where we are, so how do we know where to go?"

"You — "

"And you're 'a sort' of government?" My use of a fake British accent and air quotes encouraged an eye roll. "We're not a constitutional monarchy. We're a *republic*. For the people and by the people."

"If you think that's the truth," he shouted, "you're the stupid one."

Conscious of our escalating volume, I lowered my voice. My mother hadn't stirred. "What's the truth, then?"

Liam exhaled and sighed. "The Ordnance lobby and fearmongering controls the government. Your precious republic is for *some* people and by *a few* people."

"What does that mean, and what's a lo — "

"Military weapons, municipal firearms, hunters — it's trillions in business. A piece of that money goes to election funding, and the election winner controls how the laws pass. War profiteering. When there are tragedies, there is money to be made."

"And you're a part of that?"

Liam rested his elbows on his knees and leaned forward. "When the scales tip too far in either direction, we balance them."

"How?"

He gave me a one-word answer: power. Of course, a guy who could fly faster than a jet airplane had to have a God complex. Liam calmly explained how his organization, or collective, uses predictive measures to assess catastrophic events most likely to cause a social tipping point and allow or instigate them.

Um, what?

In simpler terms, he shared, they found crisis-causing actions to force sudden societal change — coup d'état's, political scandals, school shootings — and made them happen. He gave me an example of an African country he refused to name stricken with decades of poverty. "How would you fix this dilemma?" he asked me.

I sipped my coffee, forgetting that he might have drugged it. Spitting it out would give me away. I reluctantly swallowed and hoped for the best. "I don't know."

"Years ago, at night, we torched their agriculture and shed blood — old people, criminals, no one significant, mind you. Within a month, the United Nations sent aid. If I showed you a picture today, you'd think it was Eden." He held out his hands at an unequal level as a demonstration. "Balance."

I'd thought I was in a bad situation beforehand, but this dude had just admitted to mass murder and property destruction to accomplish his goals. How was that balance? "The UN would've sent help."

Liam counted his points using his fingers. "Eventually and to a lesser degree. Overpopulation, famine, poor agriculture — we solved this country's most widespread problems overnight. It was good work."

That didn't seem logical. "They'll eventually overpopulate again."

"No," he said in a powerful, definite tone. "They won't."

They'd figured out that problem, too. I was afraid to ask how.

"The power to control what happens in this world, Lucy, is at stake. You're in control, or you'll be controlled. We're not your enemy, no, not unless you stand against us. What happened with the 'Chicago Fourteen' years ago opened our eyes to a bigger solution.

"After your mum heals, we hope you'll join us. With you on our side, what took us hours to burn to the ground that night would've taken seconds."

I placed the cup on the glass table to my right. The writing was on the wall. "And if I don't, you'll let my mother die?"

His face twisted. "I didn't say anything about killing her, and — "

"And you didn't answer my question. You'll kill us if we don't join you?"

Liam cursed, balled his fists, and pressed them against his knees. "No. How can I get you to trust me? I saved your lives and lost good people to do it. Why would I do that just to kill you?"

Again, I fought to keep my voice down. "I don't know."

"If I wanted you dead, I would've left you inside that cave."

Fair point. "Regardless. I'm not joining your group. Point blank. Once she heals, we're out."

A smirk crossed his face. "Never say never. Drink your coffee. It's Jamaican and better hot."

His insistence made me nervous. Mom always taught me men didn't do things for women because they were nice guys. They wanted something. What did he want beyond me joining his superpowered army? What did it matter to him if we lived or died? I didn't imagine a world where Liam would come out and tell me, especially since he was getting aggravated by all my questions. I'd have to find out for myself.

I nudged the coffee an inch on the table. "I'm not really thirsty anymore. Can I have a minute to talk to my mom? Alone?"

"All right." Liam left me and disappeared behind the door we used to enter.

My feverish tinkering with my suit's Wi-Fi didn't work. Their wireless connection was strong but encrypted. I'd blacked out during our flight, and if I hadn't, I'd still have no clue where we were. He and I were high in the clouds, and I didn't recall the position of the sun. We hadn't been airborne long enough to change coasts.

Not like I could escape with Mom down. Whatever all this meant, I'd have to see it through. My pillow top bed and down comforter I yearned to bury myself inside had been destroyed in a fire. We had no home to return to.

But stay here? Be a superpowered soldier? I didn't want that. There were worse things in the world, I guessed. The image of that guy teleporting his hand through a body...I could've been next. Was what the dead guy had done worth such a gruesome death? In the heat of battle, though, I supposed you did what you had to do to win.

I stood next to Mom and rubbed the outside of her hands to rouse her, careful not to hit the IV embedded beneath her skin. She responded with a tense squeeze. Her eyes fluttered open and darted all over the place. "Easy." I didn't want to lie or tell the truth. "We're safe."

She mouthed the word "Where?"

"Military medical facility," I said. "Still on the East Coast."

The monitor measuring her pulse beeped faster. I'd never seen her panic before, and her tremoring hands scared me. I wasn't at ease, either, but I had to get her to relax. She'd spotted the blood repository and stared at it. Mom mouthed two words to me: no blood.

"Got it. Now, rest." I patted her shaking shoulders. "We're safe. I promise."

Satisfied, she shut her eyes and heavily sighed. Her pulse returned to a more normal pace. Injuries had taken a lot out of her. She'd always told me to follow my gut. Right now, my gut was rumbling with hunger and unsure how safe we truly were. I'd stretched the truth. Contrary to what he'd said, Liam gave me the impression that we wouldn't be free to leave once she healed. For better or worse, we were captives, and, when the time came, we'd have to force an escape.

Liam reappeared and signaled my alone time with Mom was up. Watching her lay there helped me understand the truth of what Old Guy told me about being used as leverage. I wouldn't leave without her. They may slow her healing process until I do what they wanted me to do. When I exited the room, I asked him, "How long will she be like that?"

"Hard to say. Until she passes concussion tests — a few days? She'll need to be careful not to puncture her lung with that rib. We'll need to do some tests and bloodwork."

"No blood," I said to him. "She has a clotting condition."

He believed the lie and notated her file. "I'll make sure they know."

His inability to give me a timeline meant we'd have an indefinite amount of time here whether I liked it or not. I decided then that I'd spend all I could right here. Liam quickly put that to rest by mentioning he'd show me to my sleeping quarters sometime after dinner, which it was now time to do.

Walking to the dining hall was halfway pleasant. By the sun's position and the outside temperature, I could tell we were, indeed, still on the East Coast. The trees were barren, and the dead grass had been finely manicured and edged. Liam told me about the immediate area, careful not to mention the state, city, name, or a landmark I'd know. The way he spoke...he'd rehearsed his phrases or had been coached on what to say and what not to say. I ignored him trying to access my suit's geotagging. Naturally, the location wouldn't come up without Wi-Fi.

"Can I call my best friend Natalee Gupta's house?" I asked him as we neared the building. "Her father is probably climbing the walls right now."

He dug his hands into his pockets and produced his holo. "Nilesh Gupta? He's dead."

I shook my head no. "How do you know that?"

A news report on his holo screen showed Mr. Gupta's workplace picture. He was dressed in a white shirt and plain red tie. He'd been missing since running into a gutted two-story house — *my house!* He must've thought Nat was still trapped inside it. The news sank my spirits, and I no longer cared to eat. Regardless of my emotions, I needed the food to function.

He opened the door for me, and I entered the dining hall. Of course, the décor was white and entirely too massive to accommodate the small number of people there. Fifteen heads besides ours, mixed ethnicities, with short haircuts if they were male, hair tied back for females. Nobody spoke to one another even if they sat within earshot. Nor did they look up when we neared them. This made it impossible for me to see any of their facial features or distinguishing marks. My peripheral vision didn't help, and Liam, with a hand at the middle of my shoulder blades, moved me along when I slowed my steps.

At the front was a luscious buffet of anything I could possibly want in a meal: medium rare steak, sautéed vegetables, lasagna, sausage pizza, shrimp lo mein, lobster tail, pasta with red sauce, king crab legs soaked in butter, and so much more. I'd missed Thanksgiving days ago, and this more than made up for it. The scents were varied and delightful. Seafood overpowered most of them except the fresh smell of yeast rolls.

I piled two plates high with everything, stacking types of food that didn't belong together to fit it all, and moved my tray to the end of the line near the desserts. Dessert! I wedged an oatmeal raisin cookie between my lobster tail and pizza slices. Considering all the rich food I'd be eating, I skipped soda and got a glass of water. Liam laughed at me, and when I glanced at his plate, it was a portion I'd have eaten if I was normal and cancer-free.

When we sat, Liam performed some sort of prayer in a language I didn't understand. I prayed, too, and did the sign of the cross. Most times, I was a terrible Catholic, but I at least did that. Though each item mixed together in my mouth, everything tasted wonderful.

Just when Liam finished, I started on my second plate. Wait, he had powers, too. Why wasn't he eating like I was? I immediately felt fat and chewed more slowly on the chunk of butter-drenched lobster tail I'd jammed mindlessly into my mouth.

"What's wrong?" he asked me.

The soft meat gushed flavor as I chewed it. "Why aren't you eating more like me? Don't you need it for your powers?"

Liam checked his wristwatch, swallowed another gargantuan brown pill, and gulped down a glass of water. "You were born this way. I wasn't. The pill makes the difference."

Anger and resentment in his voice raised my guard. Surely, if he'd poisoned all the food I'd consumed, I'd have dropped dead by now, superhuman or not, so I continued eating. "You have a stone, then?"

He nodded and stuck his thumb at his neck to reveal a reinforced chain, but I did not see the color of the emeralds. From the bumps under his shirt, he had more than one. *Way* more.

Person by person, the diners in the hall left. They did not interact with one another. In fact, they did not come within five feet of one another at any time. Too strange. There must be a rule against regulars fraternizing, which made me want to become one to break it.

Only one person remained in the front corner of the room — a girl from the look of her loosely wrapped hair bun. I didn't remember seeing her on the way. "What's her name?" I pointed my fork at the girl while gnawing on a tender piece of garlic-crusted prime rib.

He ignored me and kept chewing.

I mumbled, "Does she smell? Pick her nose? Why doesn't anyone sit with her?"

Liam wiped his hands on a napkin, crumbled it, and tossed it onto his plate. "She's a nonverbal autistic, unstable around strangers. She's able to fold distance and time with her mind, and it makes her...she's difficult to work with. Finish your food so I can show you to your quarters."

That seemed insensitive, like someone discriminating against me because of my bone cancer. She couldn't help her autism. There had to be a reason they kept her around. Her value had to outweigh her challenges. "What does she do for you?"

"Are you done stuffing your face?"

Right then, I decided she needed a new friend — *me*. During my chemotherapy, it helped to have advocates in my corner to cheerlead for me. This girl might have issues, but who didn't? Instability didn't have to be a curse. I'd finished most of my second plate anyway, and the food's richness weighed on me. A walk around would do me good. We'd walk, and I'd talk to her, and she'd listen and not say anything but appreciate the interaction.

"You're rude," I said, standing up.

"What are you doing?"

"The right thing," I told him.

Liam nearly choked on his drink. *"Don't.* What part of 'unstable' don't you understand?"

"She's a human being. Ever think all she needs is a person to be nice to her?"

Liam snatched my wrist. "You'll only get hurt."

By that stick figure? One thing was for sure: if Liam didn't let me go, *he* was going to get hurt. To make my point, I stared at his fingers and elevated the temperature of my arm to an uncomfortable level for a regular human being. He let go once the pain became unbearable, shook his hand, and rubbed his reddened palm.

"It's not going to end well."

I strode up to the girl with confidence, sat next to her, and introduced myself. I held out my hand and determined to prove Liam wrong. "My name's Lucy Sandoval. Nice to meet you."

Close up, I could see honey-brown highlights in her greasy blonde hair. I also noticed faint but raised black scars snaking across her face. What were those from, the autism? The disorder was a mystery to me. And did her condition also mean that she didn't *understand* English?

I lowered my voice and slowed my speech in reintroducing myself. She remained silent. Next to her was a small tablet computer she must have used to communicate messages. On it were ornate drawings of colorful butterflies and underneath them were their scientific classifications. I swiped through pages of them. "These are beautiful. Can you — "

She screamed in my face so loud my ears rang, and she raised her hand to slap me, which I blocked. I dodged the head butt and many of the kicks she tried as well. Once her anger appeared to cool, I let her go. She wiped the screen clear and wrote one word over and over in crooked capital letters.

DIE.

By the second time she'd written "DIE," I'd gotten up and jetted out into the courtyard. She didn't have to tell me again.

She stomped after me, screaming again, and she didn't look as if she was going to stop following me anytime soon. I didn't want to hurt her, but it was beginning to look like I didn't have a choice. I wound up and threw a fireball at her. Totally missed. The next one grazed her face. "Stop where you are," I shouted. "I don't want to hurt you. I want to be your friend!"

Liam didn't mention how antisocial she was or that she'd respond with unintelligible gibberish. Then, her face softened, her eyes welled with tears, and she reached out her hand to me. I knew nothing about autism except that there were different kinds, and it obviously didn't mix well with superhuman abilities. Up to this point, she hadn't revealed anything about what she could do, so I extinguished my hands and approached her with caution. Our fingers grew closer, and when we clutched hands, she yanked me toward her so hard I'm surprised my arm didn't break or dislocate out of my shoulder.

"Die!" Her tone made it sound like she had really said, "Why did you stay, stupid?"

She lifted me over her head and tossed me flailing across the lawn. I landed and slid face-first in the grass. By the time I flipped over, she was singing gibberish in a shrill voice, and she had almost reached me.

Enough of this.

I fired up my hands and blasted her in the stomach with flames. Her screaming changed from one of anger to pain. I didn't let up until she sank to her knees and fell over. In an instant, my blood ran cold, and I remembered the guy who I'd burned to the skeleton. My inferno had scorched the grass around us and left her cowering. I'd seared away her clothes and much of her hair. She curled, whimpering and naked, into the fetal position. The dirt cocooned in a circular pattern around her body.

A five-man crew rushed onto the scene and covered her reddened, smoldering body with what, I guessed, was a fire retardant, bright yellow blanket with a plastic appearance. One of the rescuers, a white guy with lime green eyes, broke protocol and glared at me as if I had barbecued his puppy. He had romantic feelings for *her?* Quivering lip, jerky movements...he had it bad. And I felt awful for pitying him. She couldn't communicate if she loved him back, at least verbally, and that had to be frustrating.

This time, when Liam grabbed me, I didn't make him let go. I'd neglected his warning and, had I left well enough alone, there wouldn't be a gigantic burn hole in their campus, and the autistic girl wouldn't be naked in winter temperatures. I'd done something awful, and, no way around it, it was totally my fault.

"She'll be all right, won't she?"

He rushed me to a five-story building where he used his handprint to access. "You have no idea what you've done. We need her!"

A guilt pang hit my stomach. He'd told me I'd get hurt, and I didn't listen. Meanwhile, his expression did not change.

"This isn't my quarters, is it?"

"No."

Liam's pace quickened. He pulled me down a series of hallways, all of which were white and looked the same. I could spend days trying to find my way out of this maze.

When it hit me that he was taking me somewhere I most definitely did not want to go, I commanded my body to light up. *I couldn't.* How did he do that? Nothing about Liam's arm strength suggested he had his abilities either, so I dropped to the floor and refused to move. Though I kicked with everything I had, he snatched me by the ankle and dragged me down the hallway to a specific door.

When it slid open, he pulled me inside. Unlit, except for a vented window some fifteen to twenty feet above my head, the room looked to be circular in design. There was a toilet on the far side and, I hoped, toilet paper. I found myself bound to the ground at the hands and ankles by a weight I couldn't see. I struggled to free myself. "Wait! Let me out! I'm sorry. Let me apologize to her. I can make it right."

Liam did not turn around except to say, "You nearly killed her. What did she say to you?"

The truth was on my tongue. "Check her tablet."

"You melted it."

"She wrote 'Die'."

He lowered his head. "I told you to leave her alone."

"What now?"

"Stay here."

Like I had a choice to leave. I screamed after him. "What about my mom? How long will I be here?"

He disappeared behind the sliding door, and when he did, I was able to get up. I still didn't have my abilities, and there were only two ways out — through that door or the glass above me. Mom was the flyer, not me. If I had my powers restored, all I could do was melt it away, and then what? Have a nice winter breeze blowing in? There was no climbing to that height.

I walked the cell — for that was what it was — seven times until my legs started to hurt. It was about two hundred fifty steps in circumference, and I lost count doing the diameter, and the math to convert the numbers into feet made my brain hurt. The place was bigger than any room I'd been inside. Like all the other structures, it was painted white and had the powdery fresh aroma.

I wiggled out of my bodysuit and was thankful it wasn't funky smelling. My body, however, was. The toilet worked, and, surprise, surprise, there was toilet paper. But, no shower. Things were about to get interesting.

After I washed my hands, I splashed lukewarm water on my face and hoped to wake myself up from this long and vivid nightmare.

CHAPTER TWELVE

Once it became obvious I'd be spending the night imprisoned here, I navigated a path to the toilet and practiced reaching for toilet paper with my eyes closed. In a room with nothing but a commode and my solar-powered body suit, which charged underneath the ceiling window, finding my way around in the dark seemed like the smart thing to do. Hours passed, and my confines grew more and more black and cold with the setting of the sun. My powers would've come in handy right about now with the temperature dropping.

In the moonlight, I saw slivers of the cell and relied on my memory to get around. I rolled up my bodysuit to use for a pillow and lay on my side facing the toilet. After listening to my own breathing pattern, I drifted off to sleep and dreamt of escaping by flying — *flying* — through the ceiling window. I'd soared out inside a breathtaking bluish-white flame pillar. Was burning a different color than orange a good or bad thing or even possible?

When I awoke, the temperature in the room had warmed up. However, the floor was cool to the touch. Next to the toilet was a glass door shower with towels flung over the top and a brown cardboard box with folded clothing on top of it. My surroundings appeared to be the same, and I hadn't moved. At least I thought I hadn't. One thing was for sure — those things weren't previously there. They were toying with me. I wouldn't give them the pleasure of driving away my sanity. Instead, they would get a show.

I didn't remember the last time I had a chance to bathe. My legs and arms were grizzly, and my ungodly personal brand of funk wafted up to my nose. The soap bar created thick, mango-smelling suds on my skin, and as they rinsed away, I lathered up again. Two more times, I repeated this not to eradicate the dirt and smell, but because I had nothing better to do in my prison. The razor they had provided me with was top notch. My skin was clean and hairless. The realization that someone was watching me quickened my pulse. Naked, on a wet surface, and without powers, I was at my most vulnerable. Suddenly, the water pit-pattering against the shower floor sounded weird like miniature footsteps. "Who's there?" I screamed again and again until my throat hurt.

Switching the water off, I stepped out of the shower and enveloped myself in the white bath towel. Its softness was no comfort. The thing might as well be his — my captor's — dry, eager fingers touching my body's contours. No. I dropped the towel at my feet and stood on the crumpled pile. There, he had seen me naked from my catheter scar and finger-swept wet hair to my chipped royal purple toenails. I strutted the length of the cell, lifted my hands in a flourish, and paraded my naked fat with confidence. This was what he wanted: what all guys wanted. By showing it to him, now he could not take it from me by force. And I was no longer afraid of it. There were other things I had yet to conquer — the lack of noise, the voices that weren't real, and the anxiety of it all.

Baby steps.

I'd been provided with plain cotton underwear, a sports bra, a pair of lace-up leather sneakers, and pants with a long-sleeved shirt. Everything white, of course, and in my exact size. Inside the box were toiletries: my favorite lavender lotion and hair products, high-intensity deodorant, a toothbrush, whitening toothpaste, and blue mouthwash. Whomever had scoped out my likes and needs had done their homework.

I dressed without caring who could see me or my stretch marks. The battery meter on the bodysuit said it needed more time to charge to full capacity. Rather than leave it in the cell, I slipped into it and turned on the cloaking in case they moved me to another place. Right after I finished zipping up was when the sliding door opened about a foot. My feet were glued to the floor by the same gravitational pull as the night before. A white plastic tray slid into the room, and I was able to move once again when the opening shut. Breakfast. Nothing like the delicious meal from the night before, but those sealed packages that Old Guy had given me plus a plastic container of water. This time, I recognized which to eat in the correct order, and I was satisfied. First time I remembered the man since he sacrificed himself for us. Should've paid more attention to his instructions.

Lunch followed when the sun was overhead and dinner right before it got dark. In between meals, I sang songs, did push-ups and sit-ups for exercise, meditated, took naps, talked to myself...I even prayed a little. That helped pass the first half of the day. Extra showers worked until my skin started to flake, and they wised up and let me access the water twice a day for a short period of time. After that, it became a useless game of keeping my boredom at bay without anyone to talk to or the internet to entertain me. About the time I was going to bust from anxiety, night fell.

This routine repeated — one day, two days...after that I lost track, and then, the sickness came. I tasted bile at the back of my throat and almost missed the toilet. Not a stomach virus or food poisoning. No way on earth I was that lucky. Soreness seeped into my muscles which forced me to move when necessary. Whomever had been feeding me continued sliding trays and bottles into the cell although I'd left the last four there out of pure exhaustion.

The cancer had returned.

I was going to die. Here.

Mom would be told of my demise, and she'd be alone in this world like I was now. All the time I wasted cursing at her under my breath and avoiding her. What I wouldn't do for her to hold me close and call me "Mariposa."

I licked my cracking lips and cried. "Help!" A wavering crackle came from my throat.

Once I'd spent all my energy, I drifted off to a heavy sleep.

Unaware of how much time had passed, for my surroundings were pitch-black, I blinked my eyes when the cell door opened. From the corners of my eyes, I spotted the night sky through the ceiling windows and wished for drops of rain to penetrate the glass and fall into my mouth. The trays rattled against the floor.

Someone had kicked them away.

Liam straightened my head, forced a pill down my throat, and poured water between my lips. The first swallows burned like alcohol, and some of it dribbled down my cheeks and into my hair. He patiently waited for me to swallow the pill and catch up with the flow before offering more. Inside my head, my sense of balance spun so fast that I thought he was rolling me. All I wanted to do was go back to sleep. My lips weren't moving though I had plenty to say to him for abandoning me in this hole.

He lightly smacked my cheeks and shined a light into my eyes. One by one my senses returned to normal. My hearing and ability to speak came alive after touch, sight, and taste in that order. He'd had two fingers pressed hard into the side of my neck. "This wasn't supposed to happen. Why didn't you drink? It — it doesn't matter. The pill...you swallowed it?"

He'd shoved it into my mouth. Too disoriented to think about whether he was trying to end me, I swallowed it. Immediately, I coughed to spit the thing up, but it was too late.

"It's a formula to restore your vitals and boost adrenaline production. You should've drank, and this wouldn't have happened."

A wavelike feeling like nausea stirred in the pit of my belly. My body felt as if a power switch had been flipped, and electricity crackled from my poor split ends to the edge of my toenails. I propped myself up, got to my feet, and conjured large fireballs in my hands. I was ready to rescue my mother and get the heck out of wherever I was.

"Good," he said. The green emeralds hanging from his neck gleamed in the moonlight. "There's been an incursion — "

"Incursion?" I repeated. The word was unfamiliar.

"We're in danger. All of us."

The curse words couldn't come out of my mouth fast enough. I winged fireballs at him, again and again, but he dodged them all, so I changed over to shooting flaming streams from my hands. He caught one to the leg and crumpled to the ground. He begged me to spare his life. "Please," he said, waving a hand at me. "I'm not the enemy here. *He* is."

"Who?"

"Outside, if you want to die first."

"Who?"

He winced. My fire had burned through his body armor and singed the skin on his shin. "Nobody knows. Terrorist. One of the Chicago Fourteen, I bet. Trust me."

I didn't. I'd use him like he used me. "What's the plan?"

Liam stood and hissed from the pain. The burn gave him a limp. "We get your mum and get to safety."

Sounded good to me so far. He opened the door to the cell, and we were greeted by a push of fire. "Ladies first," he yelled.

The heat would've kept a normal person out of the corridor. Not me. As I jogged through the hallway, the flames grafted onto me. Soon, my entire body was covered in orange inferno, but the corridor was clear.

Liam gave me directions from behind. "Next hallway on the left," he yelled. "Hurry!"

I turned. The sight of my mother, tubes and wires hanging from her body and slumped over the shoulders of a stranger, froze me. I couldn't move or breathe. His identity was concealed by a menacing black bodysuit and mask with odd shaped gray eyes. I couldn't attack him without hurting her, but she'd eventually heal, and I couldn't lose her again, so I shot everything I had in his direction. The stranger gently set Mom to the floor and shielded her from my flaming attack with his back.

I gritted my teeth, exhaled, and intensified the blast as I approached. His head turned to me. No, I was not going to stop coming for them.

The fire had little effect. How fireproof could his suit be? When I least expected it, he lifted Mom in his arms and turned his back again to protect her. No way was he escaping. With my right hand still shooting flames at his back, I hooked my arm around my mother's dangling neck. He'd hurt her by dragging me with them. I kicked him in the back of the knee to cripple him, and I might as well have been stomping on a piece of concrete. Holding on to Mom was my best bet.

He elbowed me in the chest with so much force my sternum had to have caved in. I flew backward, hit a wall, and lost consciousness.

However long I was out, the first thing I saw was a blurry, bloodied Liam sitting between my outstretched legs. Throbbing pain beat through my head and my neck. He reached forward and touched me on the shoulder, I think. Turning my head was torture.

"Can you walk?" he asked before spitting a stream of blood onto the floor.

Walk? I had no feeling below my neck, and I was out of breath. He figured that out after asking me a third time without a response, so he downgraded his questions to a blinking system—one blink, yes, two blinks, no. Keeping my eyes open through the livewire popping, white smoke, and thick dust swirls was difficult for me, but he was patient. Eventually, he'd gotten his answers: I couldn't talk, walk, or feel anything. But I had my own questions about the freakishly strong super being who had kidnapped my mother.

"What?" was all I could muster to mouth to him, and to move my stinging lips took an eternity.

With a mix of amazement and terror in his voice, he shouted over the sirens and dropping fragments of ceiling and frantically pointed at a giant hole in the ceiling in the middle of the hallway. Beneath it were massive chunks of fuzzy pink insulation, drywall, concrete, and silver HVAC pipes. He pointed and talked. From what I gathered through lip-reading and my stunted hearing, I learned the truth. After knocking me unconscious, the guy who attacked me had *flown through the ceiling.* Mom was gone. Sure enough, above a mound of broken rebar, cotton-candy-like shredded insulation, and crumbled drywall was a man-sized hole.

Only one thing mattered now: getting her back.

With staggered heaves, Liam dragged me to safety. Under the circumstances, lugging me by the armpits was the best he could do. As we passed broken and twisted bodies, I learned that while death has one color, it has many dank, chilling, indescribably terrible odors.

Closing my eyes and breathing through my mouth didn't help. Either my hands brushed limp, booted feet and slithered through pooled blood or I tasted debris fragments and electric smoke. I willed my arms to cross over my breasts, but no matter what I tried, I could not hold them there. I cursed myself for being weak and helpless again. Inhaling hurt. The more I avoided sucking in air, the closer I approached hyperventilation. A multitude of tears fell from my eyes and quickly dried because of the bodysuit's cooling unit. So, I cut loose and wept. Mom, Nat, wherever she was, Nat's father, my father, Old Guy, Moses — it all purged out of me in uncontrollable, ugly sobs, wails, and sniffling.

Unbothered, Liam propped me up next to a solid steel panic room door, squatted in front of me at eye level, and tried to arrange my body against the wall to make me comfortable. Good luck with that. Shooting white knives that I couldn't blink away stabbed at the backs of my eyes. My muscles burned. Nothing would change that but time, rest, and obscene amounts of painkillers. The way things were going in this place, it appeared I'd get none of those.

"I haven't exactly been straight with you." Liam unmasked me. "Our predictive measure is that girl you almost killed. We call her the Forecaster. She saw all of this, down to the moment — "

"What?"

"His people abducted her. We thought we could prevent that prediction, take measures."

I'd heard what he said, but my throbbing brain slowly processed it. "What?"

"Her last foresight was... She termed it Nuclear Winter. At first, we took it literally: an enemy attack, World War III, Extinction Level Event, end of the planet — not a *person*." He said the next sentence with a large dose of belief. "Until *you*. She meant you. You are the Nuclear Winter."

Bull crap. She should've changed her psychic channel. I meant a lot to *one* person in this world, and I'd just watched her get abducted by a flying man. Besides, if I possessed *that* kind of power, Mom would never have gotten taken, Natalie wouldn't be in a coma, and Mr. Gupta would be alive. By my count, only one of those was my fault. But I would've been able to prevent them all. Nevertheless, if he thought I was *that* powerful, and "the Forecaster" hadn't been wrong before, nothing would change his mind. I'd have to play along to make it out of this nuthouse.

The chamber had a handprint biometric lock and keypad. When it opened, I waited for Liam to drag me inside. He did not. He walked in himself and left me. I'd been used to guys walking in front of me and then standing aside to let me in first and standing aside so they could check me out without me noticing. This was not that. Dude genuinely abandoned me. What a way to treat me, the "Nuclear Winter."

I treated myself to a heavy portion of dignity and didn't follow him on my knees like a servant. I'd strut in like a queen. With a deep breath, I urged my body to move. First, I rolled to my right and put my fists on the floor. A few grunts later I was on my knees and then my feet. Liam was pressing buttons on a control panel. I'd seen elevators like this one in older buildings. They were solid metal, not clear around the sides like the ones I was used to, and they did not use antigravity technology to smooth the ride. Instead, your stomach dropped when it went down and had a tingle and rise sensation going up.

Leaning against the inside, I asked him, "Where are we going?"

"Down."

Obviously. The level we had been on was one story with high ceilings. The elevator panel had no floor indicator. Down, yeah, but how far down and to what? If Liam were going to kill me, he had ample opportunity to do so. After being dragged this far, I owed it to myself to find out where he wanted to take me.

We descended for minutes...long enough for my body to stiffen. I assumed the distance had to be at least a mile underground. At its bottom, the door slid open. In front of us was a yellow and black symbol — a fallout shelter sign. Liam led the approach, and I hobbled after him the best I could. Through a series of checkpoints, we finally reached our destination. I expected to find the president there, but I'd forgotten her name. Mom had lectured me about not remembering the name of the first woman of color president. Now, I'd meet her and would have to call her "Madam President" until someone referred to her by name.

The place smelled of mold, and everything had a coat of dust and cobwebs on it. Clearly, the place hadn't been intended for immediate use. The attack must've drove them down here. The stench of age made me cough. Looks like this hyper-technical suit of armor had its limits.

Liam had alerted the bomb shelter's residents — a strikingly handsome Hispanic man in a pressed blue suit, white shirt, and red tie. His diamond-studded wedding ring glinted in the overhead light. The freckled redhead at his side wore a black dress and a string of sparkling diamonds around her neck. My defenses came up as they moved closer.

"So, Liam, this is the Nuclear Winter?" He pointed to me and clapped. "Not a catastrophe after all. Wouldn't be the first time we'd misunderstood the Forecaster. Well then, welcome!"

His tone wasn't negative; it was...*happy*. Sincere. Regardless, I palmed two fireballs and prepared to strike. That's when the woman came to his defense. At first, I'd thought she was his younger wife. Her body language said otherwise.

"At ease, young lady. We won't hurt you."

My hands were still aflame, and I had no reason to put them out. Stories underground surrounded be three people I didn't know or trust, I'd fight my way to the surface if I had to.

"We all have an understanding about the final prophecy," Liam said. The three of them laughed. "The Forecaster said the Nuclear Winter would bring desolation."

I paused, thinking one of them would shoot me dead and this would be the end of my story. Not quite. They thought it was funny.

"Who are you, anyway?" I asked the man.

"State Representative Ramsey Mateo," he announced as if I'd won something. "Welcome to Square One."

CHAPTER THIRTEEN

Oh, great. *A politician.*

I didn't feel right calling him Ramsey, and Mr. Mateo sounded like he was about to teach me high school science. "And who is *she?*" I asked him.

He introduced the woman with the jeweled necklace as Claire, his chief of staff. There was softness in her freckled face. Not her expression. She focused on the miniature bonfires at the end of my arms. Suddenly, my flames extinguished. Claire smirked. She'd done it. The jewels around her neck were white emeralds, not diamonds, and she'd turned my powers off. All that was left of my fireballs were trails of smoke drifting up from my gloves.

When he verbally corrected her for binding my abilities, her voice jumped an octave. "With all due respect, she'll *kill* you."

"You're assuming she does not want to see the surface again, Miss Allen."

His words were more factual and less threatening — not that he wouldn't kill me if he wanted it. In consideration of that, Claire released her grip. Now I could roast them all. Fireballs returned to my hands. That little bit of freedom — the access to my abilities — eased my anxiety.

"You're not going to kill me?"

"No. Are you going to kill *me?*"

His expressions were hard to read. The wrinkled brow and the "that-is-insane" flash of whitened teeth said he didn't think I'd murder him. But nothing said I wouldn't die anyway. I wasn't a killer, at least a premeditated one.

My eyes fell on the white emerald necklace around Claire's neck. She could shut me down at any time, and it had to go.

"Why'd you all drag me down here?"

Liam interrupted Mateo. "We didn't plan to. The incursion forced our hand."

I squeezed my fists in frustration. "Use smaller words!"

"They had us under surveillance — took your mum and the Forecaster. We couldn't risk losing you, also. We're in Square One to regroup."

Claire brushed her auburn bangs with her hand and cleared her throat. The facility's invasion had bothered her. Did she know Mom?

"What's your problem?"

"With *you*?" She leaned against a dusty filing cabinet. "You're a liability."

My eyebrows raised at her bold statement. "So, *you* want me dead."

"The world would not miss you."

Both Liam and Mateo stepped between us to keep the ensuing shouting match from coming to blows — Liam pulled me aside, and Mateo tended to Claire. I couldn't hear what he said to her, but whatever it was, it cooled her off. My anger was at a boiling point. One more thing, another smart remark, and I'd turn her into a Roman candle.

Mateo explained Square One as a web of underground facilities meant to jumpstart what was left of society after a nuclear holocaust or whatever they thought I was capable of. Heads of state, politicians, diplomats, and whomever resourceful enough to save would gather in structures like this. Everyone else — the poor, homeless, working class people — were radioactive toast.

I wondered how the government could allow most of humanity to die. Then, I thought logically. Survival of the fittest: the strongest, ablest, most capable human beings to rebuild society from nothing as quickly as possible.

Having superpowers would only help. Which meant — they wanted to use me? Start over with nothing but us?

I was able to toss the fireballs in my hand at them before Claire sucked away my powers. One of them landed near her head and set the shoulder of her dress ablaze. Mateo stripped off his suit jacket and patted the flames away. It burnt away most of the material and made her white bra visible. Liam stepped behind me and, with his forearm at my throat, jammed a needle through my body armor and into the side of my neck. Within seconds, I blacked out.

∞

I found myself strapped to a metal table by the arms and legs. They'd stripped the top of my bodysuit down to my waist. Goose bumps dotted my entire torso. Thank God, they let me keep my bra and shirt though they didn't provide much warmth. An intravenous needle was embedded in the bend of my left arm, and clear fluid coursed through the tube connected to it. I hadn't eaten or drunk in *days*. Pretty sure they were juicing me up for an impromptu blood donation and that nothing about it was going to be safe or nonlethal.

Liam lay on a table beside me with a similar looking tube in his arm. *He* was going to be the recipient of the blood they sucked out of me. His body shuddered every couple of seconds. Out of the corner of my eye, I spotted Mateo standing at the edge of my bed. He placed a hand at my calf. Struggling with what little strength I had left didn't break the bonds or shake him off. "This is your fifth," he said, tapping the bag of fluid with his fingers. "You were dehydrated."

And with me well hydrated, they could drain my body of its blood like a leech.

"Are you a religious girl?"

"I'm Catholic."

"Me, too, albeit not a very good one." Mateo eyed the machines as he spoke to me. "You have to recognize the poeticism of this moment, though. Christ gave His blood for the salvation of the world, and as we speak, you are going to do the same."

I yanked at my bonds. "I didn't *give* anything. I'm held against my will, drugged, and strapped to a table by some psycho with a God complex. And, could've been the version I read, but He *chose* to do it."

"Did He?" That wicked smile again. He switched the IV feed with a different tube and forced me to flex my fingers to begin the blood flow. "Didn't His Father send Him to Earth to die? Dying was His sole purpose—the one thing forecast thousands of years before His birth—that He would die so that we might live and thrive and be *powerful.*"

All the politicians I'd ever heard of told the parts of the story they wanted you to believe. I called his plan a couple of choice words before following with "And what is forecast for me?"

"That somehow, you escape this place before we get what we need," he said, drawing and cocking an Ordnance he'd kept tucked in the back of his pants. "And you will destroy the planet. Which is why, once the initial blood transfer is complete, that is, I will shoot you in the head."

Lovely. "Can I pee first? I can let it go all over the place if that's better for you."

Mateo checked the monitors and yelled for Claire. "Bring a bedpan," he hollered. "Strip her down. I can't stand that smell."

Since I lacked my abilities, she couldn't have been far away. Sure enough, the high heels clicking against the floor grew louder. "You gave her four IV bags without a catheter?" she said, still a distance away.

Sucking his teeth, he motioned for her to come, and the reply she gave him frustrated him more. "From our intel, I thought her suit had high enough tech to have filtration systems. Will it affect the transfer?"

"Do you mind a delay if it does?" She handed him a yellow bedpan. "Sir, with all due respect, I believe my job description is 'Claire Allen, Chief of Staff to State Representative Ramsey Mateo' not 'Nurse Practitioner-slash-Phlebotomist.' Have you ever catheterized someone? I haven't. You're welcome to try."

He placed his hand over hers on the bedpan and forcefully suggested she accommodate me. Following a brief exchange, she stood at my midsection, unfastened my suit, and lowered it down over my hips. I still couldn't pull my own clothes down to go, so she unstrapped my right hand. Maneuvering stuff into the right place required some effort before I could go. Having someone watch me urinate wasn't a new level of embarrassing. I'd passed that space long ago.

"Lucy, you're going to have to listen and quickly follow my directions. Can you do that?"

Claire's tone had changed from screaming-cat annoying to a softer, commanding tone. Her ice-blue eyes focused on me. She expected a response.

"Yeah."

Her stare grew colder. I'd violated some unwritten rule. It was at that point I realized she was communicating to me through her thoughts, and I should do the same. Mateo was off in the distance but within earshot. *"Pee. I'm going to drop the bedpan to get his attention,"* she said to me. *"Grab my white beryl necklace when I bend down and toss it as far as you can away from me. Hit Mateo with fire. Unstrap yourself and we'll improv the rest. Got it?"*

I didn't understand. The chick who wanted me dead was on my side? There was no time to do anything but agree. Do what she said and die, or do nothing, stay put, and die. I nodded and readied myself to move.

Claire did as she said. The sound of sloshing pee and the clattering bedpan got Mateo's attention. He cursed at her and called her all sorts of names. When she knelt within my reach, I grabbed her necklace, yanked hard until it came off, and whipped it into the distance. Power roared through my system. I conjured fire and shot a long stream which hit Mateo in the chest. He crumbled to the floor, smoldering, screaming, and frantically patting his skin.

I unstrapped myself and yanked the blood transfer needle from my arm. Once I rearranged my clothes, I sidestepped the yellow puddle at my feet and Claire put her back to me. "No!" she yelled.

Taking her cues, I put my forearm at her neck and did my best to drag her to the elevator. The exchange, clumsy and, I imagined, fake looking, didn't matter. Mateo writhed on the floor, yelping like an injured puppy, while Liam lay motionless on the transfer table. I wasn't checking where I was pulling her, but she purposefully flailed her legs in the correct direction. *Turn me around.* When I did it, she placed her hand on the biometric board and gave a code word to override its lockdown command.

Slowly, the elevator door opened. Once we were inside it, she dropped the façade. "Sorry for the act. I had to retain cover as long as possible," she said. "Torch the place."

She wasn't commanding me to burn an empty room but to extinguish two lives on purpose. This was the moment: where I had to decide to preserve life or take it on purpose. Easy to think that when faced with a life-or-death situation that you would kill or be killed.

The application itself was much different.

Her voice tensed. "We don't have time, Lucy. Do it."

They had a sample of my blood. Who knew whether Mateo could create more super beings without the moral challenge I had in front of me? He was contemplating power or no power, not life or death or right or wrong. There was no blinking with his decisions. I wasn't a person. I was a factor in a dangerous equation he was trying to multiply.

Claire impatiently mashed the button. "Lucy! When they come after you, and they will, they will not hesitate or show mercy. You'll — "

"All right! I get it, lady."

Wouldn't a superhuman population in a wasteland be a worse consequence, and a more righteous result, than two measly murders?

I closed my eyes and attempted to steady my shaking fingers. "C'mon," I encouraged myself. The tingling in my wrist rose to my fingertips and spurted out in flaming streams. The fire caught onto Square One's surroundings and wildly spread. They'd have time to escape, right? At least that was what I planned to tell myself.

When the doors closed and the elevator began to move, Claire unzipped her dress and squirmed her way out of it. Underneath, she wore a white sheath covering her thighs, chest, and back. With a few coordinated hand movements, the suit crawled like an ant swarm all over the rest of her body, all except her face. Coolest outfit I'd ever seen.

She caught me eyeing it. "Our newest technology. I'll get you one. Good job back there."

Nothing about what I'd done should be congratulated.

"You fly, right?"

Fly? The look on my face drew a look of disappointment. Why? I should be able to fly because Mom could?

"I need a two-person extraction," she said to no one in particular. Claire patted the elevator panels and examined the ceiling. "Twitchy comms... We might have to do this the hard way."

Considering all that had gone on, I was afraid to ask about the hard way, so I didn't.

"No time to test them. I hadn't been down here... Nothing above ground is made of this alloy." She smiled and used her fingers to rearrange her hair. "No worries, Lucy. We've got this."

"Who are you talking to?" I asked.

The smile continued. This must be *bad*.

"Call me Claire. I kept my cover so long — I'm used to the name. I kind of like it."

"Who *are* you?"

Claire drew an imaginary circle in the air above her head. "Burn a hole. This size. Puncture through to the other side. Keep it shallow — don't damage the elevator. Use your eyes."

I cleared my throat and focused the energy inside of me. Soon, thin orange lasers came out of my eyes. From my viewpoint, it was trippy. My eyesight was the same; however, it required intense concentration. The slightest wiggle would send my targeting off course. I held my breath until the mission was done and a chunk of jagged metal thudded at our feet.

Claire measured the distance and jumped through the hole. The shift in weight shook the compartment. She lowered her arm through the hole and opened her hand. I was supposed to allow her to help me. This woman said I was a liability, and she thought I didn't deserve to live. One thing was clear to me — until Mom and Nat were in the clear — I was my own best chance at survival.

There were rails around the interior of the elevator, and if I was a professional basketball player, I could have leapt up to the hole and pulled myself through alone. Since I wasn't, I let her help me. The strength in her arm was outstanding, like that of a professional weightlifter. Claire curled me as if I were a hand weight. I gained my footing at the top of the elevator. A mile of darkness stretched above us. The pulleys and winches raised us into the uncertainty. Eventually, it would end, and we'd be crushed. I guessed that wasn't the plan. "Why are we up here?"

"Extraction team can't see us," she yelled over the constant whirring and clicking.

I raised my hand like I was in class and lit it up. "Now, they can."

"At this distance? You'd have to explode. We need to get closer fast. I need you to fly."

I was puzzled. "What's the rush? We'll get there when we get there."

"You don't smell the smoke?"

Come to think of it, I hadn't until she mentioned it. All I could detect was the sharp scent of electricity on the wires. I inhaled deep and caught the scent of burning. In retrospect, setting Square One on fire didn't appear to be the best idea, considering Claire's insistence that the elevator may shut down at any time. She had me risk both our lives over drops of my blood? I should've gone back and destroyed the collection bag. Since I didn't, this mile-long tunnel could become our coffin. My anxiety hit a new level.

She pulled close to me and said, "What are you waiting for? Fly us out of here!"

I blended curse words together and turned my back to her. "What don't you get? Does it look like I can fly? I'll say out loud: I can't fly! I can't fly. I. Can't. Fly."

Claire placed a hand on my shaking shoulders. "You *can*. The torque of your flames. Concentrate it into thrust from your feet and lift at your chest. And, you can fly."

Her statement brought tears to my eyes. School. Social life. Overall health. Even in super-heroism, I was a *failure*. Fine, I could fly. In theory. Not so much. I didn't want to try and fail at that, too. Here, failure meant death. "There has to be another way!"

The elevator braked. On instinct, we held our arms out to the side to steady ourselves. Beneath us, the bottom level was cooking. The smoke trickling through the open spaces was worsening. Above us somewhere was ground level. Climbing it was an option until I remembered how terrible I was at the endurance challenges at school, and that was before the cancer struck. Claire's strength wouldn't be enough to get us to the surface with me clinging to her back. I fought back sobs. Of all the ways I could've died in the last two weeks, this was it — suffocated or burned alive atop an elevator?

Claire handed me one of two small syringes full of green fluid from a pocket in her suit beneath her left armpit. "Last resort. Stick this in your jugular."

My eyes bulged. I wanted to make sure I understood her correctly — I should inject this into my neck *willingly?*

She demonstrated. For a second, her eyes flashed the color of the fluid. Then, she hissed through her gritted teeth and leapt into the darkness. I listened for her landing and heard nothing. Her body did not plummet back to the elevator, so she must've made it to the surface. The stuff she injected herself with was some kind of an energy boost. What could I do if I took it?

I'd soon find out. The elevator shook beneath my feet. I had every confidence in two things. One, it was not going to drop, and two, either Liam or Mateo had climbed up to reach us.

Against my better judgment, I looked down. Sure enough, Liam had torn a hole through the elevator floor and pulled himself through it. With his strength, he'd be next to me in seconds. Setting aside my hatred of all things related to injections, I plunged the needle into my neck.

The reaction was instant and terrible. Pain seared every single body part, and I screamed. My powers kicked into overdrive. I burst into flame and, unlike when it usually happened, I experienced every degree of heat. The next thing I knew, I focused my eyes downward and saw the elevator in the distance. I was flying, but there was no controlling what was happening.

As I reached the surface, I wanted to steer myself through the hole Claire had created but couldn't. Everything was on instinctual autopilot.

I burned through the shaft, the building's levels, and ended up landing on the roof. Thankfully, I flamed out.

Unfortunately, I'd burned through every stitch of clothing I had. Whoever found me would be getting quite a peep show. I rested my head on the rough, ridged roof material and tried to keep awake. Not like a completely naked Panamanian girl could defend herself from an attacker. There had to be injuries involved in that display and staying conscious was important.

At least I'd peed.

Two different footstep sets, one heavy and the other heavier, landed on the roof. I managed an "ugh" before a blanket covered my shoulders and was fastened above my breasts and at my navel. In the cold November night, I had the feeling that the blanket was not to keep me warm but to keep me from spontaneously combusting. The hot flutter in my stomach let me know heating up again was a definite possibility, and I had no idea what I had injected myself with. The drug's cost was heavy. I was starving, thirsty, in pain, and I couldn't cool off. Tired of fighting, I let my legs go limp and gave in to the agony.

CHAPTER FOURTEEN

The extraction was a blur. I remembered things happening at night and being nude under a fire-dampening blanket for much of it. People moved quickly, and there was the stench of rotten eggs. A teleporter. Nothing else explained how I was simmering on a roof one minute and strapped into the seat of a loud, flying transport the next. Claire wasn't around. Nobody paid me much attention once the immediate threat of combustion passed. I was freezing, and the blanket wasn't doing anything to warm me, so I unhooked it and let it fall at my feet.

Seconds after I'd been sitting there, legs and arms crossed, a skinny Chinese man with black buzzed hair took notice. "You're shivering," he shouted with a noticeable accent. He lifted the blanket and swaddled me in it. "Doesn't do much for warmth, but it's fireproof. Ironic, I know."

The rough material was like sandpaper on my skin, and activating my abilities would've warmed me up, but igniting a fire in an enclosed place was dangerous. "Protective for me or for *you?*"

"Both," he chuckled. "Nobody wants another explosion."

That explosion was me.

Details regarding how everything went down were a little fuzzy other than my body going supernova inside a secret complex. Frostbite was the least of my concern. "Where's Claire?"

"Recovering. Same as you."

Good. She made it out, too, but I doubted she was in her birthday suit like I was. My limbs were gelatin, and the only thing keeping me upright was the safety harness strapped around my shoulders and waist.

The transport's rhythmic rumble lulled me to sleep while my co-traveler rambled on and on about my fantastic display of radioactive heat and the amount of damage it'd caused.

I blinked my eyes and found myself lying on a twin mattress almost as comfortable as my own. Come to think of it, *more comfortable*. This mattress had a heating element, and the gray blanket on top of me was the perfect blend of fibers. Thankful it wasn't the color white, I buried my face into the soft pillow and went back to sleep. Whatever the world's challenges were, they could wait another couple of hours or so.

Eventually, after resting, I returned to feeling like a regular human being. That term had been relative to me since my diagnosis — regular, normal, stable, ordinary, *average*. Here, I meant I was tired of being tired and couldn't sleep anymore without some certainty as to what was going on. I'd lost any sense of time passing. Had it been days? Weeks? The wall across from where I lay was bare. So was the one at my head and the one at my back.

The corner, however, was a different story.

There was a man, a *handsome* black man, sitting in the corner and nodding off. He wore gray clothes, and a bodysuit showed beneath it at his wrists and neck. I'd seen holovision stars less beautiful than him. His skin was a medium dark shade as if it had been blended and refined in a mixing bowl. There was a strength in him beyond his build. I felt it — like lightning weighing down the air and crackling each time he breathed. It surrounded him like a cloud no one else but me could see. He had *power*, and I respected it.

Slowly, I brought myself to a sitting position and used the wall to support my back. Clearing my throat did not wake him. A pretend coughing fit didn't work, either.

Finally, I loudly said, "Excuse me," and it roused him enough for his eyes to open. When he looked at me, my heart stopped. His eyes... Had I seen him before? My mind said no, but he sparked something deep in my soul. I didn't want to believe the truth about him that gnawed at me, so I waited.

"Hi."

His throaty baritone shouldn't have startled me by its rich quality, but it did. "Hi."

He shifted his sitting position to face me. "I'm sure you have a lot of questions, so let me answer the first one. No, I did not dress you."

A sense of humor like mine. Interesting. More, please. "Who did?"

He rested his ankle on his knee and pulled it toward him. After a deep exhale, he told me the answer I'd been waiting to hear. "Your mother. She's better."

A piece of good news — a life preserver to keep me afloat through the fluid concept of what I had considered reality. "She's here? She's safe?"

"A long time ago, I guess you could call him a mentor told me that safe means you have more power than whoever threatens you."

"Old Guy? Peters?"

His eyes lit up. "Ransom, actually. You knew him?"

"I did. He died saving my life — *our* lives."

His mentor had fully lived, and he was grateful for the sacrifice he'd paid to save us. It was in the way he bowed his head and didn't talk for a moment after stating "Mine, too." They had shared a complicated history that Mom didn't tell me about, but she dropped enough clues for me to use my imagination. Old Guy Peters had not been a hold-your-hand kind of teacher but a push-you-off-the-cliff-and-you'd-better-figure-it-out-on-the-way-down guy. For whatever guidance he provided, anyone who encountered him was grateful for it in the end.

"And am I safe? Are *we?*"

He presented me with basic facts, and they spelled out simple truths I had to accept. *I had power. Radioactive, science-defying, wonderful, dangerous, fantastic, terribly awful abilities. And I couldn't control them.* In my estimation, that made me dangerous *and* a deterrent for an attack. Like an unpinned grenade a millisecond from detonating or a nuclear bomb; yes, that's how he described it, an atomic bomb inches from the ground. In my defense, these abilities didn't come with a manual or a safety switch. Whether I mastered them or not, people would die because of me. Liam and Mateo didn't know all I was capable of any more than I did.

Being the Nuclear Winter was particularly useful in that case.

He described the scene I'd left behind at the military compound, called it "a firestorm." I used to *love* rainstorms. The texture of warm, humid rain wetting my clothes and sticking to my body—it was *perfect*. What he described were dozens of fire pillars and dirty soot clouds thick enough to block the moon. The transports had difficulty taking off in it, he explained, and they flew blind for miles until the horizon cleared. That sounded like a disaster film.

"It wasn't your fault," he reassured me.

"Wasn't it?"

With a gentle hand on my ankle, he told me more. "Abilities take time to master. Claire handed you a concentrated adrenal stimulant, which you took without knowing what it was."

That's true. Still, I pushed. *"I shot it in my neck.* Doesn't that make me responsible for the damage I caused?"

He rubbed the back of his neck and groaned. I'd given him something to think about. Yeah, I wasn't an innocent little girl after vaporizing government property with my radioactive body. Having superpowers made things...*complex* he'd explained to me. I'd done a "good" thing. Destroyed the bad place that belonged to the bad people. Without my blood, there would be no more superhumans trying to influence governmental decisions.

But it was *theirs*. They had the right to do whatever they wanted to do with their property, cloning me or otherwise.

Until they tried to kill me in it.

True, Liam and Mateo had broken several laws, including attempted homicide and a few other crimes I couldn't identify. What court would prosecute a United States House Representative? Who would believe an almost fifteen-year-old girl who could set the world on fire?

"There are different laws for people like us," he said.

He stood and extended his hand to me. I lifted the blanket to make sure I had pants on, which I did. The gray clothes were like his—new but had a stiff but worn before texture to them. I didn't have the heart to examine the condition of the underwear. At least I had some, I guessed.

Satisfied, I swung my legs over the bed, discarded the covers, and placed my hand in his. The rough skin was tangible not imagined like in my dreams. I wasn't hallucinating. Without reason or explanation, I trusted him without him confirming his identity. Because, deep down, inside the marrow of my cancer-riddled bones, I knew the truth.

He was my father. He didn't have to say or prove anything to me.

I clutched his hand like a lifeline. No way was I letting it go again. I thought, no matter how hard I squeezed, I'd never hurt him. And now that he was here with me, I wouldn't have a chasm of darkness growing inside of me anymore. I wanted to be happy. I did. But *I feared it*. What happened after that? Nowhere to go but down, right? He'd die, or I'd die, or we'd die together — do superhumans even die? Old Guy did and so did Moses. I guessed we would.

And then what? I wanted to find out with *him*.

One of the rules was unavoidable: superhumans must eat. Unlike the pristine setting of Liam's cafeteria, this other space was more basic and functional with black wooden benches and tables. It had less rich food than the other place but equally as filling. We piled up the different kinds of available dishes and sat next to one another. He drank from a smaller glass than my tower of water, and it stank of alcohol. Okay, dear old dad liked brown liquor. No judgment from me.

He said a prayer, and we both did the sign of the cross. He was a Catholic, too? No wonder I loved him at first sight.

"How long have you known about me?" I asked him while chewing.

After finishing a slender fry, he said, "Four years."

I nearly choked on my next bite of cheeseburger. I was diagnosed around then. If Mom contacted him, she must've thought I wasn't going to live, and she did so out of guilt. "I'm gonna die in a few weeks."

He looked me in the face. "Let's wait and see what our medical staff has to say about that."

"And you stayed away from me because..."

"You mother and I — we had a mutual agreement. I sent Kendel, 'Claire,' to shadow you, though. That wasn't part of our agreement."

I almost choked. "By shadow, you mean..."

"Watch over you. She's a shapeshifter, so you wouldn't know she was there to protect you. *You* decide what kind of life to live for yourself," he told me. Then, for the first time ever, I'd heard my parents referred to as a unit. "No one can decide for you. Not your mom and I...nobody. What you do, from here on out, is about your choices for your life."

"What if I want to live a regular life, you know, not to be a human nuclear reactor? Can I do that? Is that possible for me?"

He didn't frown. The way he averted his eyes and slowed his eating telegraphed his disappointment in my question. He folded his hands together and answered me. "Your call, though, I may need one favor…"

"A *favor,* like…" A sparkle on his left ring finger caught my eye — a band with tech embedded in it from the look of the design. "You're *married?* I have a stepmother?"

"Divorcing. Lawyer doesn't know where to find me." He self-consciously moved his hand and ate a forkful of food. "You can't be something for someone. Truth comes forward whether you want it to or not."

For him, that hadn't worked. I received the advice in stride, but both he and my mother were crazy if they thought for a second I'd let this moment go. "Do you have any family besides her? Any kids?"

Without mentioning his estranged wife's name, he counted while dawdling over pasta salad. "I have a half-brother, Zachary, who is serving a tour overseas and an aunt who's in an assisted living facility. Two stepmothers, one across the world. I have shadows on all of them."

That's it? I had an uncle, a great-aunt, and two grandmothers? "What about your parents?"

"Mother died when I was twelve, father four years later."

I couldn't eat without wanting to know everything about this man, so I decided to keep inquiring, and, if he got sick of me, he'd let me know. Although, I had an eternity's worth of knowledge to gain in God knows how long with him. "How's your leg?"

Laughing, he rubbed his shin. "It's fine. Took a few days for the skin to totally regenerate from the radiation burns. Don't heal as fast as I used to. Plus, I have a scar for my trouble."

Add healing to the list of things I'd seen him do — super-strength and flight. I lifted a piece of blueberry pie to my mouth and let its gooey filling drop into my mouth before I bit down. This was the birthday gift I'd always pictured and never shared, not even in my journals, for fear it'd never come true. For the rest of the meal, we exchanged small talk. Until the end, when I asked for more information on what exactly it was we were doing here.

"C'mon." He wiped his hands on a napkin and tossed it onto his tray. "I'll show you, and then, you'll tell me your decision."

Funny. I made my decision the second he'd woken up at the foot of my bed. "Wait." I grabbed my tray. "What am I supposed to call you?"

He shrugged. "Everybody but your mom calls me Director. What do you want to call me?"

Director was too formal. "How about Jason?" I'd never said his name out loud before, and it sounded weirder in the air than it did in my head. "Or Dad?" Which was worse?

His twisted lips communicated the same discomfort. "Trial and error. We'll figure it out."

Sounded reasonable though my stomach knotted.

"What's wrong?" he asked me.

All these things were happening, I explained to him, and I wanted it to stop or, at least, slow down. Two weeks ago, I was minding my own business and dying of incurable bone cancer. I had one wish — to meet my father. Standing face to face with him, I openly wondered whether all the death and destruction I'd seen, caused, or been a part of was worth it. He listened to everything I said without commenting, but his eyes never wavered from mine. Near the end, he put his arm around my shoulders and squeezed me. I tightly wrapped my arms around his midsection and laid my head on his chest.

"I embraced this life. Consider what it will cost you before you do it."

His wife wasn't anywhere around. She hadn't chosen this life, and it looked like it cost him his marriage. I didn't know my stepmother or her reasons for leaving, but for me, I hadn't gone through all this hell to turn my back on him and walk away. If I died now, I'm for sure it wouldn't be alone anymore. My heart stuttered as I clutched onto him. I never wanted this exciting feeling to go away. "Dad?"

He squirmed a bit. Dad it was. "Yeah, Luciana?"

"It's Lucy. I want this."

Dad patted me on the back. "Give yourself some time to reconsider, Think about it."

This time, my tone was more insistent. I'd sign up for everything he was involved with doing. *"I want this."*

Clearly, he was the pushover parent since he didn't fight back.

"Can I see Mom?"

"Sure." He squeezed me again.

My father ushered me down a flight of metal stairs to a room he opened by biometric handprint. Inside lay my mother on a bed bigger than mine, free from wires and tubes, asleep. I glanced back at him for permission, and he waved his hand in a "go ahead" motion. Eager to rejoin her, I lifted the covers, slid in next to her, and lay down. The time display on the wall showed it was a little past midnight on December second, two days before my birthday. I wished myself an early happy birthday, snuggled next to my mother for the first time in ages, and closed my eyes.

I woke up first, but my injuries hadn't been as extensive as hers. While she slept, I studied her face close up. Without makeup on, she still didn't look thirty-two years old. Neither did my father, who was the same age. No way! Superhumans aged more slowly, too? This was too good to be true!

"Stop staring."

My mom's whispering voice cracked. She was tired, worn out. From everything, I thought. I was, too, but meeting my father gave me new life. I downplayed the excitement, but my hand slightly shook when I moved it forward to clutch hers. "Mom."

"Whisper, Luciana."

"Why?"

Mom eyed the corner of the room. I followed her gaze and concentrated on the spot. *A camera.* For surveillance or for spying — was there even a difference? She didn't know, and I wasn't sure. Everyone had secrets, and my father wanted in on those secrets. As far as I could tell, my parents wanted to protect me but in completely different ways. "Has he said anything to you like 'If you keep secrets, I can't protect you'?"

I swallowed hard. "No."

"Yeah, well, he probably will." Her eyes darted. "I don't trust him that much."

"But he's the love of your life."

Mom's eyes watered. She lay unmoving on her pillow and looked at me. I'd never thought about this before, but I was a living, breathing reminder of what they had — both good and bad — almost sixteen years ago. What kind of pain must she be in every time we saw one another? I'd never dated or been broken up with. I didn't have a reference point.

"The love...of my life." She repeated herself twice. A decade plus of hurt feelings clouded her face. *He* was the reason she didn't date guys all these years. My friends said for years she was gay. I denied and denied it, and then, I started to think maybe it was true and she was into girls and that her friends were her secret girlfriends I didn't know about.

No, she wasn't a homosexual, not that I would've cared. Just infinitely heartbroken. The irony was she was the one who broke up with him and wanted to disappear forever, not him. These were raw, years' old, self-inflicted wounds she hadn't nursed, salved, or bandaged. And I'd inadvertently poured salt in them by my mere existence.

She told me everything she remembered about the past week, my father, and her extraction. Yeah, about that — my breastbone was still sore from him elbowing me. It hurt every time I inhaled and hooked and unhooked my bra. I might have an internal injury or just one heck of a bruise. I wished I healed like my father. I didn't tell her about my injury. She had enough to deal with as it was.

Her story was filled with emotional breaks and teardrops. At the end of it, she wished me a happy early birthday, like she did every year, and I loved it.

"Thanks, Mom."

"Since you've met him." Several breaths later, she said, "I know what you're thinking."

I closed my eyes to reimagine the man and whispered, "Man, you were *crazy* to let him go."

"I was desperately in love with a fifteen-year-old boy in search of himself, and when he discovered who he was" — she sniffed — "I wasn't the person to walk with him anymore. I broke up with him so he could live the life he wanted to live...without me weighing him down."

My hand found hers as her tears dotted the pillow she lay on. By weighing him down, I wondered if she meant me, too, but, according to her teenage pregnancy warnings, she didn't know I was inside her until he was long gone. "Is he living that life here?"

"Looks like it. He's *married.*"

I argued back, *"Divorcing.* And she's not here. You are."

"Divorcing?" She paused. "Luciana, you don't know that — "

"Mom."

She squeezed my fingers and licked her lips. "Your father is Jesus Christ to you, but like anyone but Jesus Christ, he has flaws. It takes two to make a relationship go south."

"Don't spoil this for me..."

"See his imperfections and accept them and him for who he is before deifying him. That's all."

Fine. She was trying to spoil my euphoria. Good luck with that. I propped myself up and spoke way above a whisper. "Nothing you can say about him will change my mind."

Mom moved her stray hair back behind her ear as she shook her head no. "I swear, I'm not trying to. Just take some time, baby. Make an informed decision. This is your life we're talking about. That's all."

Fair. I should take time to confirm his divinity — check his hands, his feet, his side — that whole thing. Those proofs in the *Bible* were for the doubter. Though she'd introduced me to godhood in the form of these powers, now, she was the one having questions and doubts.

For years since my diagnosis, I did, too. I questioned God's existence. Really, like, who thought it was a good idea to let girls like me rot inside out from bone cancer? With these powers, in a way, I was closer to being like Him. I could start or prevent a lot of things. But I hadn't yet. Didn't necessarily mean I wanted to be uninvolved.

Somewhere, at any time, people were suffering in the world, and I had power to stop it. Was the fact I was lying here next to my mother a sign of neglect? Maybe, but I wasn't God. I couldn't be everywhere at once, and I accepted that.

Mom's door opened. Behind it was a woman with long, auburn hair. I thought she was Claire at first. "Good afternoon, Lucy, I need you first for intake and assessment."

Afternoon? My internal clock was all messed up. I kissed Mom goodbye and left the bed. I had a thousand questions, but my escort answered a great deal of them by shapeshifting her face into Mateo's Chief of Staff, Claire Allen, and back to, what I assumed, was her natural form. "My real name is Kendel," she confirmed. "I've shadowed you for the past four years."

She transformed into Murdoch, the policeman who tackled me and brought me home, and then one of the nurses who helped to administer my chemo treatments, and two other people I remembered but couldn't identify from where or when. I didn't see the need to know the details of her intrusion into my privacy. I crossed my arms and held myself around the elbows.

Kendel stepped in front of me. *"Shadow*, all right, Lucy, not a voyeur."

"What's the difference?"

"There are *differences*. We have a protocol to protect you. I didn't watch you bathe or change clothes or anything."

I studied her face for sudden changes. This was a shapeshifter, after all, and catching her slipping with a physical tell would be difficult. Her statements aggravated me. "And you followed that protocol, *Kendel?*"

"To the absolute letter. Nobody likes answering to the director, not even me."

Oh yeah. My father was her boss. "What's first?"

She explained the basics. They would take my information, vitals, measure and fit me for one of those high-tech bodysuits she and my father wore. From there, they would test the extent of my powers and train me for combat.

And I was ready for it.

CHAPTER FIFTEEN

My "shadow" ushered me to an area used for medical treatment where there were these isolated bluish glass physical examination tubes. The girls going through cancer treatment with me — I called them my "tribe" — named these machines "cocoons." It was why my mother nicknamed me Mariposa, because she thought I'd emerge as a butterfly and not die in the metamorphosis process.

I dropped my clothes behind an opaque screen and changed into a nightgown. The air conditioning in this place was spectacular but not when all you were wearing was a paper sheet and cotton underwear. With reassurance from Kendel, I stepped into the opened cocoon she pointed me to and admitted to her that I was scared.

"You've been here," she reminded me. "It's a little bigger than ones you're used to."

Didn't matter. I was being treated for bone cancer then, not a superhuman ability to burn. The examination required me to be still as death for ninety seconds. Sounded like a short period of time to anyone who had never been in one before. "It's like being buried alive for a minute and a half," I once told Mom, who insisted I exaggerated. "Closed casket burial, six feet of dirt, and silence." My tribe agreed with me. One of the girls even described it as "the suffocating vacuum of space."

I lay on the soft, padded insides. The lid's hydraulics hissed and sealed shut. There, in my two-minute death, the machine did its work. I eyed my vital statistics through the glass. I'd practiced not blinking and become a master at it. Apparently, I'd lost weight, too. I didn't remember the last time I was that close to my target. Heart rate, blood pressure, temperature, Body Mass Index, cholesterol, white cell count, cancer number — everything was ideal. The black masses were gone as well. How had my tumors and mets disappeared? Cocoon examinations were accurate 99.99 percent of the time, and if it said no cancer, then there must not be even a microscopic amount of the disease inside of me any longer.

Though it was truth to me, I dared not speak it out loud for fear it disappear on me. I leaned forward. "All good?" I asked her.

Kendel eyed the results. Must have been the ones written in code — nonsense to me and not to her. Her gaze tightened at the bottom. I'd seen concern like that before on my oncologist's face. She raised her wrist in front of her face and called for my father. He was on my side. Whatever it was, he'd defend me. He came running, with Mom close behind him, and demanded the shapeshifter tell him the truth about his daughter. Though he referred to me by title, the way he halted prior to saying daughter sounded like he was talking about a stranger, which I was. Mom and Kendel noticed what I'd called him, and it threw them off.

Dad enlarged the details on the holo screen. His face showed less concern and surprise than hers, almost as if he expected to see what he's seen. Mom, like me, was clueless. "She's a *legacy*. An extraordinary one."

Kendel added, "Her antibody and antigen levels are higher than Jade's. You can't seriously be thinking — "

"Those aren't the conclusions I'm arguing against — "

The two of them spoke over one another, each argument growing louder than the next. Mom jumped in and started cursing them both in Spanish. My parents were on my side, and Kendel was not. Matter of fact, she'd never really warmed up to me or even been cordial. Nobody cared to address my questions, no matter how much I cursed back or yelled, so I tightened my fists and set them ablaze. "Answers. Right now."

The display of my powers stopped them from arguing. "She knows what a legacy is." Mom's Spanish accent exaggerated as she explained. "And--"

Dad's booming voice shut down both Kendel and my mother. "That legacies have...*problems?"*

"You call insanity and homicidal behavior problems, Director? Your personal ties are clouding your perspective. Lucy, by all measures, you're a nuclear bomb, and if you weren't his daughter, we wouldn't be having this conversation."

My parents' extended pause told me the truth about my potential. Nuclear Winter wasn't hyperbole. I could cause damage equal to that of an atomic explosion? On top of that, Jade was an insane murderer? "Should I grab a razor and get in a warm bath now or later?"

"That's not funny, Luciana."

I fake laughed. "Wasn't joking, Mom. I can blow up, and all the others like me were psychotic, right, Kendel?"

"You're not wrong," she answered. She talked about me as if I was a rodent or a swarm of insects. "Power at that level must be *eliminated*."

I shrugged and turned to my father. "Or controlled. Teach me."

He cupped my chin in his hand. "I'm not a teacher. But I know someone who is."

Kendel stormed off, mumbling about "abandoned directives." Meanwhile, Dad led Mom and me to the grooming and outfitting area, where we threw the clothes we'd slept in into the laundry, chose new clothes, and showered. I washed my hair for there was no telling how long it'd be until the next time I'd do it. Following that, we ate a full breakfast and walked to the armory, which had racks of Ordnance, ammunition, and other equipment. The weapons were familiar, but the only time I'd seen artillery that heavy was the attack at my house.

He opened a tray display and handed each of us a disc small enough to fit in the palm of my hand. "Place this at the back of your neck and press it down until you feel it attach."

After lifting my hair, I did what he said and jumped when the disc clamped onto my skin. It didn't hurt, but it tickled a bit. Mom did it faster than me, and the process didn't surprise her.

"Our newest, kinetic-powered armor interacts with your lower brain functions. Heads-up display in your mask shows vitals and damage. Includes heat, air, underwater breathing up to fifty feet, healing apparatuses, and cloaking tech. Fits over your clothes, however thick or thin."

I wanted to see it work, so I "called" my suit into action. In seconds, I was covered, and I saw everything he was talking about. When I activated my powers, the suit registered a severe temperature and radiation warning. Dad waved a small machine over my head and, I assumed, recalibrated things so that the warning wouldn't happen again. Mom tried her suit out as well and seemed impressed. "Who made these?" she asked him.

"Sasha."

Her eyebrows raised. "She's here?"

"She was." His words were short. I didn't think he wanted any more questions about Sasha, whoever she was. "Ready for training?"

Zhang Minh, the Chinese guy from the transport who saw me naked, was my trainer. Apparently, he hadn't shared *that* part with my father. I wouldn't tell either. He may be sensitive about a grown man seeing his nude teenage daughter or be one of those weirdoes about virginity and sex and things like that. Zhang was gentleman-like and kind, and he trained me with patience. We worked on healthy breathing patterns because, and I hadn't known this at all, but I held my breath several times while using my powers. It hadn't affected the intensity of the fire the way I thought it did. My flames were larger, longer streamed, and more intense when I steadily breathed.

Zhang showed me to an open circle room like the cell Liam had dragged me into. That fact alone set me on edge. "What's this, Zhang?" I asked him.

"Target practice. Remember to breathe, and nothing in here can permanently hurt you." He gave the command for Ordnance to be set to *stun*.

"But it can hurt me?"

"Not unless I want it to," he replied with a smirk. "I'll be in the staging area watching with your parents. Feel free to talk to me over comms. Only I can hear you."

I grinned. A chance to show off to my father. "Can you set it so I can hear what they say?"

My trainer winked at me and left the room. The lights flickered, and the next thing I knew, a flash of blue light whizzed past my head. Live Ordnance fire. I threw flame at my attacker. Before I had time to verify the mechanism had indeed met its doom, the attack intensified.

Good. Give me more.

To conserve my energy and better my accuracy, I narrowed the stream from my hands and shortened the bursts. I struck every target, and if it wasn't a direct hit, the proximity and temperature of my heat burst did enough to disable it.

"Hey." My father's voice was distant in my ears. He wasn't talking to me.

Mom's response was shallow and cold like she strictly said it out of courtesy. "Hey."

Keeping my concentration with live Ordnance fire shooting in my direction was difficult. Doing it while eavesdropping on my parents' conversation was near impossible, but I did it.

"You look amazing."

Mom pretended the compliment didn't hit her ego. "You're...yeah. You, too."

I knew so little about the two of them, as individuals and as a couple. I had to know more. When they chatted, I ducked behind blockades they had given me to simulate real life objects to eavesdrop.

"She's beautiful."

"She's never had a man tell her that, which is why she doesn't think it. Tell her."

No, I didn't, but, at least, I'm self-aware. My nose is too blunt, and I could use thinner thighs. Who couldn't? Anyway, guys don't focus on my lower body, at least, not my legs.

"Of course, she doesn't. We didn't at her age, either. She looks like you."

"And *you*. Did you think she wouldn't?"

"I... It's been fifteen years, and I..."

"And what? I've never been with another guy, and besides, how many superhuman fifteen-year-old girls do you know? She's obviously your daughter."

I wished Mom would tell him how she really felt about him. Not that it'd make a difference. He was tied down to the stepmother I had never met.

"You owe me a conversation or a thousand."

She made a sound that made me angry for him. "I don't owe you anything, Jason."

My father's voice spiked in volume and pitch. "Of course, because Rhapsody doesn't need anyone's help to do anything. Next time, rescue yourself."

"Nobody asked you to interfere or to send anyone after us."

Dad cursed at her. "I'll remember to say that when I notify the families that their loved ones died saving mine."

"Don't be afraid, Lucy." Zhang was on to my delay tactics. "I'm setting your cover to dissolve and regenerate."

I wished I could tell my parents to shut up without letting them know I was listening to their conversation. Their back and forth was really screwing with my concentration. I didn't expect him to be overjoyed to see me or for her to be so combative — hardly the warm, family reunion I had envisioned for myself.

"You have thirty seconds. Go."

Sure enough, the digital transport became nothing. I sprinted to an imaginary wall and watched as it, too, disappeared, but the transport reappeared. I counted to twenty in my head and timed my counterattacks. Soon, I had disabled or melted the Ordnance. With my hands on my hips, I stood proudly and faced my trainer and parents. "Do I get to enter my name as the high scorer?"

"We're going again," Zhang said. "Higher armament rate and less cover."

I made a "come here" signal with my hands to my father, which I'd soon regret. "Bring it, baby."

"Director override. Set to injure-slash-maim."

Mom came to my defense and cursed him. "Are you crazy? You want to injure or maim *my* daughter? I'll ghost down there — "

"And *what*, save her? What about when you're not there? That's what we're training for in the first place."

"I'll *always* be there," she said. Meanwhile, the course had reset itself.

Dad argued back. "Like Peters was? Courtney, Hughes, Camuto are all gone, Rhapsody, and you know as well as I do that day will come when neither of us will be here to defend her."

An Ordnance burst hit me in the back. Searing pain traveled up my spine. I said a few words I wish I could've taken back, but from the laughter over the comms, Zhang didn't think my injury was serious. This armor was trash if it couldn't block a shot like that.

"Cancel it," Mom said to one of them, "or I'll do it for you."

Dad tried to reassure her after she'd done something I couldn't see. "Rhapsody, don't. Give her a chance."

I quickly located the offending Ordnance and fried it. This time, the transport lasted fifteen seconds. I practiced stopping the actual Ordnance blasts with walls of flame. Once I nailed the right temperature, I erected a wall of flame high and wide enough to block incoming fire and hit all the targets I located. More came up behind me, and I managed those, too.

"See," he said with joy in his voice, "she did it!"

Mom didn't say anything else. She was wrong, and she didn't have a leg to stand on.

I had a feeling Dad wanted to level up one more time, but my mother wouldn't have it.

Last training module today was flight. I enjoyed this training the most because there was one spectator for my failures. I asked for that. The constant bickering got in my head, and I wasn't the greatest fan of towering heights.

Zhang and I walked to the end of wherever it was. During the trek, I asked him, "What was going on up there?"

"At the end of your last session?"

I nodded since I couldn't see into the viewing area.

"Your mother quantum tunneled her hand through my chest and was threatening to yank out my heart if I didn't shut down the simulation."

To think my mother possessed that kind of savagery — the same woman who baked red velvet cupcakes for my third-grade class on my birthday and watched holovision shows with me could ghost her hand through another human being — made me believe the side of her I knew nothing about was a side I didn't want to know. She was, in many ways, a stranger to me.

"You weren't afraid of her?"

"Not really."

There was apparently more to Zhang, too.

"Your mother has killed before. It's an instinct there behind the eyes, but she didn't want to murder me. She also did not want you to die."

"So, what stopped her?"

Zhang smiled. "The director touched her hand. Anyway, here we are."

My father kept her from killing him with a *touch?* What was that?

We ended up in front of what amounted to a sparkling glass tower. Its size and circumference gave me claustrophobia. "I'm supposed to get into that and do *what?*"

Zhang opened its door. "Fly, of course."

Huh. "Come again?"

"Don't be afraid. You're not in any danger."

Inside it, I was able to stretch out my arms without touching anything all the way around, and though air freely flowed inside of it, the suffocating feeling was real. He put an arm around my back, rubbed my shoulder to comfort me, and reminded me to breathe. Crazy how I had to be reminded to do something to keep myself alive.

"Your powers are intuitive. They shape themselves around your personality like an extension of who and what you are. Think of your abilities like you would a talent or gift, playing piano or such. Let them flow from you and guide them to where you'd like them to go."

"Okay."

He pointed to the tube. "Step inside and fly to the top. Levitate yourself there, and then descend."

"How am I supposed to do that?"

Zhang said six words. "Focus, breathe, control. Lift and thrust."

The chamber closed. Almost immediately, I started hyperventilating. Okay, I didn't get the breathing thing, which sounded ridiculous.

Rather than close the chamber, he clearly mouthed "relax" and "breathe." I accomplished that, eventually, and pictured myself rising to the apex of the chamber.

Then, I channeled my powers through the soles of my feet and reached my arms upward. Slowly, I ascended about four feet off the ground then five. He shut the chamber. Soon, I was halfway up the tube.

I was doing it!

My progress brought a smile to my face. I increased my speed and got to the top quicker than I had anticipated. I was supposed to levitate there, but the middle ground between on and off was harder for me than just on. Fighting off the urge to look was unbearable.

"Breathe!" Zhang yelled. "And don't look down!"

I peeked and immediately panicked. The back and forth cut my powers in and out some fifty feet in the air. As I plummeted downward, my powers yanked me between flying and falling. I screamed and tried to regain control of what my body was doing to no effect.

The last thing I remembered was blacking out in midair.

I woke up in the twin bed I thought they had assigned me alone. The corner chair was empty. My father directed this entire facility. It was naïve of me to assume, after meeting me half a day ago, he'd discard all his responsibilities to be there for me like Mom had done for most of my life without pause.

Cool massaging sensations traveled my spine, and a cushion at my hips kept me from rolling onto my back. That added up. Numb from the back of my neck down, I wiggled my toes, tested my legs, and swiveled my hips — all functional. "Not in danger, huh?" Zhang had lied to me, and it'd be a while before I trusted him so much again.

Getting up was a chore. I gathered myself and maneuvered to a sitting position, my rubbery legs dangling over the bedside's edge. Little by little, my nerves tingled, and then feeling returned. The massage pad beneath my clothes was too hard to reach. Its work continued while I eased out of the room and down the hall to where I had been training.

Out of nowhere, Zhang teleported in front of me. God, that sulfur-smelling green cloud was awful. "Don't worry," he said, fanning the fumes away from his face with his hands. "You never get used to it. Good evening. What are you doing out of bed?"

I pointed to my back. "I'm starving, and I can barely walk, thanks to you."

He explained, using big, scientific words, that the security measures worked, and my falling velocity had strained my back muscles. Didn't make me feel any better. I had to stay off my heels to walk with minimal pain. "So, you're my trainer *and* probation officer?"

He showed me a flashing red light coming from the device on his wrist — a tracking device. "You don't know your way around this place yet. I had to take precautions."

I put my hands on my hips. "Isn't that what Kendel is for? Where is she, anyway?"

Zhang avoided my eyes. "Yeah, well, it's me again today. Do you mind much?"

His accent sounded less harsh to my ears, and I was getting used to his perfect smile and unmoving buzzed black hair. "No, I guess not."

"Good." He took me by the elbow and tried turning me. "Back to bed. You need to heal."

"C'mon, Zhang. I only turn fifteen once, and it is about to be my birthday, isn't it?"

"In another half day, yes."

I thought about how to avoid confinement until morning. "Do I get an early birthday wish?"

"Sure. I have just the thing." He plucked two, yellow, pebble-sized tablets from his suit. He held them beneath my face. They smelled sweet, like a mixture of flowers, perfume, and candy. I sniffed them, and they vanished from his hand. Had they flown up my nose? I squeezed my nostrils and exhaled.

Zhang laughed his head off and teleported me to a part of the place overlooking a marvelous cliff. I swallowed, thinking, in moments, I'd be vomiting all over myself. No nausea, though, and no sulfur. He'd given me the gift of keeping down my last meal. I asked him why we were here. He hushed me and instructed me with his hands to look straight down. I wished I hadn't. My stomach dropped at the sight below us — a cliff formed of shadowed mud and brown rock, and from this perspective, its ledge did not look large or secure at all. Ahead of us, I loved the view. The sunset was beautiful, and it colored the distance a palette of oranges, reds, purples, and blues. I could watch this every evening for the rest of my life.

Someone swooped in from our left and landed on the rock. From this distance, I couldn't tell the person's identity, but Zhang let me know it was my father. Shortly afterward, another flyer joined him from the opposite direction — a woman. It had to be Mom. After he made sure my comms had been turned off, Zhang let me in on the secret. "At sundown, every night, the director comes here. No one else knows this place except the two of us, and now, you and your mother."

"Why do *you* know about it?"

He accessed a panel and changed several green-colored levels with his fingers. "For emergencies. I'm the only other one in the complex who can reach it. Now, listen."

My father thanked my mother for coming, and she said, "This view is gorgeous."

"I came to a place like this with Sasha the day of your funeral," he said. "She thought it's how you'd want us to remember you."

"Jason, I'm sorry. I — "

He raised his voice. "Is it? Is *that* how you wanted us to remember you?"

"Yes," she admitted.

The surveillance levels were fantastic. We could hear them like they were in the room with us, minus any wind or background noise, and they could not hear us. Dad was hurt by what she had done, and he did not hesitate in letting her know. I didn't blame him. Letting me think whatever about my father for fourteen years and three hundred sixty-four days was messed up on many fronts. But, this was supposed to be a private conversation. Otherwise, they wouldn't have chosen that place to meet. "Should we be here?" I asked Zhang.

"We can go if you want."

He'd have to teleport me away against my will to get me to move especially once it started getting good. "I'll let you know," I said halfheartedly.

"Jason..." Mom continued. "Did you invite me here to attack me?"

"No. I want answers."

Without their mannerisms and facial expressions, eavesdropping on them was like watching holovision when the projection crystal goes out.

"After I left you," she said, "I changed my mind about leaving three weeks after Oregon. Halfway to Walsh, I found out I was pregnant. And, I stopped and headed east."

"Why?"

She gave the obvious explanations — they hadn't finished high school and she was confused. With a pregnancy, she'd never know if he'd want her for her. "You'd have dropped everything and married me in a second, and I would've given you a yes before you even asked," she said through sobs. "I wanted you to want me with or without Lucy."

They moved closer to one another. Were my parents about to get back together? Was this happening? Dad was divorcing, and Mom hadn't dated since they broke up.

"How many people have we seen die, Jason? How many have died at our hands?"

"I stopped counting."

Wow.

"We were around Lucy's age when we got these powers, and we've made decisions nobody we know ever had to consider."

Dad gestured toward her. "But she *wants* it, Rhapsody, she — "

"She *thinks* she wants it, but what she really wants is *you*. She wants her father and whatever that means for her. If you decided to pour concrete and collect garbage tomorrow for a living, she'd be right by your side. I know that."

"How do you know?"

"Because I would, too."

They kissed, and my heart leapt. I notified Zhang, and he immediately teleported me into my mother's room. Under the covers, I smiled and fell asleep.

My parents were back together. Happy early birthday to me.

CHAPTER SIXTEEN

When I awoke in Mom's comfortable bed, I discovered she hadn't returned from the cliff. Her side was smooth, undisturbed. Back home, in our "normal" lives, where she held to a tight routine, I'd have panicked. By this time, eight o' clock on a regular Monday morning, she'd be dressed and fixing her second cup of coffee. Maybe she was doing that in the galley.

I left the bed and stepped into the hallway. Where was the galley? I walked as if I knew. The third time I'd passed the same restroom, Zhang found me wandering and cursing to myself.

"This way," he waved. "Happy birthday."

"Thanks!"

On our approach, the scents of fresh pastries, cooked meat, eggs, and brewed coffee grew stronger. I momentarily gave in to my hunger, snatched a cherry Danish the size of my hand, and devoured it. Not that I trusted Zhang much, but he was smart to feed me first. I stacked two plates of food and dove in. He sat across from me, and we did not talk. Too much chewing going on.

My parents arrived while I was halfway through my second plate. Their body language toward one another was *different*. Mom didn't hesitate, and my father constantly smiled. She gently touched his shoulder, and they shared a laugh. This interaction continued throughout the food line. Whatever they were both on to get them this happy, I wanted some. My back had healed, but I wasn't in a good mood. Mom had been out all night long, and I had worried.

" — and a giant, poisonous octopus started singing with me."

What was Zhang talking about? "Huh?"

"You haven't heard one thing I've said, have you?"

I shook my head no and refocused on my parents. "No. At least I'm honest." Mom sat with me and my father across from me and next to Zhang. "What's so funny, Mom?"

She pointed to a spot on her right calf where a nasty pink gash had healed over. She never explained to me how she'd gotten it besides a "clumsy accident."

"When he had just gotten his powers," she said, pointing her thumb at my father, "he dropped me on a roof, and I landed on a rusted nail. That's where I got this."

That wasn't funny. Had to be there, I guess?

Zhang's wrist beeped with a notification. He and my father stepped away from us and out of earshot. I leaned over to Mom. "Fell asleep waiting for you. Late night?"

She didn't respond.

Pressing for details, I kept with the questioning. "You were on a mission? That's what they're talking about over there?"

She nibbled on a square of fresh watermelon and dried the juice on her lips with a napkin. "Where do you think I was, Luciana?"

She avoided my questions, so I played along. "You weren't alone, right?"

Mom continued eating and didn't divulge details. If my dream of my parents getting together was happening, I needed straight answers. Part of me wished for that as far back as I could remember although I had no clue who my father was until now. My fists melted divots into the table. "Stop ignoring me!"

"Don't forget who you're talking to. Fifteen or not, you're the child here, not me. And happy birthday."

The silence was telling. Sorry I asked. I choked on whatever I had last put into my mouth, and Mom patted me on the back. Regarding certain things, especially *that,* she was never a good liar. That was why she was one hundred percent honest with me regarding most things and why she kept dodging my questions. "Are you two back together?"

Her metal fork clanked against her plate. "It's ancient history."

"And?"

"New. *Complicated.* Inappropriate to talk about with a fourteen-year — "

"Fifteen-year-old."

"Last night was last night, and I'm still trying to wrap my head around...Look, he's not the boy I fell in love with anymore. And I'm not the paranoid, love-struck girl, either."

The men returned to the table. Mom violently jabbed her fork into her spinach and mushroom omelet and tore off a piece. Don't bother her any further. Okay. Got it.

"Eat and prepare for the day," my father said. "Kendel will train you."

I'd grown comfortable with Zhang more so than Kendel, and I'm sure the feeling was mutual. "I don't want to train with her. Zhang can do it."

"She's your shadow, not Zhang." Dad's answer was firm, unyielding. "He'll be handling another matter with me."

"Another matter like you had with Mom last night?"

My wisecrack sucked the air out of the galley, and all conversation stopped. I sat back. A whole, boring day of throwing fireballs at unmoving targets and failing to fly instead of doing something, *anything*, important. I guessed I'd have to locate the Forecaster in this fortress and get her to predict when I might have something interesting to do.

My father laid his rough fingers on my hand, which should've put me at ease but didn't.

"Give her a shot, and if it doesn't work, quit. Nobody here will judge you."

She was *that* bad of a shadow, huh? I hardly believed him, but I told him what he wanted to hear. Mom let out a sound. She knew my say-what-he-wants-to-hear-so-he'll-leave-me-alone tone well and wasn't buying my answer. But, to my surprise, she didn't snitch.

We finished eating and went our separate ways — me to the grooming area and my parents and Zhang to wherever they were going. After my shower, Kendel met me. Pulling the white cotton towel tight under my arms, I rustled my hair with my hands. My broken ends tickled my shoulders. That was an inch or so of growth since I stopped chemotherapy.

"Hi."

"Hey." She sounded totally thrilled to be on babysitting detail. "Here. Research and Development modified it for your powers."

Kendel presented me a new bodysuit disk. I twisted the old one at the back of my neck until it detached, gave it to her, and replaced it with the new one. The process was a little painful like popping a pimple. She turned her back while I moisturized and got dressed.

Once I slipped on my underwear and bra, both of which fit uncomfortably well, I asked her, "What's first?"

Kendel clicked her teeth. "Battle training with live targets."

Interesting. "Like against actual people?"

"Yep."

"For how long?"

"Until I say stop."

We didn't exchange another word until I was fully dressed. Fighting naked sounded like an idea for a guy's holovision show, not something I should be doing in a grooming area. Without being obvious about it, I measured her up. In her regular form, she was a head taller, skinnier, and narrower in the hips and chest than me. Who knew if muscle mass and weight changed when she shifted forms? I had no intention of finding out the hard way.

I could bring the heat, though. If she tried me, I'd fry her.

Mom had always told me eye contact was a sign of respect. Respect was not the emotion I was having toward this chick. Still, I faced her to hear the truth — see it come from her thin, pink lips. "What's your problem with me, anyway?"

"You *exist*."

I thought my armor into action, and the sleek, black metal snaked across my clothes. It had a heavier weight than the old one Peters had given me. "So, try to kill me."

Kendel didn't bother activating her armor. Instead, she patted me on the shoulder and said, "No thanks."

She led me past the training center where I'd been yesterday to a wing in the facility I had never seen before. Bottling my aggression toward her was near impossible and walking to an unknown destination didn't help. *That's it. I'm done with secret places.* "Where are we?"

"Go." She pointed to an open room. "She'll tell you what's next."

Ugh. I hated surprises like this. Inside the bare room were two black padded chairs — one of them occupied. The occupant stood — a skinny woman with brown, curly hair. She wore a comfortable-looking beige turtleneck sweater, brown leather pants, and modest heels. Was she in her forties? Fifties? Hard to tell. The gray hairs in her bangs could have arrived early.

"Hi, Lucy." she said. Her voice was soft music. "My name is Susan. I've been expecting you. Welcome to your psychological evaluation."

My stomach dropped and rumbled. "Why?"

"Part of the process, I'm afraid. Would you like a drink? A soda or maybe a water? And happy birthday."

I'd been around people like her before. "Thanks. Just read my mind, and I'll be on my way."

"That's not the kind of work I do, Lucy. I'm not one of you."

"You're normal?"

Her hair bounced as she shook her head no. "Normal is a relative term. Will you sit?"

I put her to the test by thinking a stream of nonsense she'd have to respond to. Susan didn't flinch. She was telling the truth or had an out-of-control bluff. "How do I know I can trust you?"

She tapped the right arm of the chair. "We trust one another. That's how therapy works. Everything you say is confidential unless you intend to hurt yourself or others."

Therapy. Therapy meant a label. *Damaged.* I claimed the seat across from her. We sat for a moment. Susan's ocean-blue eyes tightened on me. "The speed and honesty with which you answer my battery of questions and follow-ups, the faster this is all over. Whatever you say beyond that is up to you. I'm evaluating you for the field, Lucy, that's all."

"Field?"

"To use your powers in a more comprehensive, open, and controlled manner in sanctioned situations. We call those situations 'the field'. Oh, I forgot about this." Susan handed me a metal bracelet with five studded white jewels. "Can't have you tossing my front door into the ocean."

"What?"

"Never mind. It's strictly for safety purposes. Mine and yours. The bracelet suppresses your powers while you're with me. I'll release it when we're finished. Are you ready?"

I slid the bracelet over my wrists and immediately noticed the difference. "Do I have a choice?"

"Let's start out simple. Describe the extent of your abilities and the times you used them."

I explained to her about the fire, and it might or might not be radioactive, and I could fly with help. I'd used them first starting at the house. There was the guy in my hallway — no, I had stabbed him through with a knife not burned him, and the guys in my house who I'd given burns, and the practice with Old Guy, the car explosion...

And the guy who I unintentionally *incinerated.* I didn't count Mateo, because I couldn't confirm his death. Pretty sure Liam was still breathing.

Susan tapped a glowing blue module hooked to her right ear. I'd seen one of those before used to record notes. "You've used lethal force more than once."

"Yep. So?"

I sighed and anticipated the next question. How did I *feel* about the ability to kill? I rubbed my right wrist — the one I had to shake loose from a charred skeleton hand. I'd never thought about responsibilities attached to having this degree of power. Part of me saw power as a curse and hated it. A different part of me loved it.

"How does that feel?" she asked me. "The ability to control whether someone lives or dies."

The rigid coldness of the bony fingers on my wrist haunted me. "Complicated," I admitted to her.

"That's fair."

"How am I supposed to feel?"

Susan rested her chin on her hand. "No right or wrong answers here, Lucy. You're either ready for the field, or you're not. No judgment either way. Your parents only know the end."

"Fine."

"I'm going to push you a little bit. I need you to explain complicated to me."

For a moment, I thought about how much I wanted to share with her. Whatever I said was being transmitted through her headset to cloud technology — confidential to a point. Who was to say my parents weren't listening? "Good and bad, like good about the bad, bad about the good, I don't know. That's wrong, isn't it?"

"Try not to think of my evaluation in a binary fashion." She repositioned herself in the chair. "Not good or bad, right or wrong, black or white. It is what it is, and the fact you feel a sense of wrong isn't a negative thing. Do you want to go into the field?"

My heart thumped. What was I supposed to say? Yes, I wanted to go into the field, fight for the right cause, and beat the bad guys. Or no, I wanted to be a normal girl who could light her entire body on fire. There was no more "normal." My parents had decided that for me years ago when they had a relationship and conceived me. I told Susan the truth.

"All right," she responded. "I can work with that. Let's proceed."

The questions continued, but the interview went forward more like a conversation between, say, a teacher and an uncomfortable student. As Susan talked to me and shared personal stories of her own — she'd split with her husband after she started work here — she got me to talk. We discussed everything irrelevant, from holovision reality stars to current events, over hot coffee. Had therapy been like this when Mom had taken me, I wouldn't have blown it off.

Then, she fired kill shots in the form of a word association game. Easy rules. Respond to her prompts with the first word or words that came to my mind. "Elayna Sandoval."

Simple. "Mom. Kind of a stranger lately."

"Try to stick to fewer words. Jason Champion."

Hmm. "Handsome stranger."

"Life."

I relaxed a bit. This wasn't so bad. "Short."

"Death."

"Shorter."

Susan paused for a moment, and she focused on the tip of her square-toed, brown leather shoes. "Natalee Gupta."

Natalee was my best friend who was wasting away in a coma somewhere in Nowhere, Ohio. Whom I couldn't stop from getting shot, and who was being tended to by a person with one name who might or might not be an actual doctor. My world grew dark and hot. Every place on my body tingled with energy. The bracelet was doing its job. No flames.

"Natalee Gupta, Lucy."

In all the mayhem of my life, I'd forgotten all about her. She could have died on Isabella's table a week ago, and I wouldn't have known the difference. Nat was my best friend, my *only* friend, and I'd been self-centered and stupid and I...

"Pass."

"Why do you want to pass?"

I stood and tossed my chair aside. Heat seeped along my neck and the front of my chest, and the bodysuit's cooling system did little to fight it. Neither did I. The bracelet weighed on me. Digging my thumb beneath it, I yanked and pulled, but it had locked shut. "I quit," I shouted. "I'm not playing anymore. Don't try to make me."

Susan's voice didn't raise or waver. "Natalee Gupta."

I cursed her and flung my arms in the air to overcome the bracelet's control and burn everything to cinders. "No!"

She invited me to sit. I crossed my arms and tapped my foot instead. Whatever I had to do to escape this room I would do even if it meant hearing whatever nonsense she'd come to understand about me. The trash receptacle in my brain had been full of advice from teachers, counselors, therapists, police officers, and general adults about what I needed to do. What was one more person pointing out what was wrong with me and advising how to fix it?

When Susan said Natalee's name one more time, I broke down into tears. All I could think about was how Nat had gotten shot and how I hadn't prevented it. I said the words out loud. "Guilty." I sobbed. "Helpless. Dead. My fault. Responsible. Are you happy?"

She handed me a box of facial tissues. I took one and dabbed at my eyes.

"Why do you think it's your fault, Lucy, when you were under duress and unable to control the fire?"

"Because...what kind of good can I do out there if I can't even save my best friend?"

"There are eight billion people on the planet right now," she told me. "A few million in this state. Somebody, somewhere, is going to need help, and you're not going to be able to give it to them. That's not your fault or theirs. People die, Lucy. You have to be able to cope with the inability to save everyone."

I continued sobbing. "I don't know if Nat's alive or dead. Do you?"

Of course, Susan didn't. She couldn't tell me if she did. Therapists and doctors were sworn to confidentiality unless they felt you were a danger to yourself. And with this bracelet on, I wasn't a threat to anyone. I'd gone through enough tissues for the time being. I offered her my wrist. "Are we done here, Susan?" I sniffed.

She tapped her ear to complete recording and unlocked my bracelet. My energy level immediately spiked. "I have enough information to render a decision, yes."

"Which is?"

Her shoulders sagged, and she exhaled. "Do you want to go into the field, Lucy?"

I gave her my best response. "Yeah. My parents want me to, don't they?"

"All right. Say you're in the field."

"Okay."

"One of your enemies is threatening to kill Natalee. Another enemy says he is going to kill me, a woman you barely know, and you can only save one of us. Who do you save?"

My heart said Natalee, without a doubt, but my brain said Susan. Then, Susan added more qualifiers — only I could save either of them, and she had two young sons at home. That made Susan the right choice, didn't it? But I loved Natalee. She was my best friend, my *only* friend.

How could I let her die and have her family mourn both her *and* Mr. Gupta?

Of course, under pressure, I'd go with my heart. Anyone would. And, I'd leave two boys without their mother. Either choice was impossible and cruel. She knew that when she posed the question. There was one truly fair but heartless answer. The words hurt to say, but I forced them out. "I do nothing. You both die. And I cut myself to deal with the pain. Is that what you wanted?"

Susan's blue eyes widened. I'd shocked and surprised her. Wasn't what I was going for, but who cared? It was an answer, and my evaluation was over. She tenderly reached out to me. "Lucy..."

The tears were already falling. "No. I've failed, and now, I can be normal, right?"

I ran out of the corridor. Susan called after me, but by then, I was down the hallway. She followed me, but the click of her heels slowed when she couldn't see me. I'd rounded a corner and ducked behind a wall. After a couple more steps, her shoes tapped against the floor in the opposite direction. I'd lost her. She'd finally given up on me.

Evaluations like hers were why I never cared about tests.

Try or not, I *always* failed them.

THE NUCLEAR WINTER   207

CHAPTER SEVENTEEN

In case Susan doubled back, I smashed my body against the door. That way, I'd only be visible to a person immediately in front of me. My breathing slowed enough for me to hear faint tapping at the metal. Slowly, I turned. A pair of crazed brown eyes stared at me through the open window. The heavy locks grinded open, and I conjured fireballs, unsure of the horrors on the other side.

Standing in the center of the room, Kendel greeted me. "Welcome to Training Room Four."

Incredible. I'd run away to the one place I didn't want to be. After extinguishing my hands, I examined my surroundings. The area was much smaller than the other training room — narrower with a lower ceiling. The floor had a rugged, grooved texture I felt through my shoes. My body craved rest or an escape from expectations to produce results. I'd not get any of that here. The one exit I knew about had locked.

Looked like the only way out was through.

Kendel dropped a holographic display in front of me and manipulated its definition — the results of my body scan. "Before you get into the field, you need to know the fullness of your powers. Her armor crawled across her and formed a shiny second skin. The texture looked lighter and more flexible than mine. "Watch it, and then, try and hit me."

The presentation started with a diagnostic description of my powers using words, like: thermodynamic, nuclear, propulsion and antigravity, concussive fission and fusion, and access to the radioactive spectrum. The rest were terms I needed a college degree to pronounce.

What I understood was that I was a walking, talking, thinking nuclear reactor with the untapped ability to fly. My flame blasts weren't radioactive unless I wanted them to be. In that case, anything I touched would have *an undetermined half-life*. And my powers were *inextricably linked to my cancer*.

Use my abilities and no bone cancer. Skip the powers and die.

Got it.

I squeezed my fists tight and felt power course through my veins. The next part was strategy. I'd be moving through a simulation cityscape with panicking civilians and powered aggressors. Protect the civilians. Eliminate the aggressors. Seemed easy enough.

Kendel lifted the hologram, and I viewed the realistic downtown area. Transports had been overturned, civilians ran, screaming, and the aggressors weren't obvious until they made threatening gestures. Before I processed everything that was going on, a teleporter slashed my neck with an intangible knife, ending the simulation. I'd forgotten to reactivate my suit.

"Stop!" Kendel yelled. Her irritation put me on alert. "Are you ready *now*?"

My suit slithered over my clothes. "Yes."

This time, I was prepared for the knife-slashing teleporter, but he did not appear. I stepped forward with fireballs at the ready. A trio of civilians at my right screamed for me to help. Chasing them was the teleporter, who noticed me and disappeared and then reappeared in my face. Bursts of flames erupted from my eyes and vaporized him. At my feet was a pile of blackened ash. I reminded myself this was just practice and moved on. Using my eyes worked better for crippling small targets with accuracy.

I zapped everybody who I thought would cause a problem, until I came to a police officer who fired her

Ordnance at my chest. The armor shielded me from the brunt of the blasts, but they hurt like a small bee swarm stinging my chest. I threw a shock of fire with enough force to send her through a storefront window but not kill her.

Then, Natalee rushed to my side and grabbed my wrist. "Sandoval!"

We embraced, and I didn't want to let go. "What are you doing here?"

Nat stabbed me in the shoulder with a knife — a *real* knife. I gasped as the blade exited the wound and blood soaked my clothes. Before she had a chance to strike again, I sent flames all over my body, and the knife clattered to the floor. Around me, the simulation faded, and Kendel shapeshifted from my best friend to her original form. Her mask melted away from her face, and I sensed real fear in her eyes over my reaction to being stabbed.

I growled at her. Fire suppression steam hissed around me. I thought of it as a dare to outlast it, and my anger fueled my ability to do so. Though my fire had dampened a little, it was still an inferno. She'd used my guilt against me, and she'd pay for that.

"Back it down, Lucy," she begged me. "You're compromising the integrity of the building. You'll kill us."

"Maybe you should've thought of that before sticking a knife into me."

The air cooked with heat. Kendel sprinted toward the exit, and I sent a ceiling high wall of flame to block her. She started this, and she'd have to end it. "Enough, Lucy," she told me, holding an object I couldn't see in her left palm. "You were supposed to block my blow. Control it."

"What if I don't want to?" I asked her.

"Then your parents will lose their only child."

Could she do that? She spoke as if it was a definite possibility, like the object in her hand was some sort of protection against what I could do. I flamed out. Then, the pain from the stab wound heightened. I'd probably need stitches to get the flesh to close.

The damages I'd caused around me were considerable. For one, I straddled a gaping hole in the floor. I'd burned clean through, and *I had been levitating* above the piping and insulation beneath me. My armor was smoking everywhere, and I was afraid to retract it because I had probably torched my clothes. If that weren't enough, much of the ceiling had caught fire and fallen to the ground in blackened, wet lumps, and the door to the room had melted shut.

We were trapped.

At my foot was the knife stained with my blood. Kendel and I breathed heavily and stared at one another. I wouldn't be the first one to speak, but if I had any choice in the matter, the last word belonged to me. The throbbing in my back worsened. Stinging wetness oozed down my back. I dropped to the floor in pain and gritted my teeth.

"Deactivate your armor so I can examine your wound."

And give her an opportunity to finish the job? No way. I'd stall until we were found and rescued, and *then* I'd drop my guard. I told her what she could do to herself. The heads-up display under my mask analyzed the damage to my shoulder. The blade had come close to severing a nerve. That explained the burning numbness and why I didn't want to move the fingers on my left hand. Kendel moved closer, and I kept her at bay with the threat of a fireball. "Come any closer" — I grunted — "I'll turn you to ash."

"I'll take my chances."

When she approached me, I tried manipulating the heat in my hand into a deadlier version. The agony in my shoulder blocked my concentration. Soon, the fireball flickered and extinguished. Nothing worked to reignite it. Kendel knew exactly how to incapacitate me — shapeshift into a person I loved to get close to me and wound me in a way to block my powers. I didn't get it. Not only did she *sound* like Nat she *smelled* and *moved* like her, too. She'd shadowed me for God knows how long. There was no telling what she'd seen and heard and practiced how to do. Whoever they were fighting against out there could have similar strategies.

Kendel manually deactivated my armor, and, as I feared, my powers had incinerated my clothes to shreds. It didn't take her long to examine my shoulder and arrive at the same conclusion I had. She clamped her right hand over the wound to staunch the bleeding. "We need help."

Obviously. I eyed the melted metal clump blocking our exit. "Push the door open."

"I can't. The director will be here soon enough."

Fire extinguisher fluid dripped from the ceiling sprinklers onto the floor. The tapping drove me nuts, so I played along with small talk. "How do you think he'll feel when he finds out you stabbed his only daughter and threatened to kill her?"

Her hand squeezed a little harder, and I winced in pain. "It's my responsibility to get you ready for the field. He doesn't question Susan's methods. He shouldn't question mine."

"Then don't stab people!" I shouted.

Kendel switched hands. The fingers on her right hand dripped with blood — my blood. I started feeling woozy and nauseated. The loss was getting to me. "Too bad Liam isn't..." I slurred. "H-he could have...as much...as he wants."

With a hand wave, she summoned a portion of the wall the size of a suitcase that floated over to us. Many of her quick movements were hard to track, but the wall unit had compartments, and Kendel had no trouble accessing what she needed. She cooled and numbed the stab wound with a swab and injection and forced four staples into my flesh. I heard the metal *click* and *snap* into place and felt the separated parts of my skin knit back together.

Following that, she swabbed the area clean and handed me a large vitamin. "Chew this," she said. "It'll increase your blood pressure and production. The shot will suture the muscle and nerve damage. You'll be sore for a day or so."

I did as she told me to do and immediately noticed the difference in how I felt. Energized, I reactivated my suit and got to my feet. As I did, I noticed the simulation had restarted and the hole I'd burned into the floor had almost reconstructed itself.

"Shapeshifters must be convincing imitations," she said. "I watched the real Claire Elizabeth Allen, day in and day out, for two weeks before assuming her identity. I had to know every detail from her preferences in men and makeup down to her favorite chai tea blend. Our enemies study us, too. They may even know our armor's weakness above the arm."

I hadn't been keeping time, but a considerable amount of time had passed, and there had been no rescue efforts. "Do you know how many of us got injured our first time in the field? *Ninety-seven percent.*"

No way. "Even — "

"The director is near invulnerable, so we don't count him."

This — me losing control, the stabbing, the patching up — it was all part of her plan? Betrayed and infuriated at the same time, I cursed at her and asked why she hadn't healed me sooner.

Kendel did not seem bothered in the least. She sent the wall piece back into place and masked up. "When supplies are available, they take an average of four minutes and thirty-six seconds to arrive without a teleporter for extraction. I gave you treatment thirty seconds early. You were bleeding too much."

Things started to come together. She'd told the truth about leaving the training room. I was stuck here no matter what I did. "Nobody's coming to free us, are they?" I asked her.

"Not when they see my name on the simulation room log. Not even if I call for them."

How were we supposed to get out? My face must have conveyed my confusion.

Kendel pointed to the imaginary cityscape's end. The only way out was through.

"Now, concentrate. Make it hot," she said to me, gasping. "Level down the kRads."

Focusing on the melted wad of metal blocking the exit, I shot a tunnel of flame from my hands. I bored through quickly to minimize the smoke curling from the hole. By the end of the fifth time, we'd been through the full simulation, I'd become adept at adjusting the radioactivity levels of the flames, their dimensions, colors, and intensity. I couldn't fly, though. A moment, thirty seconds of subconscious levitation, was the best I could do.

Kendel's double-barreled-Ordnance-under-the-chin-style training got me this far. I wouldn't call us friends though. Less than enemies and unlike strangers worked for me. Once the liquefied metal stopped dripping onto itself, we stepped through the opening and into the hall. The passageway reeked of burnt metal and sweat. Okay, the sweat was probably ours. We'd exercised for hours, and I was so hungry I swore I could've eaten for a day straight.

She cracked a dirty joke about how our suits must smell, and I smiled. She'd been a jerk to me for most of the time I'd known her, and I hated that I didn't hate her anymore. My father had been the one to push Kendel onto me, and perhaps, he knew more about me than I thought he did. With Zhang, I might've "girled" my way out of being useful to anyone. With her training me, the possibility of getting to Nat myself? Not an impossibility.

Kendel's wrist beeped with an urgent-sounding alarm. She tapped it with her finger twice. A white beam streamed from her arm into her right eye.

"What is it?"

She waved me off with her hand until she had a chance to process the information. Then, without a word, she broke into a full run ahead of me. Whatever was going on, it had to be serious. I struggled to keep her sprinter's pace, but I followed her into the armory. There, she pointed me to the center aisle, third row, first locker, and told me to wait. A panel verified my identity and popped open. The inside had fresh sets of clothes, a new bodysuit disk, and a couple things I didn't recognize.

"Your suit is damaged," she said from a distance. "Change."

She unlocked her own bodysuit disk and shed the clothes I'd singed. I'd never seen a naked woman besides my mother, and she was far leaner and muscular than her. I redirected my attention to my own situation. My body had a terrible smell — like body odor and ashes — but there was no time to remedy it. I changed, closed my locker, and met up with Kendel. She kept a pace closer to jogging this time. After not moving for a few minutes, my legs were liquid.

"What's the problem?" I asked her, nearly out of breath. "Silence on my comms."

After fanning her hand at me and waiting a beat, she said, "It's on another, secure channel — Liam survived, and he located the cave."

Okay, that wasn't much to go on. "What cave?"

She didn't answer me until we were in the staging area — a large, round room where my parents, Zhang, and every other person in this place had gathered. There weren't many people — twenty or so — I kept losing count trying to catch my wind. All were masked and of similar height, which made it harder to tell who I had already counted.

"The largest dormant beryl deposits on the planet," she whispered. Once she read my "and?" look, she whispered," Certain beryl gives powers to anyone who wears it.

Mateo found it. Yeah, that was problematic. "How much time do we have to stop him?"

From the way everyone moved, not enough. Without access to the secure channel, I had no clue as to how they — *we* — were combatting Mateo and Liam. Yes, I corrected myself to think "we." The simulation had to have prepared me for this although I was winded and wouldn't turn down a short nap right now if you paid me to.

The chaotic scene slowed for me once I found my father. He paced, arms behind his back, on a raised circular platform surrounded by rotating holographic displays — maps, graphs, and body scans. He paused in my direction. Was he staring at me? No, *through* me. He fidgeted with the band on his finger until the center glowed ruby red. The thing calmed him but agitated Kendel. She pursed her lips and sighed the way Mom did when a restaurant messed up her order, and she stormed into my father's space. He ignored her until she pushed away the holograms to confront him.

"With all due respect — "

"You know why."

He reloaded the displays, and she cleared them again. *"I'm* a decent strategist. I can — "

"Read and assess nine different situations simultaneously? You think I'd willingly make this call for any other reason? *Any* reason?"

Kendel didn't dare answer. My father had tremendous physical strength and offending him could be dangerous.

"Besides," he said in a calmer tone, "there's no guarantee it'll work."

She stepped off the platform and waved me to follow. Her quick pace was difficult to keep up with, but I managed to do it. "What were you talking about?"

"You need debriefing."

We stopped in an infirmary. Kendel stuck a rectangular object into a compartment on her left arm bend. I picked one from the same cabinet she'd taken hers and snapped it into place. A needle pricked me in the skin. Couldn't be a drug I'd been injected with. Whatever it was, I felt amazing. I kept my arm straight and allowed whatever it was to flow. "Then debrief me."

The story was a science fiction spy film. A border agent had notified my father about a man fitting Liam's description who had touched down on the West Coast close to a crystal cave my father had been surveilling. They had three hours at best to intercept, and there was scientific-sounding talk of a space-collapsing pocket dimension, a powered person who could open and close it, and how Liam could make the beryl crystals active without natural X-class solar flares.

"They," not "we." Great.

My face betrayed me, and Kendel chuckled. "You thought you'd be going."

"I-I trained... You trained me, and I — "

"Thought they want you for your winning personality? They need X-class solar flare radiation for the crystals to turn malignant. A targeted radiation blast."

I could do what my shadow wanted me to do — stay on the sidelines. Or... "I won't go."

My answer caught her off guard, but this time, I centered my emotions. "You're serious?"

"Nat's dad is dead, and when she wakes up, she'll need a friend. Besides, tomorrow's my birthday. I wanna see it."

Kendel's right eye spasmed, just a quick twitch. Enough to warn me and reveal the truth.

CHAPTER EIGHTEEN

They had captured Natalee for leverage---her life for me activating the crystals. I'd never been more important to anyone. Ironically there was no decision for me. I knew which side I belonged on.

Before I could respond, Kendel told me to let Natalee die so the world would spin on unaware but ultimately appreciative of the sacrifice. A monstrous suggestion to say the least. Thinking of my best friend's death for the rest of my life when I could've prevented it was not an option. I stomped behind my trainer to the secured dock where they would launch a counterattack. "She's my *best friend*. My *only* friend!"

"None of us have best friends," she muttered over her shoulder as we arrived at the dock. "Saving loved ones are life-and-death decisions where we don't control the entire narrative. Loss is all we know and what we live. Better not to have them at all. Susan isn't one of us, and her husband understood this."

Spare me the lecture. One life for the whole planet. Honestly, all the calculus pointed in this direction, but up to this point, my life story had been handwritten by everyone but me. "Lucy was a failure, a screw-up, and destined to die." Except to my mother and Nat. The little drop of faith they had in me kept me going some days though they didn't see it, and if Nat was going to die fighting, she would not do it alone.

"Nobody controls me," I told her. "Help me or get out of my way."

Kendel announced her intentions by shoving me to the ground and putting her mask on.

Saving Nat meant going through her. So be it.

I summoned heat into my hands. My suit warned me it could not protect me or my surroundings from this level of radioactivity. I imagined Kendel's skin sizzling beneath her bodysuit and large sweat beads forming on her face. The spike in temperature hit me, too. Moisture dripped down my neck despite the bodysuit's air conditioning. My fists throbbed and tingled, and now, I could only glance down at them briefly because of the light...Oh, the shockingly beautiful *light!* The rippling, bright orbs around my gloves stung my eyes, and I could taste the current — like licking the terminals on a battery. The sensations were addictive and too overwhelming to devour all at once, so I didn't rush through consuming them.

"Liam will slit her throat and make you watch." She coughed and groaned while sinking to her knees. "He'll force you to listen to blood pool in her throat as she gasps for her last breath."

"Open the dock, Kendel."

"Loss is all you'll know!" she screamed.

"Open it!"

From the floor, she asked me was I willing to kill her if she didn't do what I asked. Her tone of voice suggested she doubted I would. Inside, I questioned it myself. But backing down, at this point, wasn't an option for me or her. Nat's life hung in the balance, and so did the lives of many more. But *killing* her to prove my point? Would that make me better or worse than Liam? He believed he had the right to do so, too. I did not have that right either, but I'd push Kendel to the brink of death to get my way.

The radiation I wielded, which had little effect on me besides the temperature hike, brought tremendous pain to my shadow. She scratched at the black tiled floor, rolled back and forth in pain, and whimpered like a gravely injured animal left on a roadside. Her condition bore a close resemblance to my post-treatment symptoms. It made sense. I was dosing the room with enough radioactive waves for torture and not to destroy her.

Her mask dissolved, and she pulled out a small clump of her hair. Her trembling fingers sorted through the feathery red mass in disbelief. "Enough," she groaned, crawling to the biometric panel. Then, her appearance changed. She rolled over and had become my father's identical twin. For a split second, I shut down — long enough for her to activate the security door, roll underneath it, and toss up a whitish security grid between the two of us.

She stared back at me with my father's face, and for a moment, it dawned on me what had happened. Everything she'd prepared me for was for *nothing*. The mission had been planned and run its course while she occupied me with training I'd never use. She'd done it at the command of my father. Probably in the name of "keeping me alive."

He had no faith in me, and why should he have? I was his daughter — a total stranger who'd met him days before and remotely looked like him. Beyond my tanned skin and existence, he hadn't been involved in my life. Why should he now? Still wearing my father's form, Kendel smirked at me. His lips were thicker than hers, but the way they twisted was unmistakably Kendel's. Behind her, the dock opened to a peaceful night sky with a bubbling light source in the distance — the wormhole held open by the Forecaster. "You'll be safe here," she said in his voice. "It's what he wanted for you."

Screw what he wanted. I threw everything I had into breaching the shield she'd put around me, but as soon as she nabbed a jetpack, activated it, and flew through the wormhole, the shield fell. Great. I could go after her if only there was a three-hundred-yard-long ladder I could use to get to the wormhole. I cursed my father for being such a protective jerk and myself for not being able to fly. I ran to the dock's edge and kneeled so the gusting winds would not knock me over. Down below the sloping rocks was darkness and certain death.

The wormhole was still open. I couldn't see that far away. Maybe my suit could? "Enhance visual display," I said. The magnification increased tenfold, and I needed it a couple thousand-fold. Increasing it to maximum magnification helped a lot. Every head movement exaggerated my view, so I slowly lifted my chin. The Forecaster was the one holding the wormhole open. The strain had caused blood to flow from her eyes, ears, and mouth. However her powers to fold space and time worked, they were killing her, and I had to act.

Kendel had nabbed the last jetpack, and all that was left were parachutes. The flight-capable vehicles probably did not include instruction manuals or, at least, how not to crash them. No one was around. If they were, they had strict orders not to help me. The Forecaster couldn't extend the wormhole forever, and we were running out of time.

I strapped a parachute to my shoulders, secured it the best I could, did the sign of the cross, and stepped to the edge of the dock. Though I had a death grip on the threaded ripcord, I lost my nerve and backed away. I'd flirted with death all this time, and I'd been close enough to smell it creeping up behind me. Jumping off this dock and plummeting to the cavern bottom was suicidal. I talked myself into it. *I have a parachute. I'm not going to die.*

I ran as fast as I could, and the second I left the platform, I screamed at the top of my lungs and switched my powers to the hottest I'd ever burned. Though wind whipped past my head and alerted me of my free fall, I hoped I'd slow down. A second later, I surrendered hope and yanked the ripcord. My fire had burned the parachute off my back, and I cursed myself for not thinking that through.

Soon, I was praying to God in Spanish anything I could think of to say. I told Him to let my mother I know

I gave her crap, but I loved her more than I'd ever loved anyone else. And my father that I forgave him for leaving me behind. My racing heart skipped beats. I descended into total darkness. In another moment, I'd be completely shattered. I closed my eyes, and when I opened them, I'd be in whatever existed after this life. Hardly the end I'd have authored for myself. Then again, I wasn't the one writing my story in the first place.

I cracked my busted right eyelid which was one of the only things that didn't feel broken. Thinking was agonizing, and the pain wouldn't release me into either sleep or death. And, according to the diagnostics in my suit, my spine was broken in five places, so I probably shouldn't move. Except I *couldn't* move. My right lung was punctured. That explained the knifing in my chest. Didn't feel like I lost teeth, but I tasted blood. Instinctively, I spat, forgetting my mask was still on. Retracting it wasn't an option either. There had to be insects or wildlife down here. I wouldn't let my last breaths be muffled screams while creepy, crawly things ate my eyeballs. Reading a bloodstained display wasn't worse than being plastered across the floor of a canyon.

Mom's voice crackled through my audial comms. "Lucy!" she screamed. "Lucy! What did you do?"

All I mustered in response was a tortured groan. I'd failed again.

She yelled for my father using his full name. His middle name was "Ray," and he was a junior? I couldn't hear his response, but I knew it had to do with the mission and the senator since she told him what he could do with them.

Moments later, she escaped the transport. The rush of wind in the connection gave her away. Not long later, a floating projection of her arrived in front of my face.

Hysterical and speaking Spanish so fast I couldn't understand beyond *mi pequeña niña*, she reached out for me. I wiggled my fingers and felt nothing. She wasn't next to me, which meant the wormhole was closed. Then, the Forecaster must be dead.

Tears burst from my intact eye. *I tried, Mom, I tried. And now, I'm going to die on my birthday.*

"Mariposa." Her voice trembled. "Baby girl, I need you to get up."

My throbbing, aching brain must be tricking me. Mom told me to get up? Bleeding to death with a broken spine and God knows how many powdered bones? She was the delusional one. "Just let me die in peace" I wanted to say. All that came out was a gurgling whimper. I'd written out my intentions long ago — a nontraditional burial near the ocean in a place called Xobai. She'd told me about it and shown me images. The place was heaven-like with clear water and golden sand beaches. The view from its cliffs was heaven.

We'd put off a cross-country drive there many times, I never knew why, but the timing was always wrong for us. Not anymore. She'd invite no family members. We had nobody but each other. Every person at Penn High, including the faculty, either hated or pitied me. No crowds. Nobody to satisfy their piqued curiosity. Just her and a priest. After my last rites, she'd spread my ashes in the rippling waves, and we'd swim together one final time.

My father might want to show up. Fine. With my death here, I'd finally have his full attention.

What had she said to me again? *Stand?* My legs didn't work — they couldn't — with my spine in this condition. Everything hurt. I moaned in agony. *Leave me alone. Let me die. Stop with the expectations. I'm average. Sub-average. Human. Dying.* A spasm in my left eye cracked the eyelid. The three-dimensional scan of my torn body turned green at my right arm. Was it an error from a broken computer? Feeling returned in the fingers. I flipped it over to have my palm facing the uneven cavern floor. How? Bones and veins mend over weeks, months — not minutes. I bent my elbow, raised it above my wrist with my palm at the ground, and violently pushed to flip my body over. The impact knocked the breath out of me. Hand at my throat I gasped for air. The suit's red display sensors blinked and sounded warnings. I already knew — my oxygen supply was desperately low. I slapped, scratched, and clawed the cavern's surface until the sensors stopped, and I could inhale and exhale. My lungs had healed themselves, too, and I smelled fuel in the air. Overhead, an enormous shuttle flew toward the loading dock. Didn't look like one of ours. In enhanced visual display, I saw they were not our guys. Wait...the attack across the country was a smokescreen! The real target was inside the fortress, and without a wormhole, my parents would take hours to return. *Nobody* could stop the powered attackers.

The strength behind my voice surprised me. "Mom," I said through tears. Dull soreness lingered in my muscles and reset bones. Best I could tell, everything functioned again.

"Get up, baby," she said to me as the hologram connection failed. "Stand and fight them."

I propped myself to a sitting position and then rose to my feet. Unbelievable. How deep was this canyon? Ten football fields? The mask showed me how off my math was. Eight thousand feet was about *twenty football fields*. I'd fallen that far and *survived*. Forget osteosarcoma. If those two couldn't kill me, what could? Or, more importantly, how could I get up to ground level before Christmas? Climbing trails on foot would take days, and the search for whatever they were after wouldn't take near that long. No, I'd have to find a quicker way. The suits were made for protection of the weapons. *We* were the weapons.

Leveling the canyon wouldn't work. I had to *fly,* and should I fall, I'd have to try again until I flew up the mountain. But *how?*

This was nothing like my other life failures. Eventually, I'd get the results I wanted, but I just had to figure out how to do it fast enough to stop Liam and Senator Mateo's plans. The *whoosh* of the flying transport engines had faded to nothing. They'd landed, and assuming they were powered, nobody left inside the complex could face them and win. I rubbed my gloved hands together. "Think, girl, think," I said to myself. "Physics, which you are failing, lift, drag, thrust... What's the other one? Gravity?" Pale blue flames gushed from my palms and fingertips, and the force pushed my boots across the pebbly rock like I was roller skating. Turning my palms downward, I elevated to my tiptoes. With a little more push, I levitated a bit. Keeping my balance was hard. Either I wobbled too far forward or too far back.

Kendel called my powers "intuitive" like they had a nature, a mind, all to themselves. Anything like that wouldn't want to be trapped unused in a dead person's body. Its best interest would be to help me do whatever I needed to do, right? My chest's center started tingling. Instead of focusing on it or ridding myself of it, I allowed it to grow and spread throughout my body. The blasts increased at my foot soles and palms, and I was *airborne.*

Despite my better judgment, I looked down and saw nothing but darkness below me. The falling sensation I'd feared dissipated. I was flying and in total control of myself. Not a parent. Not bone cancer or some rule or law. *Me.* I let out a primal roar loud enough to resound in my own ears. I soared higher and faster — so swift and sudden that I pierced the upper sky and discovered myself surrounded by clouds. Like performing a high dive, I tilted downward and descended at breakneck speed toward the dock. The mask display identified five hostiles gazing up. They fired Ordnance at me although I guessed, at this speed, no human eye could accurately target me. My heart beat overtime as I tried to slow my landing. Instead of landing with grace, style, or, I don't know, on my feet, I hit the surface with a *thud*.

They fired Ordnance kill shots — I could tell by the burn degree. Stun shots felt like a hundred honeybee stings. Kill blasts were another level. The electric shocks popped in my teeth fillings and burned the back of my eyes. I writhed and screamed, but I was *alive*. Ordnance couldn't destroy me. Understanding that, I crawled out of the hole I'd made and pointed bare fingers at them. Pink spurts of energy jumped from my hands and dropped them.

Good. I had time to catch my breath. I peeled back my mask, inhaled deep, and pushed myself to stand. Ouch. Whatever didn't hurt or wasn't numb was sore — even my eyes. I'd burnt through the suit's gloves and boots, down to the tan padding, and the layer of silver mesh armor's serrated edges pierced my knuckles and calves. Hobbling forward on aching ankle and knee joints, I doubted I could walk farther. Suppose I could? This place was a complex puzzle inside of a maze, and where would I go? Senator Mateo wanted me for my powers, but the crystals he wanted were on the West Coast. Unless...

"This is Tactician Anderson. ID number 124534113902. I am fourteen-point-five clicks northwest. ETA five minutes. Does anyone copy? Over."

The woman's hostility shook me. Was it a two-way display? Could she see me? Beneath the designer eyeglasses, her perfectly-shaped eyebrows pointed downward toward her nose in criticism. I didn't want to answer. She was the most beautifully angry African-American woman I'd ever laid eyes on. Still, Tactician Anderson's three-dimensional appearance and rushed vocal delivery weren't the things that intimidated me about her. No, it was the information she continued rattling off and whether I could trust her. Anderson repeated herself, claiming she was two clicks closer.

However long a click was. I responded, "Yeah. Yes. I'm here."

"Who are you? You sound like you're twelve, and this is supposed to be a secure channel. Over."

Should I use a fake name? "I-it's secure. I'm Lucy...*Champion*."

I'd paused in using my father's last name. Mom had taught me about taking a man's last name, and it indicated protection. Never in my life had I felt so out of control, on my own, and unprotected. Yet, I was a *Champion*. Didn't feel much like a real Champion or a Sandoval. Too late to pull it back now. I'd put it out there.

Anderson covered her shock by asking me to repeat myself and asked how old I was. I gave her my full birthdate. My birthplace? Told her that, too. Then, she wanted me to reveal my mother's name. I said nothing. Her holographic eyes scanned my face. She knew my mother — not Elayna Sandoval — *Rhapsody Lowe*. I didn't press her for details though the tremble in her voice made me think she took it personally. "You're alone," she said.

"Far as I know. I'm not sure. Can you — "

"No, I'm telling you. I've tried all the compound's satellite and cellular channels, tracking, even the analogs, and you're the only answer. No biometrics are on my scans but yours. Over."

What's the big deal? Nobody answered. I could've been one of a million things: bad Wi-Fi signal, spotty connection, destroyed tower...

"It's just us, Lucy, and I've just arrived. I need you to come to me. Can you do it? Over."

Was everyone dead? Anderson sounded that way. Silence. Her face had frozen beyond an occasional blink and facial movement. Finally, she spoke. "Your prototype suit gives off a traceable signal. I'll walk you through the steps to shut it off."

I followed her directions and did as she said. Without it, my parents may think I'd been killed, too, but the enemy's ability to track me may make it true. I'd had basic training with Kendel, and Anderson didn't seem at all impressed although I may have played the melt-the-door-off-the-hinges episode too cool. Plus, I didn't know how to get through the compound to the entrance where Anderson had parked her transport. I'd have to sneak my way through.

Anderson directed me to do the opposite. "Get here fast. Kill anything in your path. Over."

CHAPTER NINETEEN

A clear directive. Destroy. Murder. Stain my soul with blood. How many rosaries do I say, confessionals do I go to, and candles do I light for *considering* that? These people weren't innocents. They were *murderers*. But maybe they were weekend killers, and during the weekdays, they had families, loved ones. Perhaps, they had no one. Did I care? The right answer for now was no, but was it wrong in the eyes of God? Would I spend eternity thinking about the lives I was about to take?

Anderson had walked me through the plan. Blast the dock walls, around the northwest perimeter, and to the front corridor. Then what? She didn't say. Here was the kicker — keeping my kRad level down to keep the compound from becoming a nuclear disaster site.

Concussive blasts not fiery burns.

Right.

She and I needed help in the worst way. My parents were on the other side of the US. How fast could they get here without the wormhole? The crimson, rippled opening had closed a while ago, and the Forecaster was certainly dead from holding it open. This suicide mission was not one of a trillion ways I'd ever pictured myself dying.

Should God look down at me and see me *erasing human lives with a flick of my wrists*, what would He think? There's a teenage superpowered soldier doing My work! Little girl murder dog on the loose! I wiggled my dirty, bleeding fingers and toes and cleared my throat a little. Crazy. The whole thing was nuts, and, according to Anderson, the only way to — what was it we were supposed to be doing once we found one another? She wouldn't say. Hopefully, it involved lots of fleeing in the opposite direction.

I paced through the corridor which was clear of conscious hostiles. I didn't have the stomach to eliminate them. Until I stepped too close to one of them and his fingers aggressively scraped at my naked toes. His flesh and muscle melted from his wrist down like hot butter dissolving on a stove. Consciously, I hadn't tried to maim him. But something dark, nasty, and *primal* had taken over my mind.

What had I done?

I wanted to apologize. Didn't he deserve an apology? Did superhumans have a code of ethics, a set of laws, a border or demarcation line between what they would and would not do? Maiming had to be high on that list, right in front of death. I'd crossed — something I couldn't *uncross* — but, I didn't hate it. Part of me died with the hand. That was wrong. No, no more maiming. Wait, but what if I *had* to destroy a hand to save my life? Ugh. I puffed out my chest, pushed it off, and forged ahead in the darkness. "What's next?" I asked her.

She told me to pace one hundred steps forward and blow a hole in the bay door with *force*. Heat had less thrust. Had she accounted for that? She assured me she had and rattled off the math behind her figures. Okay, I didn't understand it, but I got it. She had the figures to back it up. All I had to do now was to *do it*. Pretty simple. I stopped at ninety-eight steps, fired up my hands, and shoved a heat stream into the open blackness. The metal opening gave with a *boom*. Shards flew back in my direction, and a piece the size of a man's fist struck my head. I pulled my mask back to clear the cobwebs and silence my ringing ears.

I must've blacked out for a minute. No amount of blinking or wishing wiped the haze away. My fingers wandered to the blazing gash in my forehead and stopped short. A steady blood stream flowed down my face.

Popped my jaw, blinked my eyes...nothing helped. With a deep breath, I pressed my right palm against the wound. *Oh God.* I used to think nothing felt worse than chemo or chemo recovery which was true until just now. My painful moans echoed in my head. Was Anderson on line with me, or had the connection dropped? "Hello?"

"Why do you sound like that? Proceed on the route. You haven't moved in minutes. Over."

"Debris," I managed to say. "Caught debris."

She sighed. Yes, I admitted to her, I'd screwed up and shorted the distance prior to blowing up the opening. Everyone makes mistakes, I explained in words broken up by wincing, and perhaps she made approximate calculations. Sprinkled with several curse words, she rattled off the formulas she'd used and said her math was always, *always* perfect and that I should trust her to help save my life. Whatever. I didn't have energy to argue or debate with a well-educated stranger. According to her, there was a voice-activated analgesic inside my suit, which I used. The medicine was powerful, quick acting, and it allowed me to think. Next, I had to get to the control hub or what she called the central corridor. From there, I'd head northeast down the main hallway to the entrance, access the biometric panel, and let Anderson in.

My pathway was sparsely lit. I squinted my right eye, and the crusted blood made it difficult to reopen it. In my left eye, a strange thing happened. Although it was pitch-black, I saw everything outlined in white like an X-ray. My body was a skeleton, and so were the walking people in front of me. They had heavy Ordnance, and the random way they moved — they couldn't see! I could walk past them without being noticed. My right side was compromised because of my still-healing eye. I didn't feel safe, and using my powers would give me away. They were prepared, trained to kill me.

I had to be ready to do the same.

Slow steps. I rolled my feet. The first guy passed by close enough to lean in and kiss me on the cheek. I paused and waited until he was too far gone to shoot me. Two more guarding the access to the central corridor. I ripped a piece of armor from the sleeve of my suit and tossed it behind me. The soldiers charged in search of the sound's source. Once they passed me, I broke into as close to a full sprint as I could, placed my palm on the biometric panel, jumped through, and closed the door behind me. I used my powers to weld the metal shut.

I was in the central corridor, and now, I didn't have far to go to meet Anderson. "Anderson," I said, my voice spiking with excitement over my victory, "I'm in the central corridor." She didn't answer me. The Wi-Fi connection must be spotty again. "I said — "

I circled around mid-sentence. Five skeletons trained heavy Ordnance on me. Unsure of what to do, I remained still. They shot me anyway.

I awoke, lying flat and fastened to a table by the wrists, waist, and ankles. Stun shots. They'd stripped me down to my clothes. The bodysuit meant what, comfort? I couldn't have a little comfort and not basically be dressed for an exercise class before they murdered me? Except, they *couldn't* murder me. Not before I did whatever they wanted me to do or Anderson rescued me first. Liam stuck the bend in my right arm with an input tube like the kind the doctors attached to my old Broviac catheter for chemo meds. The intravenous bag had opaque liquid in it clearly *not* for my benefit — not anesthesia or vitamin boosts. The wound above my right eye had been cleaned and treated. The dressing felt like a pie crust baked onto to my face.

"What's that?" I croaked.

He told me that it was a concentrated adrenal accelerant to activate my powers, so, in a few minutes, they wouldn't have to ask me to do anything. That stuff would make my body shoot out radiation like an out-of-control firecracker. My target was the largest, golden, football-shaped stone I'd ever seen. The thing had to be longer and wider than two of me set head to foot and weigh as much as two transports. Though the ceiling lights were bright enough to be halogen, the stone was dull and cloudy. My father, or someone, had supported the thing in a massive chamber.

Practically bouncing on his heels with excitement, Liam waved at it and said, "Largest chunk of heliodor on the planet, a *provenance*...makes sense he'd keep it close... it's a Fountain of Youth — the proverbial seed of an immortality tree which *you* are going to plant."

The stream of consciousness rambling had a point. The senator had sent up a huge smokescreen. *This* was the jewel, and not the ones in the mountains, he wanted me to activate. In the cabin, my mother had told me the powers one got from them were benign, but the longevity and invulnerability were not. With this on his side, Mateo could reshape the planet how he pleased and construct an invulnerable army to rule it.

"Over my dead body," I mumbled.

Liam smiled. His teeth were perfect from flush pink gums to bleached white caps. "The accelerant will send your bodily systems into failure," he said, tapping the bag with his fingers. "You *will* die."

His attempt at being menacing made me laugh. Terminal cancer kind of made one immune to death threats. I've contemplated dying and the transition of death to the Great Beyond so much that philosophies about it were starting to make sense. They always did from a certain perspective. I supposed admitting and accepting it was another deal.

Liam reached into the waistband of his black dress slacks and produced a silver handgun with an off-white handgrip. I'd seen these before in movies before the conversion to holograms took place.

"Ordnance gives a clean shot. No gunpowder on the hands and minimal kickback on kill setting." He brandished the weapon over my face so that I could get a good look at its workmanship. Liam backed away and unloaded a shot. A terrible jolt ripped through and exited my left thigh. My adrenaline spiked, and my powers surged beyond my control. I fought it as best I could. The second I thought of closing my eye, the irresistible urge to release energy overtook my mind and raised my lids. A bright flood of yellow energy erupted from my eyes, burning the dressing on my face, destroyed the ceiling directly overhead, tunneled through layers of earth, and blasted into the open sky. Anything in its way was likely to be vaporized.

Liam tilted me downward, and the streams sliced through electric wiring and steel until I faced the crystal. Then, the yellowish-red fire struck the crystal's center. I screamed until my chest and throat ached. The stench of livewires and burning metal hung in the air like a rain cloud too stubborn to open its arms. No one was coming to help me, and even if they could, at this point, I might have been too explosive to stop. Darting my eyes to avoid the crystal would've worked, but Liam had thought of that. He'd rolled me so close that the thing's dimensions were too wide and long for me not to look at it. So far, the center of the jewel where I'd struck it glowed like the sun — its heat warmed my naked feet.

He'd donned protective shielding over his face and slid close to the provenance. Liam turned his head to me, and I knew there was a perfect grin meant for me under the blast shielding. Heliodor shards, splinters, and dust spurted from one of the two holes I'd created in the stone and landed between slabs of ceiling, charred rebar, and cooked aluminum tubing. The moment he'd been waiting for. Liam knelt outside my sight range and reached into the debris piles, instantly jerking back. Aside from the accelerant burning my insides worse than the aftermath of a chemo treatment, the room temperature was like that of a warm, summer day to me. For him, it had to be like roasting inside of a nuclear reactor. His gloves caught fire as he hurriedly gathered all the fragments he could find and dropped them into a bag. Wasn't much, but he'd have a dozen superhumans to start with. No way was I going to die for this.

At that time, I felt a rhythmic chopping overhead. A transport with rotating blades, too slow to have a fusion engine, flew low enough for me to notice movement inside the dark cabin. He'd brought reinforcements. Had I gone with my first thought, I'd have shot it out of the sky. First thing was first, and that was to protect the provenance heliodor until *my* reinforcements arrived. Whatever the men in the transport had prepared for me, I thought I could handle it with ease. So far, that had been the case.

Rather than stop my abilities altogether, I needed them to defend myself, so I focused on allowing them to flow throughout my body. The table, its restraints, the needle in my arm, and the remainder of my bodysuit and clothes burned away. Being naked was the least of my concerns. The light I gave off and its brilliance was blinding, even to me — I couldn't stand the sight of myself. So, I looked ahead and stepped through the molten pools I'd created. Liam batted away the flames on his body and backed away from me on his hands and feet. How did I appear to him? He shot his pistol at me, and the bullets evaporated before striking me. Right after I sent a direct volley in his chest was when I heard a sound of rushing liquid.

I didn't have time to dodge. Ice-cold white foam poured down on me. The temperature drop consumed all the energy I was giving off and reduced it to sizzling steam with the thick, strong scent of chemicals. While my heart rapidly beat, and I still felt the jitters from the adrenaline spike, I had no powers to show for it. The wound in my left thigh throbbed with my heartbeat, but the coldness seemed to help keep me from bleeding out.

Any hope of gathering more crystal shards had been drowned in whatever they'd used to suppress my abilities, but he had enough. The chopping grew more distant. The transport was searching for a place to land.

I wiped my stinging eyes clear of the stuff, which was rapidly solidifying, and all I saw was a haze of whiteness. Liam was in front of me and reloading his weapon. I heard it *click, snap*, and shift into place. I deeply inhaled. The explosion of his next two shots coincided with pain shooting through my ribs beneath my breasts. The rounds punctured my chest, and it was impossible to breathe.

A few more seconds and I'd be with all the relatives my mother said I'd never get a chance to meet, including her mother, Ruby, whom she'd almost named me after. Thank God she hadn't. And my grandfather, George, who I reminded her of. Mom wanted to save me from choosing this life, saving the world, but it seems that, in the end, I didn't have a choice to begin with. Maybe I never had. I'd never put myself intentionally in harm's way. I just wanted a chance to meet my father.

Loss. Kendel was right. I'd be losing so much in death.

I braced myself for the last shot and heard it but experienced no additional pain. The blast sounded different, electric, not gunpowder. I blinked and, while nothing was clear with regular vision, I could see the yellow X-ray like I had before. From the shape of the skeleton and the small set of bones in its stomach, it was a pregnant woman. No, two pregnant women, side by side. Three. Four. They were multiplying, or I was hallucinating. Altogether, there were *nine*, all armed and on my side. One of them put a finger to her teeth and closed her mouth. I shuddered from the cold and the lack of oxygen. The foam helped more than it hurt, but it wasn't permanent. Pink streaks oozed from my chest and leg. I'd bleed out soon.

"Don't move," one of them said. I thought she sounded like Tactician Anderson.

Liam's next shot was quick and nicked my right shoulder, but hers hit his shooting hand. From the way he waved his hand and cursed at her, she'd shot to kill. Sure enough, when I got a good look at his body, two of the fingers on his right hand were missing. His entire skeleton disappeared, reappeared, and disappeared. The women fanned out and encircled me facing outward. One of them approached me from behind, cleared the foam from the back of my neck, and attached a new bodysuit. It materialized across my skin beneath the chemical encasing and immediately started diagnosing and treating my wounds. My limbs trembled. Although my body's systems were failing, one by one, my powers and senses slowly returned to me.

Mindful of her delicate condition, I said, "Get out of here," to the lady guarding my back. "I'm radioactive, and —"

"It's the life," said the woman. I realized she didn't sound like Anderson; she *was* Anderson. They all were. The mannerisms were all slightly different, but they were her. That was her ability — to multiply herself — and fighting like a freaking martial artist.

After silencing me, she and the others shot randomly around the room. The chemical scent couldn't cover the golden puffs of smoke that smelled of rotten eggs. I caught a glimpse of him near the provenance crystal then across the room and back to the stone. He was...*teleporting?* He could do that, too? Well, Mom flew, and I was a walking nuclear disaster. Why not?

Wherever or whenever he arrived, he'd stay a second at a time before popping out. I conjured a fireball in my palm, but by the time I grew it to a throwable size, he'd disappeared multiple times. Though he vanished and reappeared, it didn't look as if he'd mastered it. We'd have to stop him before he did.

I dropped the fireball at my feet and lost my breath. I was dizzy, as if the room was a top, and my stomach cramped. My forehead was blazing, and if the heads-up display was right, I had dehydration along with a 105.3-degree fever, ongoing blood loss, and kidneys on the edge of shutting down.

"Help," I managed before collapsing to my knees.

Anderson's clone helped me stand and continued shooting. The mask couldn't filter out the horrible stench anymore and I dry heaved. Nothing came from my mouth because there was nothing in my stomach to give, not even liquid. Another sound rattled the building, louder than anything I remembered ever hearing, and it stopped just as quick. Two people in bodysuits like ours dropped through the hole in the ceiling that I'd created. *My parents!* Anderson absorbed her clones all at once, which was strange, and nodded to my father, who was pleased.

"You came," he said to her.

She pointed to his left hand where the glowing ring had been, and said, "You called."

"Thank you."

Their interaction was awkward, topped only by the strange and sterile way she and my mother hugged one another and separated. I doubt their bodies even touched — just arms. Everyone knew each other except me. Who was Anderson to them? She'd called Mom "Rhapsody," so, she did know her from the past. What was that she called Anderson...*Sasha*? *Anderson was "Sasha," my father's wife*?

My powers were back and no longer suppressed but multiplying quicker than before. Everything turned bright white around me, and while I could not see much or feel anything, I could hear — all except for a faint buzzing that distorted their voices.

Anderson stated what all of us had figured out to some degree. My powers were growing too dangerous — nuclear bomb-like levels. After spewing out mathematical calculations nobody understood, she said the best way to minimize casualties was elevation as high as possible before detonation.

"Detonation," I said over the buzzing, "like I'm going to *explode?* Won't that kill me?"

"No," she said. "Your power flushes out of you and replenishes itself, like a rechargeable battery. You'll probably absorb much of what you output."

But she said *casualties,* so I wouldn't die, but people were going to die? *Because of me.* How many? Could she give me an estimate? Did she even know?

"Mom," I called out into nothingness. "Mom, get as far away as you can."

"I'll stay with her," my father said. Had he not been my hero before he said it, that right there probably clinched it for me. "I've been through this before. Remember the pit?"

"Not with this wide range of radioactivity you haven't." Anderson turned to me. "She can fly by herself, elevate to a safe distance...you can fly, Lucy, can't you?"

The buzzing in my head got louder and shriller. "Not really, I mean, I can't steer or direct myself...can we move this along a little?"

My father argued back. "There's a city of twenty thousand below us. Without shielding, the radiation will hit the coast. Underground, maybe, one of the mines?"

I interrupted him. "Dad."

"Consider *all* of the variables, Jason," Anderson said. "You can't do everything, not after flying to get here. You can hardly catch your breath. And the mines? She'd cause earthquakes and poison the ground. She's better at a high altitude, below the ozone layer, and we cross our fingers."

Mom put her hands up and joined the argument. "She's not a statistic or a *variable*, Sasha, she's a human being," She yelled and pointed at me. "*My* daughter, *our* daughter."

"Okay, so I'm not a parent, so I don't know anything."

"I didn't say that, but — "

"But what, Rhapsody? She's a variable and a human being who will survive, no matter what," she shot back. "Who or what are you willing to sacrifice to save her?"

The pain intensified. This debate had to end. "Máma," I cried on my knees. "Help me."

She joined me on the floor, wrapped her arm around my waist, and whispered, *"Hasta el final"* in my ear. I bent my left arm and grasped her hand. That's when it happened. We vaulted through the hole I'd seared into the roof, past the transport Kendel piloted, and *whoosh*ed into the night sky. I fought back, but her clutch tightened. In the thin air, among the clouds, my voice was little more than an echo inside my mask. "Let me go. You'll die!"

Apparently, becoming a human nuclear bomb meant you could not sob. I wanted more than anything for her to live and for me to die. My father's presence made Mom's face light up in a way I'd never seen her smile before and would never see again. She removed her mask. I did the same. What I wanted took a backseat to what was happening now. We looked at one another, and the light within me illuminated our space in the sky. Without air to breathe, Mom passed out first. I held her until it grew to be too much and closed my eyes.

EPILOGUE

SIX MONTHS LATER

My stepmother, who I now called by her first name, cooked a hot breakfast that morning, like she had pretty much every Tuesday since my fifteenth birthday last year, also a Tuesday. The day I incinerated my mother.

Belgian waffles, sausage, eggs, and coffee. I smelled it all, and my stomach barely grumbled.

Same as the other twenty-six Tuesdays, I had no interest in eating that meal, the two afterward, or a snack of fresh fruit in between. I supposed it wouldn't have made much of a difference to her if I went downstairs and kept up appearances. She did wake up overnight to nurse a newborn — the baby I'd seen in her womb that my father didn't know about and who had survived radiation.

They'd been estranged. All it took to bring them back together was a secret daughter and an Extinction Level Event. That and my mother disintegrating into the molecules that formed her. Sasha explained it to me like this. "She existed," she'd said with her hands in fists, "and then" — she opened her hands — "she didn't. No pain. She went from light to light."

Sunlight made me think of her smiling down on me. The nuclear winter afterward made sure I didn't see light for a while. I imagined a priest would've told me it wasn't my fault she died, that God had a purpose in everything He did. I guessed so. There was no rational explanation why the atmospheric changes spread across three state lines. On the holovision, the falling flakes from the sky where I'd detonated were chalky gray, like burnt paper.

With the 4-D holovision setting on, I'd felt them and shuddered with the memory.

Nothing, besides my mother, the compound, and a chunk of the mountain had been incinerated, but the nation was on continuing terrorist threat alert. International flights inbound shut down indefinitely. The Americas had become the world's largest islands.

I pried myself out of bed, forced my feet down the sprawling staircase, across the carpet, and into the kitchen. My breath hitched in my chest. I hadn't been in it in so long that I'd forgotten I'd insisted my father build a kitchen identical to the one in my old house down to the Italian marble tiles. Sasha had opened the kitchen drapes for the morning light to shine in, as if she knew.

So many memories. And loss.

"C'mon, Sandoval, I can't eat all of this by myself," Natalee said over a heaping plate of food. She had become my roommate, at least until her uncle and aunt could get a workable visa situation and take her to India. She'd never been, and her father's brother was what she called "India rich," which, I guessed was different than American rich? Either way, the paperwork was delayed, and I was glad. Otherwise, I'd be cooped up in this house by myself, and someone else would have to help me do online schoolwork. Mom always had said she'd regretted never giving me siblings, and now, I had *two*.

My father didn't mind her being around, and neither Sasha. Isabella, the doctor she'd taken Nat to, had given Nat a transfusion of radiated blood to keep her alive while I was busy blowing up. Thus far, she hadn't shown any positive or negative side effects or superhuman abilities. If she did, Liam had murdered Isabella, so we were on our own. My parents wanted to be sure of both before she left.

She'd tried to pull me out of my depression with everything she could think of, Sasha and my father, too, but nothing worked. Telling a psychotherapist that I was the cause of the nuclear winter on the East Coast and half the free world's problems right now would be dangerous. Not like they could commit me to a hospital that could hold me.

Without thinking much about it, I tore a waffle section off and ate it. It was perfectly sweetened without syrup, and I happily chewed it. I was hungry after all. I finished the other quarter and then the other half, some bacon strips, a handful of blueberries, and a glass of orange juice. Nat and I treated it like a competitive eating contest which, of course, I won. She got a lot closer to beating me than I thought she would. I'd dropped a dress size or two since the New Year, and she looked the exact same. Not fair.

My father entered the kitchen, kissed my stepmother, and looked at me with shock. "Hey. Good morning, girls."

I nodded and waved, my mouth stuffed full of eggs, and ignored Nat. She thought he was hot, and the youth in his face made her forget he was thirty-two-years old.

"Have you seen the news out of Beckley this morning?" Sasha asked him. "Residents claim they found glowing precious stones like gold diamonds buried in the soil."

All noise in the kitchen ceased. The area around the provenance heliodor was still so radioactive no regular human being could approach hit. But, if part of it had exploded, and we did nothing, superhumans would be running all over the place. My father placed a black circular disc next to my right hand. "You won't shred this one," he told me. "You in?"

I wrapped my fingers around the disc and shed my bathrobe.

THE END

ACKNOWLEDGEMENTS

TO: My Lord and Savior Jesus Christ for the ideas and the drive to finish.

My wife and business partner Heather and our three daughters. Your sacrifice of time and support is everything.

My parents, Bradley and Barbara, my stepmother, Debra, for her inspiration, and my editor on this project, Kelly Hartigan of Xterra Web (www.editing.xterra.com)

This novel marked a new beginning of sorts. Thank you to my BETA reading team and those who advised me on content and names: Pam Alexander, Claire Allen, Makayla Baker, Tiandria Cotton, Julie Druckman, Alan Fowler, Greg Freeman, Marché Scott-Jenkins, Gina Johnston, Beth Lowe, Donna Mengel, Jackie Rodriguez, Jhoseline Sanchez, Susan Scherrfel, Michelle Sutton, Meredith Talmage, Laramy Wells, and Jean Williamson.

A special thank you to Christine Mayfield, Amy Purcell for "Gail's Law," Jeff and Diane Ransom, Richard and Virginia Dietrich, Phyllis Conway, the Lowe family, Kendel McAuliffe, Allie Petree, Angela Shamsid-Deen, and April Canavan.

Discover more by Brian Thompson

The *Reject High* series chronicles the journeys of Jason Champion, Rhapsody Lowe, and Sasha Anderson from high-risk kids tossed away by the system to confronting dangerous foes and finding a power all their own.

Reject High ISBN: 978-0-989-10560-6 * Paperback * 270 pages

Sophomore Freak ISBN: 978-0-989-10563-7 * Paperback *258 pages

Forgotten ISBN: 978-0989105644* Paperback * 300 pages

Champion Immortal ISBN: 978-0989105668* Paperback * 294 pages

Available in print/electronic format at www.amazon.com
www.greatnationpublishing.com